"Sara?"

Slowly, reluctantly, Adrian lifted his mouth from hers. He raised one hand to tangle in her hair while with the other he stroked the length of her back. She could feel the intensity in him as he urged her soft thighs against the hard planes of his lower body.

"I believe you said this was supposed to give me something else to think about?" Sara murmured gently.

"I don't know about you, but I may have given myself a little too much to think about tonight. Forgive me, honey, but I've been wondering for a long time what you would taste like." Once again he lowered his mouth to hers.

Sara felt her lips being parted and then he was deep in her unresisting mouth, exploring her with such intimacy that she trembled. For countless moments time stood still for her there on the narrow path. She gave herself up to the intriguing, captivating touch of a man who qualified as a near-stranger and wondered why he seemed so right to all of her senses. . . .

For Ann Maxwell,
who understands the fantasy

——— ö ———

JAYNE ANN KRENTZ
is also the author
of these novels in
Temptation

UNEASY ALLIANCE
GHOST OF A CHANCE
WITCHCRAFT
TRUE COLOURS
THE TIES THAT BIND
BETWEEN THE LINES

THE WAITING GAME

JAYNE ANN KRENTZ

MILLS & BOON LIMITED
ETON HOUSE, 18–24 PARADISE ROAD
RICHMOND, SURREY TW9 1SR

First published in Great Britain in 1987 by
Mills & Boon Limited, Eton House, 18–24 Paradise Road,
Richmond, Surrey. TW9 1SR

© Jayne Krentz, Inc. 1985

ISBN 0 263 75918 0

21-1187

Printed and bound in Great Britain by
Cox & Wyman Ltd, Reading

Chapter One

Sara Frazer paused in the act of searching Adrian Saville's desk and told herself for the hundredth time that what she was doing was illegal and potentially dangerous. And while she had her faults, as her family had only recently pointed out to her in some detail, she had never, until that moment, sunk to the level of doing something of this nature.

But Sara was concerned, worried, anxious and more than a little suspicious of the stranger whose study she was going through with such haste. Besides, she told herself with her customary impulsive enthusiasm, the opportunity had been too good to let pass. The door to Saville's isolated home had not been locked when she had arrived twenty minutes earlier. And she had, after all, no intention of stealing anything. She just needed some answers.

Impatiently Sara scanned the room as she closed the drawer of the desk. The study was a clean-lined, orderly room. It was a quiet, solid, masculine room, and she couldn't help wondering how accurately it reflected its owner. Hardwood floors, simple, substantial furniture and a great deal of shelving were the main features. If the den did mirror its owner with any degree of accuracy, she would be in trouble should Saville happen to walk in the door. Something about the place seemed to resist and resent her intrusion.

A greenhouse window that overlooked the cold, dark water of Puget Sound provided the main source of light. Dusk was settling in on Bainbridge Island, where Adrian Saville made his home, and across the expanse of water the lights of Seattle began sinking into life. Sara didn't dare turn on a lamp for fear of alerting a neighbor to her presence. The house was tucked away by itself amid a stand of fir and pine, but one never knew who might pass by on the road outside. It was late summer and she ought to have enough fading twilight to get her through the rest of the search.

She was turning away from the desk, intent on exploring the bookshelves, when she noticed the apple. Startled, Sara reached out to pick it up. In that moment she was forced to acknowledge that she might have been mistaken in her suspicions of Adrian Saville. After all, she had an apple just like this one and there was only one person who could have given it to Saville.

Sara held the object up to the fading light and studied it intently. It was not just any apple, of course. It was fashioned of heavy crystal, and the stem with its leaf was of intricately worked gold. The person who had made a gift of the apple believed in substantial things such as gold, Sara knew. Small bubbles had been captured inside the apple by the artist. They reflected the light in an intriguing manner, making anyone who held the object want to examine it more intently.

All in all, it was a very attractive paperweight, and the fact that it sat on Adrian Saville's desk put a whole new light on the situation. Sara stood still, turning the apple so that the crystal caught the light, and wondered what she was going to do next.

"Offer me a bite."

The deep, graveled voice came from the doorway. Sara chilled for an instant as fear and embarrassment washed through her. She nearly dropped the crystal apple as she spun around to face the man who was lounging calmly against the doorjamb. Frantically she struggled for self-control and a reasonable explanation of her presence in his study. Unfortunately the situation did not do wonders for her presence of mind. Sara found herself wishing very badly that she had never succumbed to the temptation his empty house had provided.

"I'm sorry," she managed, stumbling over the words. Vaguely she realized that her hands were trembling. "I didn't hear anyone. I mean, there was no one at home when I arrived, and the door was unlocked. I had no business wandering in to wait for you, but it seemed pointless to sit outside in the car and I—" She broke off abruptly as something occurred to her. "You are Adrian Saville, aren't you?"

Eyes that were either unusually colorless or else were washed of color by a trick of the dim light swept curiously over her. Sara had the feeling that the stranger had taken in every detail in that brief glance.

"If I'm not Adrian Saville, this situation is going to get even more complicated, isn't it?" he noted softly.

Sara's fingers tightened on the paperweight as she forced herself to sound reasonably cool and collected. "It would mean that there are two intruders in Mr. Saville's home instead of just one. Yes, I would say that would complicate things. But I don't think that's the case. You are Adrian Saville."

Arms folded across his chest, the man regarded her with mild interest. "What makes you so sure?"

"You're leaning much too casually in that doorway, for one thing," Sara retorted. Whatever he was thinking, he didn't seem intent on doing her any immediate harm. Actually, he really didn't look like the sort of man who would harm someone unless greatly provoked. The fear died away, leaving only the embarrassment. "Look, I can explain this, Mr. Saville."

"I can't wait to hear the explanation."

Sara felt the warm flush paint the line of her cheekbones. Carefully she set the crystal apple back down on his desk. It was a relief to have an excuse to look away from that strangely colorless gaze. "Then you're going to acknowledge your name, at least?"

"Why not? This is my home. I might as well use my name," he murmured easily.

"I'm Sara Frazer," she said quietly, turning her head to meet his eyes once more. "Lowell Kincaid's niece. I have a paperweight just like this one at home."

"I see."

She hadn't expected the silence that followed. It made her feel uneasy and awkward. Hurriedly she tried to fill it with further explanations. "I came looking for you because I couldn't locate Uncle Lowell. I just arrived from his place in the mountains late this afternoon. I caught the ferry here to the island and by the time I found your house it was getting quite late. There was no answer when I knocked on your door, and when I tried it, it was unlocked. I'm afraid I just came on in to wait for you," she concluded with a tentative smile.

"And wound up searching my study as a means of passing the time?" He didn't return her smile but he didn't seem unduly upset.

Sara took a deep breath. "I happened to notice the paperweight," she lied politely. "It really is just like the one I have. Uncle Lowell gave it to me a few months ago. I assume he gave you this one?"

"Umm."

Sara decided the noncommittal sound was an affirmative. "They're quite beautiful, aren't they? I have mine on my desk at home."

He ignored her determined chattiness. "What were you looking for, Sara?"

Something about the calm manner in which he asked the question convinced her that Adrian Saville wasn't going to accept her explanation of why she happened to be in his study. Sara exhaled slowly, considering her options. This might be a clear-cut case of honesty being the best policy, she decided ruefully. Folding her arms across her small breasts in a subtle mockery of his own stance, she leaned back and propped herself against the edge of the desk. She met his gaze with a level one of her own.

"I was looking for something."

He nodded as if it were the most natural thing in the world. "For what?"

She shrugged. "That's the problem. I don't know. Anything that might give me a clue about where my uncle is."

Adrian continued to regard her with solemn interest for another long moment. This time Sara resisted the impulse to fill the silent void with attempts at explanations. She could be just as remote and laconic as Adrian Saville could, she promised herself.

"What makes you think I might have some answers for you?"

"I'm not sure you do. But Uncle Lowell once told me that if anything ever happened to him, I was to notify you. He gave me your address several months ago, shortly before he sent the apple, in fact."

"And you think something has happened to Lowell?"

"I don't know," Sara admitted. "I only know that he's not at his home up in the mountains."

"Perhaps he's taken a short trip. Was he expecting you?"

Sara swallowed uneasily. "Well, no. I just showed up on his doorstep unannounced, I'm afraid. I did try to call but all I got was his answering machine."

"Then why the concern?" Adrian pressed quietly.

Sara looked at him searchingly. "How well do you know my uncle?"

"Well enough."

Not much to go on, but she might as well see what happened when she told him the reason for her concern. "His neighbor said he went hunting."

Adrian Saville greeted that bit of information with more silence. Then he straightened away from the door. "Have you had dinner, Sara?"

Sara frowned as he turned away and started down the hall. "Wait a minute! Don't you understand?" she demanded, hurrying after him. She caught up with him just as he rounded the corner and walked into the small, rather old-fashioned kitchen. "They said he went *hunting*."

"And Lowell Kincaid doesn't go in for blood sports. Yes, I understand." Adrian opened the refrigerator door, examining the contents with a wary eye.

"It's because of his old job," Sara said quickly. "Before he retired he worked in a rather violent world, you see."

"He worked for the government, you mean." Adrian finally decided on a plastic-wrapped chunk of cheese. He removed it from the refrigerator and set it on the counter. Then he opened a cupboard and reached for a box of crackers. "I know what your uncle used to do for a living, Sara."

She blinked, watching him carefully. "Oh."

"You didn't answer my question. Did you have any dinner?" Adrian began slicing cheese with smooth, methodical strokes of a knife.

"Uh, no, I haven't had time," Sara said vaguely. Her mind was on other things and had been all afternoon.

"Neither have I. Cheese and crackers and some vegetables okay?"

"Look, Adrian. . .Mr. Saville. . .I'm really not very hungry. I just came here to see if you knew anything about Uncle Lowell."

"And stayed to rifle my study." He nodded. "Sorry I can't offer anything more interesting. But it's kind of late in the evening to start something more elaborate. And I'm really not that good a cook in the first place."

"I didn't rifle your study!" Sara exploded, beginning to lose her patience. She didn't have a great deal of that commodity in the first place. Life was short enough as it was, she felt. What good was an excess of patience? "Now, about Uncle Lowell. . ."

"There's some wine in that cupboard next to the sink. Why don't you open a bottle while I slice up a few carrots and some broccoli?"

"But I don't want any wine!"

"I do." He glanced back at her over his shoulder, a faint smile playing at the corner of his mouth. "I'm celebrating, you see."

That stopped her. "Celebrating what?"

"The sale of my first novel."

Sara stared at him, astonished. "Are you really?"

"Umm."

Again she assumed the noncommittal sound was a yes answer. Her enthusiasm sprang up, as usual, out of nowhere and rushed into her voice. "Adrian, that's fan-

tastic! Absolutely fantastic! A once-in-a-lifetime event.
I can't believe it. I've never even met an author before.''

"Neither have I," Adrian said dryly. He finished slicing the cheese and opened the refrigerator to pull out a
handful of carrots. "Choose whichever bottle of wine
you want."

A little bemused, Sara found herself obediently reaching into the cupboard and selecting a bottle of Oregon
Pinot Noir. She'd heard the Northwest wine industry
was starting to flourish but she hadn't yet had much experience with the products. They hadn't yet become chic
in California. "You must be very excited."

He thought about that. "Well, it was a relief to make
the sale," he began consideringly.

"A relief! Why, it's marvelous! Terrific! Thrilling!
What's the matter with you? I should think you'd be doing handsprings or something."

"I imagine it's easier to get excited when there's
someone else around to get excited with you," he murmured, arranging raw vegetables on a platter and putting a dollop of mayonnaise in the center. "I did go out
and have a beer down at a local tavern. That's where I
was when you arrived, in fact."

Sara poured the wine and handed him a glass. With a
smile she raised her own glass in a grand salute. "Congratulations! And here's to nice, fat royalty checks."
She sipped her Pinot Noir with attention. It was good.
She made a mental note of the fact. There appeared to
be a future in Northwest wines. Then she remembered
belatedly that she didn't have to worry so much
anymore about being on top of the latest culinary
trends. "Too bad you can't tell Uncle Lowell. I'm sure
he'd be very happy for you."

Adrian regarded her over the rim of his glass as he

took a deep swallow. "Yes, I think he would be quite satisfied."

Sara smiled at him quizzically. "Did he know you were writing a book?"

"He knew."

"Then you really are a close friend of his?" she went on doggedly.

"Umm."

Sara shot him a narrow glance. "Can't you just say yes or no?"

"Sorry. Yes."

"Then you do realize that it was odd he would tell his neighbor he was going hunting?" she continued more seriously.

"Is that exactly what his neighbor said? That Lowell said he was going hunting?" Adrian picked up the platter of vegetables and led the way into the rustic living room. He set the plate down on a low wood-and-brass table in front of the couch and went over to the old stone fireplace. Going down on one knee, he reached for a handful of kindling. Although it was still technically summer and the day had been sunny and warm, the first hint of the coming fall was in the air tonight.

Sara sat down in the corner of the worn black leather couch, studying the man in front of her. "That's what the woman who had the cabin near his said. Her exact words."

Adrian didn't respond, his attention on constructing the fire. Sara sipped her wine and continued to watch him. There was a certain fluidity to his movements that intrigued her. There was also a definite logical precision to the way he built the fire. A coordinated, controlled man. He was dressed in a pair of faded jeans and a black denim workshirt. The clothing molded a lean, tautly built body that seemed totally balanced. On his feet he wore a pair of dusty, soft-soled canvas sport shoes. Now that she had a moment to think about it, she decided the strange eyes were really a shade between blue and gray. In the right light they might appear as silver.

He was a friend of her uncle's and that took the nervousness out of contacting him, even if he had caught her going through the contents of his desk. Although he gave the impression of being easygoing and very friendly, Lowell Kincaid was actually quite cautious in his friendships. He had worked too long in a world where few people could be trusted. If he liked Adrian Saville, then Sara knew she, in turn, could trust the stranger in front of her. Her uncle had always been an excellent judge of people. Sometimes his life had depended on those judgments. The fact that he had survived and been able to retire at the normal age was evidence of just how accurate his analyses of other people had been over the years.

Adrian set a match to the kindling and the yellow flames leaped to life. He crouched for a moment in front of the fire, making certain it had caught properly, and the flickering light illuminated the hard line of his profile.

He was far from being a handsome man, Sara reflected. The planes and angles of his face had been carved with a dull knife, not finely chiseled. But there was a primitive strength in the aggressive nose and the austere cheekbones. He wasn't the kind of man who would smile easily; the grim set of his mouth wasn't shaped for such expressions. Sara guessed his age at somewhere between thirty-five and forty; probably closer to forty.

She thought she saw something of the fundamental sureness and strength in him that her uncle must have seen before he decided to make Adrian a friend. Lowell Kincaid was sure of this man and therefore Sara knew she could be sure of him, too. She relaxed even more and took another sip of her wine. She sensed she had done the right thing by seeking out Adrian Saville.

She just wished he'd show a little more interest in her concern for her uncle. But then, a man who had just sold his first book probably had a right to be thinking of other things at the moment.

"What's it called?" she asked as he got to his feet and paced back to the couch.

"My novel?" He seemed to have no trouble following her abrupt shift in the conversation. Adrian picked up a cracker with cheese on it and downed the whole thing in one gulp. *"Phantom."*

"Is it a horror tale?"

He shook his head slowly, his eyes on the fire. "Not in the sense you mean. It's what's called a thriller."

"Ah, secret agents, espionage, plots and counterplots. That sort of thing. I read a lot of thrillers." She smiled. "Are you writing under your own name?"

"I'm writing under the name Adrian Saville."

"Good, then I won't have to jot down your pseudonym. You'll have to autograph a copy of your book for me when it's published. I'm sure Uncle Lowell will want one, too."

"Lowell's already seen the manuscript," Adrian said quietly. "Because of his, uh, background, I thought he might be able to give me a few ideas that would make *Phantom* sound more authentic."

"Did he?"

"Umm." Adrian stared into the fire. "He was very helpful. You're really worried about him, aren't you?"

Sara resisted the temptation to say "umm." "Yes. My uncle doesn't hunt. He doesn't even like to fish. Why would he tell his neighbor he was going hunting and then drop out of sight?"

"Beats me." Adrian swirled the wine in his glass. "But don't you think you may be overreacting? You should know your uncle can take care of himself."

"He's in his late sixties now, Adrian. And he's been out of the industry a long time."

Something close to amusement gleamed briefly in Adrian's eyes. "The industry? You sound like an insider. Lowell uses words like that."

Mildly embarrassed, Sara's mouth turned down wryly. "That's how he always referred to his government work. I guess I picked up the term."

"And some of the skills?" he asked too blandly.

She looked away, reaching for a carrot. Sara knew he was referring to the fact that he had found her prowling around his study. "Obviously I didn't pick up the skills. If I had, you would never have caught me the way you did this evening. How did you sneak up on me so quietly, anyway? Must be those sneakers you're wearing. But I was certain I'd hear any car pulling into the drive."

"I walked back from the tavern. The car is still in the garage behind the house."

"Oh." Chagrined, Sara chewed industriously on her carrot.

"You'd better practice checking out those sorts of details if you plan to follow in your uncle's footsteps."

"Don't worry, as much as I like my uncle, and in spite of the fact that I happen to be in the market for a new career, I do not intend to go into intelligence work.

I can't think of anything more depressing and grim. Imagine living a life in which you couldn't trust anyone or anything. Besides, I like to limit my close association with violence to reading thrillers,'' she added with a small smile. "It's okay on a fantasy level but I certainly wouldn't want to make a career out of it."

"If you feel that strongly about it, you'd better give up the habit of going through other people's desks. You could have just as easily turned around and found yourself facing an irate homeowner holding a gun as a friendly, trusting soul such as myself."

She eyed him thoughtfully for a moment. "Actually, you did take the whole thing quite calmly."

"You didn't look that dangerous," he informed her gently. "In fact, you appeared rather inviting standing there in the twilight, gazing into the apple. Besides, as soon as you said you had one just like it, I knew who you were."

"You were certain I was Uncle Lowell's niece?"

"When he gave me the crystal apple he told me he'd given a second one to you. He had them made up specially for us, you know."

"No, I didn't know. That is, I didn't realize he'd had a second one made until I saw it sitting on your desk. When I spotted it, I decided I probably didn't have any reason to go on being suspicious of you," she added apologetically. "Unfortunately, I came to that brilliant conclusion a bit late. You'd already snuck up and found me in what I guess qualifies as a compromising situation. You really don't know where Uncle Lowell might have gone or why he would say he was off hunting?"

"No. But I do think Lowell can take care of himself. My guess is he'd want you to stay out of the way until he's handled whatever needs handling."

"Then you do believe something's happened to him!" she pounced.

"I didn't say that," Adrian protested mildly. "I only meant that he probably had his reasons for disappearing. Maybe he just wanted to take off by himself for a while. Maybe he's got a woman friend and didn't feel like explaining all that to his neighbor. There could be a hundred different reasons why he's not at home, none of them particularly sinister."

"I don't like it," Sara muttered, feeling pressured by the logic.

"Obviously, or you wouldn't have taken the trouble to find me. So Lowell told you to look me up if you were ever worried about something having happened to him?"

"He said you'd want to know, or something like that. I wasn't exactly certain what he meant. He doesn't have a lot of close friends. I assumed you might be one of them."

"But you weren't sure where I fit in so you decided to take a quick look around my desk drawers while you waited for me to return. Are you always that impulsive?"

"It seemed prudent, not impulsive, to take the opportunity to find out what I could about you before I confronted you," she said cautiously. "Some of my uncle's old acquaintances aren't the sort with whom you want to get involved on a first-name basis."

"You've met a lot of them?" Adrian inquired politely.

"Well, no. But Uncle Lowell has told me about a few of them." Sara shuddered delicately, remembering one particular tale. "He's got a great collection of stories and personal recollections, although he always changes names and locations to protect the guilty. I suppose he's mentioned a few of the more colorful characters to you if you used him as resource material for *Phantom*."

"We've shared a few beers and talked on occasion," Adrian admitted.

"You see a lot of my uncle?"

Adrian moved his hand in a vague gesture. "He doesn't live that far away. I get out to his place once in a while and sometimes he makes it over here. What about you? See a lot of him?"

Sara grinned. "Not as much as I would have liked over the years. I'm afraid Uncle Lowell has always been considered the black sheep of the family. As you can imagine, though, I found him quite fascinating. He was the unconventional relative, the one who had the mysterious career, the one who showed up when you least expected him. He was unpredictable, and kids like that, I suppose. The rest of the family thought he was a bad influence on me and, of course, that made him all the more interesting."

Adrian leaned back against the sofa, slanting her a glance. "Why did they think he was a bad influence?"

"Because he always encouraged me to do what I wanted to do, not what my family wanted. And he had a way of understanding me, of knowing what I was thinking. He told me two years ago, for instance, that I wasn't going to be happy for long as a mid-level manager in a large corporation. Said I didn't have the proper corporate personality. He was right. I think I knew it at the time but everything seemed to be on track and running smoothly in my life. I was living the perfect yuppie life-style, and to be honest, it had its moments."

"Yuppie? Oh, yes—" Adrian nodded "—Young Urban Professional."

Sara gave him another laughing smile. "I was into the whole scene down in California. I had a lifetime membership at the right athletic club, dressed for success, had my apartment done in the high-tech look and kept up with the trends in food. I ground my own coffee beans for my very own imported Italian espresso machine, and I can tell you the precise moment when pasta went out and Creole cooking came in, if you're interested."

"No, thanks. I eat a lot of macaroni and cheese. I don't want to hear that it's 'out.' So Lowell advised you to dump the yuppie life?"

"Macaroni and cheese does not count as real pasta," she told him forcefully. "Yuppie pasta is stuff such as linguini and calamari or fettuccini Alfredo. And, yes, Uncle Lowell did advise me to dump the yuppie life. Along with the yuppie males I was dating at the time," Sara confided cheerfully. "I think he thought they were all wimps. He said none of the ones I introduced him to would be of any use in a crunch. I explained I didn't plan to get into any crunches but he just shook his head and told me to come visit him when I came to my senses."

Adrian regarded her assessingly. "And that's why you went to his place today? To tell Lowell you'd come to your senses?"

Sara stirred a little restlessly on the couch, tucking one jeaned leg under her as she shifted her focus back to the fire. "Something like that. I quit my job last week. I think I'm going through a mid-life crisis."

"You're a little young for that, aren't you?"

Sara ignored the underlying trace of humor in his question. "Don't patronize me. I just turned thirty. As it happens, I've been through several mid-life crises and I know them when I see them. I'm ready to make some changes in my life again."

"You're sure that change is what you want?" Adrian got to his feet to throw a bigger log on the fire.

"Oh, yes," she whispered with great certainty, "I'm sure."

She sounded quite resolute, Adrian decided as he fed the flames. He'd heard that quiet certainty in Lowell's voice from time to time. Must be a family characteristic.

For some reason, Sara Frazer wasn't quite what he'd expected, though, even if she did have some of Lowell's iron-hard determination. Adrian toyed with the flames a moment longer, considering the female who was curled on the couch behind him. When a man had waited nearly a year to meet a woman, it was perfectly natural that he would have developed a few preconceptions.

The few expectations he had, however, had never been fully formed. Lowell had given him some vague, odd bits of information about his niece but little that was concrete enough to build a picture in his mind. Just like Lowell to deliberately leave a great deal to the imagination. He was, after all, a man, and he knew what a man's mind could do when it went to work on a mysterious woman.

Adrian realized that he hadn't expected Sara Frazer to be a flaming beauty and in that regard he'd been correct. Taken individually, her features didn't add up to those of a beautiful woman. What surprised him was that the hazel eyes, long light-brown hair and slender figure somehow went together to create a subtly appealing combination.

On second thought, it wasn't the collection of physical characteristics that made for that appeal. There simply wasn't anything that unique about eyes that hovered between green and brown or about hair that was worn parted in the middle and clipped casually behind her ears. The red knit top she was wearing emphasized small, pert breasts rather than lush voluptuousness.

Adrian turned the matter over in his mind for an instant longer before he decided that Sara was somehow more than the sum of her parts. There was intelligence, ready laughter and more than a dash of impulsiveness in those hazel eyes. And when she had learned of the sale of his first book, her spontaneous enthusiasm had been very real even though he was a stranger to her. It was her inner animation that somehow pulled the ordinary together and made the total package strangely intriguing.

He'd been consciously and unconsciously anticipating her arrival for several months but the end result had still taken him by surprise. He simply hadn't expected to feel such an immediate and compelling attraction. He hadn't thought he'd react to the reality of Sara with such intensity. It was unsettling but he'd lay odds that Lowell would probably say "I told you so" the next time he saw him.

Satisfied with his analysis, Adrian turned and moved back toward the couch. He'd long ago accepted the fact that for some things there were no answers but he still preferred situations that could be taken apart, analyzed and understood. He liked to have a handle on things, Adrian told himself. No, it was more than that. He liked to know he was in control of his environment. Having everything accurately assessed and properly analyzed gave him the only real sense of security one could have in this world. Sara Frazer was a new and disturbing element in his environment and it was good to know he was already beginning to comprehend her. More importantly, he was comprehending and accepting his reaction to her. He rather thought Lowell Kincaid would be pleased at the progress of the situation.

"It's getting late," Sara mused as she munched the last

cracker. "I suppose I'd better be on my way. If you really don't have any idea of where Uncle Lowell is, there's no point imposing on you any longer."

"Where were you planning on going tonight?" Adrian sank back down on the couch, aware of an unexpected and totally irrational sense of disappointment. She had just arrived. It didn't seem right that she should already be planning to leave. That wasn't the way it was supposed to be. A part of him was disturbed that she seemed oblivious to the fact that things were different now. Clearly Kincaid had not given her any idea of what he'd had in mind when he'd set about engineering a meeting between Adrian and his niece.

He wondered how much to tell her about her Uncle Lowell's plans for her. He wondered how she would take the news. She might be furious or she might treat the whole thing as a joke. Women were tricky. It occurred to Adrian that in spite of being nearly forty years old he didn't know nearly as much about them as he should. It would probably be better not to bring up the subject of Lowell's plans this evening. On the other hand, Adrian found himself fiercely reluctant to let Sara go without putting the first delicate tendrils of a claim on her. Something elemental had come alive deep within him, something hard to deny.

"There's an inn on the outskirts of Winslow. It's only about a mile from here. I'll stay there tonight and be on my way tomorrow."

Adrian frowned. "You're planning on returning to California?"

Sara shook her head vigorously. "Not until I satisfy myself about Uncle Lowell. I'm worried, Adrian, even if nobody else is."

Adrian rolled his empty wineglass between his palms.

"I don't think you have anything to be concerned about."

"Maybe I've got an overactive imagination. People are always accusing me of it." She lifted one shoulder in careless disregard for the fact. "But Uncle Lowell's former career must have contained some loose ends. And I know that at times he was involved with some dangerous people. There was one in particular he once told me about—" She broke off abruptly, eyes narrowing.

"What do you think you can do about the fact that he's not available at the moment?" Adrian asked reasonably.

Sara gave the matter some thought. "I think I'll go back to his cottage in the morning and break in. Maybe he left some notes or something on his desk." Her eyes grew pensive with the plans running through her head.

Adrian looked down at the glass in his hands. "The last time you tried that trick you got caught."

She laughed. "Well, no harm done if Uncle Lowell comes home unexpectedly and catches me in his house. In fact, it will be a great relief. The mystery will be solved, won't it?"

Adrian experienced a flash of amused amazement. "You're going to do it, aren't you?"

"Why not? Maybe I'll get some answers."

"I think you'll be wasting your time."

Sara grimaced. "At the moment I have time to waste. As I explained earlier, I'm unemployed."

"There are probably more productive things you could do with your newfound time," Adrian suggested dryly.

"I know. Such as look for another job. But I think I'll see what I can find out about Uncle Lowell first."

"Are you always this impulsive and stubborn?"

"Just since I turned thirty," she told him with benign menace, her eyes mirroring an amused challenge.

Adrian found himself smiling back at her. Her gaze went to his mouth, and he realized she was very interested in his expression. Did the smile look that odd on his face? "Well, if you're intent on another act of breaking and entering, I suppose I'd better go along with you."

She was startled. "Why? There's absolutely no need for you to come with me."

"You're wrong," Adrian said gently. "There are several good reasons why I'd better tag along, not the least of which is that Lowell Kincaid would probably nail my hide to the wall if I didn't."

"Why on earth should Uncle Lowell care?"

"You're worried about him to the point where you're willing to break into not one but two private homes. Lowell would expect me to take your concerns seriously, I think. He'd also want me to make sure you didn't get into trouble. What if a neighbor saw you going through a back window and called the law? You'd have some difficult explanations to make. Messy. Lowell likes things neat and tidy." Adrian paused a moment. "So do I."

"Well, I still don't see why Uncle Lowell would expect you to take the responsibility of keeping me out of trouble," Sara declared firmly.

Adrian deliberately kept his voice casual even though he was oddly aware of the strong, steady beat of his own pulse. "Don't you? The explanation's simple enough. Lowell Kincaid has plans for you, Sara. You've arrived a little ahead of schedule. I think he was planning on you coming to visit him in a couple of months, but the timing doesn't change things."

For the first time since he had caught her in his study, a degree of genuine wariness flared in Sara's gaze. Adrian immediately wished he'd kept his mouth shut. But the strangely primitive desire to let her know she wasn't quite as free as she assumed was pushing him.

"What plans?" she demanded suspiciously.

He'd already said too much, Adrian decided. In a way it was alarming. He'd allowed his unaccustomed emotional response to push him in a direction he'd guessed would be awkward. Odd. He usually had a much better sense of discretion. Having gone this far, however, he was committed to finishing the business. He couldn't take back the words he'd already spoken. The next best thing he could do was concentrate on keeping his tone light and whimsical.

"Didn't your uncle tell you that he has decided to give you to me? You're my reward, Sara. My gift for finishing *Phantom* and a couple of other things that were hanging fire in my life."

Chapter Two

"Uncle Lowell has always had an odd sense of humor. If you're really a close friend of his, I imagine you know that by now. I've always thought he would have made a good cartoonist. Between his constant doodling and his offbeat notion of what's funny, he'd have been very successful."

An hour later Sara lay in the unfamiliar inn-room bed rerunning her response to Adrian Saville's casually outrageous remarks. She decided she'd handled the scene reasonably well. She would have suspected Saville of having a warped sense of humor except for the fact that she knew her uncle. It was entirely possible that Lowell Kincaid had "given" her to his friend. He'd told her more than once that she didn't know how to pick her men. It was Lowell who had the fractured sense of humor, Sara decided grimly. What worried her was that under that trace of whimsy, she sensed Adrian might have taken him seriously.

She turned onto her side, bunching the flat pillow into a more supportive shape, and thought about what her uncle had done. It was annoying, irritating and totally in keeping with Lowell Kincaid's somewhat bizarre way of arranging things. His affinity for the unexpected was probably some sort of survival trait. A good secret agent couldn't afford to be too predictable, Sara thought with a sigh. Normally, however, Lowell didn't allow his penchant for the unique approach to infringe too much on the lives of friends and family. He knew intuitively where to stop.

But he'd let himself go overboard this time, and Sara found herself wondering why. Couldn't he see that Saville was a man who took life seriously? You didn't play jokes on people like that. They either got mad or hurt. There was always the possibility that Lowell was deadly serious about handing her over to a man of whom he approved, of course. He'd made it clear often enough he didn't think much of her own choices in male companions. Yes, Lowell might have been very serious in his intent. In which case she would be sure to give him a piece of her mind when he showed up again.

Sara watched the shadows behind the gently blowing curtains. The window was open a few inches, allowing the fresh, crisp night air into the room. She knew a lot about her uncle's sense of humor. Over the years she'd seen enough examples of it. Strange that he was such good friends with Saville. No one would ever accuse him of having much sense of humor, warped or otherwise. The faint flashes of amusement she had seen in him that evening disappeared so quickly she might have imagined them. She had the impression that when they did appear they surprised him as much as her. Saville was a controlled, quiet man who not only seemed quite different from her uncle but who was also a perfect opposite to the kind of men who circulated in her world.

Her ex-world, Sara reminded herself. Yuppiedom was another ex-world to add to the pile of such interesting experiments. It had been fun, but she had known when she'd gone into it that it wouldn't be permanent. Sara knew she would recognize the life she wanted to live on a permanent basis when she found it. Until then she played games with the world. She wondered if she was getting a little too old for games.

Restlessly she switched to her other side and plumped the pillow again. Still, she had learned some useful skills during the past few years. For example, she knew how to slide out of a socially awkward situation such as the one that had occurred tonight. A light laugh, a wry expression and an easy comment.

Adrian had accepted her withdrawal from the topic, although he had insisted on accompanying her to the inn in her car. He'd offered her a bed at his house but had not seemed surprised when she politely declined. There was no sense complicating an already complex situation, Sara had told herself. As much as she had been intrigued by Adrian, she had been a little wary of him toward the end of the evening.

She was accustomed to men who didn't take anything except their careers, their running and their new Porsches seriously, men who knew the socially acceptable vocabulary of the new male sensitivity by heart but who didn't really know how to make commitments. Sara knew how to handle men such as that. She wasn't so sure about Adrian Saville. She sensed he took a great deal in life very seriously.

There was more age in his eyes than on his face, she thought. And there was quiet, implacable strength in that pale gray gaze. She thought she understood why her uncle liked him. But she could also picture her unpredictable uncle trying to lighten the somberness that surrounded the younger man like an aura. She could just see Lowell Kincaid laughing and telling Adrian that his niece would be good for him and that he could have her when he'd finished his novel.

Sara made a rueful face. Perhaps her easygoing uncle hadn't realized just how seriously a man like Adrian Saville would take such an outrageous comment. Ah, well. She would do her best to keep things light and easy between herself and the budding author on the drive back into the mountains tomorrow. And when this was all over she would give Lowell a lecture on interfering in the private lives and fantasies of his friends. Assuring herself of that, Sara finally drifted off to sleep.

It was sunny and warm the next morning as Sara showered and dressed for breakfast. Accustomed to that kind of weather in San Diego, she didn't think much about it. She buttoned the wide cuffs of the over-sized men's-style shirt she had chosen to wear and fastened the yellow belt that clasped the tapered olive-green trousers. Hastily she clipped her bluntly cut hair with two clips and wondered if Adrian Saville would be on time for breakfast as he'd promised. She decided he would be. Authors were entitled to be erratic in their habits, Sara felt, but Adrian was the kind of man who would be exactly where he said he would be at the specified time. Dependable.

She hurried downstairs and across the street. The coffee shop Adrian had pointed out last night when he'd escorted her back to the inn was full of people who weren't nearly so inclined as she was to take the local weather for granted. There seemed to be a kind of desperation in the air, as if everyone was determined to grab the last of summer before the Northwest winter took hold. Everyone from the hostess to the busboy commented in a dazed fashion on the fact that the Seattle area was getting another day of sunshine.

"Yes, it certainly is marvelous weather," Sara agreed politely as she was seated. Privately she thought that no one in San Diego would have even bothered to comment on it. "By the way, I'm waiting for someone." Something made her glance back toward the doorway. "Oh, there he is now. Would you show him to my table?"

The gray-haired, middle-aged hostess chuckled. "Sure." She waved energetically at the man who stood in the doorway surveying the room. "Hey, Adrian. Over here."

Not just Adrian but everyone else in the room looked around. Sara experienced an acute twinge of embarrassment. She should have guessed that in a small community like this everyone knew one another. Determinedly she smiled as Saville walked toward her.

Striving for a casual pose of polite welcome, Sara was astonished to realize that she was actually mildly fascinated with Adrian's approach. His stride was a deceptively easy, flowing movement that covered the distance between the doorway and her table very quickly. He had a coordinated, masculine grace that went beyond the kind of athletic motion her male friends developed by running or working out. Sara had a feeling Adrian's physical control and smoothness had probably been born in him, the way a cat's coordination was.

The pelt of dark hair that he obviously kept disciplined with a scissor was still damp from his shower and combed severely into place. He wore jeans and a cream-colored button-down shirt. On his feet were the usual sneakers, Sara noted in amusement. The shoes made his progress across the coffee shop quite soundless. If Sara hadn't been watching him, she would never have heard him approach the table. Just as she had never heard him come down the hall to the study last night, she reflected as he greeted the hostess.

"Good morning, Angie. How's it going today? Looks like a full house this morning."

The hostess nodded, pleased. "Give these Northwest folks a little sunny weather and they crawl out of the woodwork in droves. We've been doing real good this past week. Real good. Have a seat with your lady friend here and I'll send Liz on over for your order." Beaming impartially down at Sara and Adrian, the hostess bustled off to find the waitress.

"Lady friend!" Sara winced. "I've always heard that in small towns people pay a lot of attention to what their neighbors are doing but I hadn't realized they were so quick to jump to conclusions! Better be careful, Adrian. When everyone finds out you've gone off to the mountains with me for the day, you'll be a compromised man."

"I can live with it." He appeared unconcerned, turning his head to greet the teenage waitress as she hurried over to the table.

"Morning, Adrian. Coffee for both of you?" Liz began filling Adrian's cup without waiting for confirmation and then glanced inquiringly at Sara.

"Please." Sara smiled.

"Ready to order?" Briskly Liz whipped out her pad.

"Try the scones," Adrian suggested before Sara could speak.

"Scones?"

"Ummm. Homemade. They're great," he assured her.

"Well, I usually just have a croissant and coffee," Sara began uncertainly.

"You're leaving that yuppie life-style behind, remember?" Adrian pointed out seriously.

Sara felt a wave of humor. "All right. An order of scones and a poached egg," she said to the waitress.

"Got it," Liz responded. She glanced at Adrian. "The usual for you? The number-three breakfast without the bacon?"

"Fine, Liz."

Liz giggled and hurried off toward the kitchen.

Sara stirred cream into her coffee and slanted a glance at Adrian. "Okay, I give up. Why the giggle over your order of a number-three breakfast?"

Adrian's mouth twisted wryly. "Because a number three without bacon is really a number one. The first time I ate here I didn't notice the difference on the menu and just told Liz I wanted the number three minus the bacon. For some reason she's made it into a standing joke between us."

"I see. You don't like bacon?"

"I don't eat meat," he explained gently.

Sara was instantly intrigued. "Somehow you don't look like a vegetarian."

He leaned back against the cushion of the booth and picked up his coffee cup. "What do vegetarians look like?"

"Oh, I don't know. Maybe like leftovers from a sixties' commune or like a member of some exotic religious cult. Do you avoid meat for health or moral reasons?"

"I avoid it because I don't like it," Adrian said too quietly.

Feeling very much put in her place, Sara managed a faintly polite smile. She knew when she was being told to shut up. "I guess that's as good a reason as any other. So much for that topic. Let's try another one. When will you be able to leave for the mountains? I'd like to start as soon as possible, if you don't mind."

Adrian's dark lashes lowered in a thoughtful manner and then his steady gaze met Sara's. "Was I rude?"

"Of course not," she assured him lightly. "I should never have pried. What you eat is entirely your own business."

"I didn't mean to be rude," Adrian insisted.

"You weren't. Forget it. Here come the scones and they do look good." Sara flashed her best and most charming smile. The one she reserved for cocktail parties and management types.

"Don't."

She blinked and arched a brow in cool question. "I beg your pardon?"

"I said don't," Adrian muttered as his plate was set in front of him.

"Don't what?"

"Smile at me like that."

"Sorry," Sara said rather grimly. Perhaps she would go to the mountains without him.

"It looks like something left over from your yuppie days," Adrian explained carefully. "Kind of upwardly mobile. A little too flashy and not quite real. I'd rather have the real thing."

Sara couldn't resist. "Choosy, aren't you?"

"About some things. I can leave right after breakfast if you like."

"Actually," she began forbiddingly, "I'm on the verge of changing my mind."

"About breaking into your uncle's cottage?" Adrian slid a piece of egg onto a piece of toast.

"About taking you with me," Sara said sweetly.

He glanced up, surprised. "Just because I was a little short with you a few minutes ago?"

Put like that, it did sound rather trite. Sara was at a

loss to explain exactly why she was vaguely reluctant to have him accompany her, but the feeling had been growing since she'd awakened that morning. She didn't really have a valid excuse for refusing his companionship, however. After all, she was the one who had sought him out and she had done so precisely because Lowell Kincaid had advised it several months ago. The sense of ambivalence she was feeling for Adrian was a new emotion for her. Sara drummed her berry-tinted nails on the table and decided to lay down a few ground rules. Normally she didn't think too highly of rules, but there were times when they represented a certain safety.

"I suppose I can't stop you from coming with me, although I'm not at all sure it's necessary. But I would appreciate it if you would keep in mind that this whole plan to get into the cottage is my idea."

"Meaning you're in charge?" Adrian munched his toast, watching her with intent eyes.

"Something like that. Forgive me if I'm jumping to conclusions, Adrian, but I have this odd feeling that you might be the type to take over and run the show." Even as she said the words, Sara realized the truth of them. Perhaps that was the source of her vague wariness regarding this man.

"Think of how nice it will be to have someone else along to share the blame in the event you get caught breaking and entering."

Sara's eyes widened. "Not a bad point," she conceded. Then her sense of humor caught up with her. "What did you do before you became a writer, Adrian? You seem to have a knack for getting what you want. Were you a businessman?"

He considered the question. "I guess you could say I was sort of a consultant."

"A consultant?"

"Umm. Someone you call in when things go wrong and have to be fixed in a hurry. You know the type."

"Sure. We used a lot of consultants in the corporation where I recently worked. What's your area of expertise? Engineering? Design? Management?"

"Management."

Sara nodded, familiar with the field. "Get tired of it?"

"More than that. I got what is casually known as burned out."

"I can understand that. I think that in a way that's what happened to me. Uncle Lowell is right. It takes a certain type of personality to be really happy in corporate management. I guess neither you nor I is the type."

A slight smile edged Adrian's hard mouth. "Maybe we have more in common than you thought. We're both in the process of changing careers and we both like Lowell Kincaid."

Sara laughed. "Do you think we can keep each other company on a long drive given those two limited things in common?"

"I think we'll make it without boring or strangling each other."

An hour and a half later Sara was inclined to agree with Adrian. The drive east of Seattle into the Cascades had passed with amazing swiftness. There had been stretches of silence, but the quiet times had not been uncomfortable. Adrian was the kind of man a woman didn't feel she had to keep entertained with bright conversation. In fact, Sara was privately convinced that Adrian would be disgusted if he thought someone was deliberately trying to entertain him with meaningless chatter. It was rather a relief to feel so at ease with him in this area, she realized. Her early-morning tinglings of ambivalence faded as Adrian guided the car deeper into the forest-darkened mountains.

When they did talk, the topics varied from the spectacular scenery to speculation on Lowell Kincaid's whereabouts. In between they discussed Adrian's fledgling career as a writer and the turning point Sara had reached in her own life.

"Are you in a hurry to find a new job?" Adrian asked at one point.

He had calmly assumed the role of driver and Sara had acquiesced primarily because she suspected he would be excellent behind the wheel. She was right. His natural coordination and skill made her feel comfortable at once. He had insisted on using his car and Sara couldn't complain about that, either. The BMW hugged the curving highway with a mechanical grace and power. Normally Sara wasn't particularly enthusiastic about being a passenger in a car being driven by someone whose driving techniques she didn't know well.

"I've got enough of a financial cushion that I can afford to take my time," she told him, her eyes on the majestic mountains that rose straight up from the edge of the highway. Small waterfalls spilled over outcroppings of granite. A crystal-clear stream followed the path of the highway on one side. Heavily timbered terrain stretched endlessly in front of the car. It was hard to believe such mountain grandeur lay so close to the heart of a cosmopolitan city. "But I'll get restless if I sit around too long trying to make up my mind about what I really want to do with my life."

"Any ideas?"

"Well..." She hesitated, realizing that she hadn't

discussed her tentative plans with anyone else, not even her family. "I've been thinking of going into your old line of work."

Adrian's head came around in a sudden, unexpected movement. "My old line?"

She nodded, smiling. "That probably seems odd to you, but to tell you the truth, I think I'd be a fairly good management consultant. I'd like the opportunity to be my own boss, though. I wouldn't want to work for a firm of consultants. And I'd pick and choose my contracts. I know it sounds like a contradiction in terms, Adrian, but even though I don't like working within an organization, I do have a flair for management techniques that work in an organization. It's one of the reasons I hesitated so long about quitting my last job. I was good at it in a lot of ways."

Adrian's attention was back on the road ahead. "I don't think it sounds like a contradiction. A lot of people can give objective advice about things they wouldn't want to make a living doing."

"It would take a long time to build a clientele," Sara said slowly.

"I know the feeling. It will take a long time to build a writing career."

"But I do have some good contacts who would be glad to recommend me to companies looking for a consultant," Sara went on more enthusiastically.

"And I've sold my first book. Sounds like we both have a toehold on the future," Adrian said with the first hint of a smile that day.

Sara grinned. "Assuming we both don't wind up in jail because one of Uncle Lowell's neighbors sees us breaking into his cottage!"

It was shortly after noon by the time Adrian pulled

into the drive of Lowell Kincaid's mountain cabin. They had stopped for lunch at a small roadside café en route.

The weatherworn house was one of a number of such cottages scattered about the forested landscape. Many were filled with summer visitors but a few, such as the one just over the next rise, were owned by permanent residents. Lowell Kincaid liked his privacy, however, and had purchased a cottage that was not within sight of the next house. Unless his nearest neighbor happened by on a casual walk, no one would notice two people jimmying the back window, Sara told herself.

"Have you ever done this before?" Adrian asked blandly as he climbed out of the BMW and stood surveying the cottage.

"I got into your place, didn't I?" Sara reminded him.

"The front door was unlocked, remember?"

"You should probably start locking it," she told him seriously. "You can't be too careful these days."

"I'll try to remember to do it," he said dryly. "Now, about this little business..."

"Well, I'll admit I have no direct experience of prying open a window, but how hard can it be? People break into houses all the time."

"And occasionally get shot doing so."

Sara gave him a bright smile. "Maybe we should knock on the front door first, just to make certain no one's home."

"Good idea."

Adrian strode to the front door of the cottage and pounded loudly. There was no response. There was also no sign of Lowell's car.

"Looks like we'll have to do this the hard way," Adrian observed morosely. "We'll probably wreck the window and Lowell will send me the bill."

Sara started around the corner of the house looking for a window at the right height and of the right size. "Don't be so pessimistic. I brought you along to help and to lend moral support, not to paint a picture of doom and gloom."

"It's just that I have this image of Lowell coming home and finding his window broken. He won't be pleased."

"I'll leave a note," Sara offered as she stopped in front of an appropriate window. "What do you think about this one?"

Adrian frowned and stepped forward to examine it more closely. "I guess it's as good as any of the others. We'll need something to jimmy it with. Maybe the jack handle in the car. I'll go see what I can find." He swung around and then halted abruptly, staring at the next window on the side of the cottage. "Well, hell."

"What's wrong?" Sara turned to follow his gaze. "I don't..."

"Looks like someone else has been here ahead of us," Adrian said softly.

Sara peered more intently. "Do you really think... oh." For the first time she felt a distinct chill of unease. It was obvious the window had been crudely but effectively forced open. The frame was badly marked from whatever instrument had been used, and the window itself was still half raised. "Vandals?"

Adrian was examining the damage. He didn't look around. "Surely you're not going to be satisfied with the notion that a couple of young punks broke into your uncle's house. Not after all the exotic mischief and mayhem you've been imagining."

"Don't be sarcastic. What are you doing?"

"I'm going inside to have a look." Adrian shoved the

window completely open and casually swung a leg over the sill.

"Wait!" Sara grabbed for his arm. "What if someone's still in there?" she hissed.

He glanced inside the house and shook his head. "The place is empty."

"You can't be sure. It's very dangerous to corner burglars in a house. You're supposed to go call the cops before going inside."

"Is that right?" Adrian said vaguely. Then he swung his other leg over the sill and dropped lightly to the floor inside.

Annoyed, Sara leaned through the window to lecture him further. But the words caught in her throat as she took in the chaos of the room. "Oh, my God."

"Umm." Adrian walked past a bookcase that had been ransacked and came to a halt in front of the old roll-top desk.

Feeling stunned, Sara followed him through the window. Inside the house she stood staring in speechless dismay as Adrian examined the desk. She remembered the desk well. She had helped Lowell select it at a junk shop in Seattle. Her uncle had spent hours refinishing it.

Now the surface was a jumble of strewn papers, books and magazines. The drawers had been unceremoniously hauled open and emptied. Folders of personal business papers had been tossed on the floor along with a notebook of Lowell Kincaid's sketches.

Infuriated more than anything else by the way the sketchbook had been dumped on the well-worn Oriental rug, Sara bent down to retrieve it. "Stupid bastards," she muttered as she tried to smooth the pages and close the cover. "Whoever it was just wanted to make a mess. I thought we had all the mental flakes down in California."

"We have a few up here in the Northwest." Adrian walked slowly through the living room into the adjoining kitchen. "Looks like someone really enjoyed himself."

"It's sick." Sara wrinkled her nose at the smell of decaying food. The contents of the refrigerator had been thrown against the walls. "Absolutely sick."

"Or else someone wanted it to look that way," Adrian murmured slowly.

Sara swung around to stare at him wide-eyed. "Good heavens, I hadn't thought of that. That's a possibility, isn't it? Whoever broke in might have deliberately tried to make it look like the work of vandals. That way no one would be able to figure out what he or she had been looking for."

"On the other hand, it might have really been a couple of genuine vandals." Adrian shrugged, moving on into the single bedroom.

"Make up your mind!" Sara hurried after him.

"How can I? I don't know what's going on here any more than you do."

"Good point." Sara couldn't keep the sarcasm out of her voice. "Given that basic fact, I guess we'd better go find the local police or sheriff or whatever passes for the law here."

Adrian paid no attention to her. He was looking at the phone-answering machine that still sat on the table beside the bed. Whoever had gone through the room yanking open drawers and closet doors had ignored the telephone. The red light was gleaming, indicating a message had been recorded.

"The message on there is probably from me," Sara said quietly. "The one I left when I called him a couple of days ago to let him know I would be arriving. There was no answer, so I just kept driving."

Adrian pressed the button that rewound the tape. The first voice on the machine was Sara's, as she had predicted.

"Uncle Lowell? I'm driving up from California to see you. Just wanted you to know I took your advice. Mom and Dad are in a deep depression over the whole thing but I think they'll survive. Maybe they're getting used to my life-style changes. Personally, I feel great. You were right. See you tomorrow."

Sara caught her breath when she heard the next voice on the tape. Her uncle's easy growl was as unconcerned and laconic as ever.

"Adrian, if you and Sara are the ones listening to this, then you'll have realized I have a small problem on my hands. I can't explain everything just now but don't worry. We'll talk later. Pay attention to me. This isn't anything I can't handle but I need a little time and privacy. Some unfinished business regarding your wedding present, I'm afraid. It's tough enough to find just the right gift for a special couple like you and Sara. I didn't realize it would be even harder to protect it. Do me a favor and don't bother the local cops. This is a personal matter. Oh, and Adrian, Sara tends to have a rather vivid imagination and she doesn't handle waiting very well. A distinct lack of patience in that woman at times. I heard her message on the tape when I phoned in to leave my own. I know she's on her way here and when she doesn't find me she'll probably look you up. Which, of course, explains why you're standing there listening to this tape. Aren't you impressed with my wondrous logic?" There was a rough chuckle. "Take care of her for me and keep her out of trouble until I get back. I'll see you as soon as I can."

The tape wound on into silence while Sara stood utterly still, staring at the machine in astonishment and dread. "Wedding gift?" she finally got out very weakly.

Adrian punched the stop button. "I told you Lowell had plans for us," he reminded her dryly.

"Adrian, none of this makes any sense!"

"Yes, it does." Adrian turned to look at her. His light eyes were unreadable, but the set of his harsh features was intently serious. "Lowell says that whatever's going on is private business. He'll take care of it. He doesn't want any help or he'd ask for it. And he wants me to keep you from getting involved. I'm supposed to take care of you. It all seems clear enough to me."

"Don't be ridiculous. There is nothing clear about this mess." Sara spun around and stalked back into the living room. "Damn Uncle Lowell anyway. Why couldn't he have left a simple straightforward message or called you and told you exactly what was going on?" She headed toward the rifled desk. "Just like him to leave a lot of questions lying around for us to try to answer."

"He says it's a private matter. He doesn't want us involved. He probably didn't call because he didn't want to alarm us unnecessarily. On the other hand, he figured if we got this far he'd better leave some sort of message." Adrian followed her on silent feet, stopping to examine the stack of books that had been stripped from the bookcase.

"If it's such a personal matter, what was that business about protecting our wedding present?" Sara shot him a scathing glance as she began picking up the scattered magazines that had been spilled from an end table. Lowell Kincaid was an inveterate magazine reader. Sara had frequently teased him about the number of subscriptions he maintained.

"You know your uncle. There are times when he simply can't resist throwing out a teaser." Adrian seemed unconcerned.

"It's his unfortunate sense of humor, I suppose." Sara sighed and shuffled a stack of insurance papers. "Adrian, this whole thing is going to drive me crazy. How are we going to know he's all right?"

"We won't until he gets back. But I've told you before, Sara. Your uncle can take care of himself."

"I don't like that comment about 'unfinished business,'" she went on unhappily. "It sounds dangerous. Like something from his past coming back to haunt him."

"Lowell was right. You do have an active imagination."

"Well?" she challenged. "How would you interpret that message?"

"Like something from his past that has come back to haunt him," Adrian admitted in resigned tones. He picked up a stack of books and put them back on the shelf. "The real problem is that food on the walls in the kitchen. That's going to be a mess to clean. It's going to take quite a while, too."

"Stop changing the subject! This is important. We have to figure out what's going on." Sara frowned intently down at the papers in her hand. Predictably enough, many of them, even the most important-looking ones, contained small sketches and doodles. Lowell Kincaid was forever covering books, papers and notepads with his drawings. He did them almost unconsciously, Sara knew. He could be talking about one thing and sketching a totally unrelated subject. She remembered once having coffee with him in a restaurant and discussing her growing dissatisfaction with her latest job. Lowell had carried on a detailed and logical conversation while making comical character sketches on a napkin of the people in the next booth. "What do you suppose whoever did this was looking for?"

"That's something we can't even guess until Lowell shows up."

"Except that we know it has something to do with our so-called wedding gift," Sara muttered in growing annoyance. "What in the world could Uncle Lowell have been talking about?"

"If he'd wanted us to know, he would have told us."

"You're awfully casual about this, Adrian." Sara glared at him over her shoulder.

"I know your uncle very well, Sara," Adrian said. "He doesn't want us getting involved."

She ignored that, her sandaled foot tapping impatiently under the desk. Thoughtfully Sara stared out the window toward a stand of fir. "He said he'd already gotten the gift. Now he has to protect it."

"Something like that." Adrian reshelved another batch of books.

"So whoever did this must have been looking for whatever Uncle Lowell calls our wedding present."

"Are you going to give me a hand cleaning up the kitchen?"

"You know, Uncle Lowell once told me he believed in that old theory that the best hiding place was the one that was in full view. People really do tend to overlook the obvious. He says answers are always quite clear when you know where to look." She glanced around the room with narrowed eyes. "He'd had some experience along those lines. He ought to know what he's talking about."

Adrian went into the kitchen. "If whoever made this mess didn't find what he was looking for, the odds are

you won't find it, either. It may not even be here. Or
Lowell might have removed it and hidden it somewhere
else. Or this chaos might really be the work of casual vandals who happened on an empty cabin. A coincidence.
Sara, we don't have a clue. There's no point beating our
heads against a stone wall. Let your uncle take care of his
own business."

Sara heard water running in the kitchen sink. Reluctantly she put down the stack of insurance papers and got
to her feet. Adrian was right. They should clean up the
kitchen first.

"Uncle Lowell said he was thinking of putting in a fancy alarm system. Too bad he didn't get around to it in
time to prevent this," she commented.

"I know. I was going to help him install it," Adrian
said from the kitchen.

Sara took a step forward and her toe brushed a thick
sheaf of papers that had been lying on the floor beside the
chair. The pile of neatly typed pages was still bound with
a rubber band. Automatically she leaned down to pick it
up. Halfway down the first page a single word, under-
lined, leaped out at her. *Phantom*.

"Adrian! Here's a copy of your manuscript," she
called, aware of a surging sense of interest in what she
held. Curiously she flipped through a handful of pages.

"I think I mentioned that I had given a copy to Lowell," Adrian said softly from the doorway of the kitchen.

"Would you mind if I . . . ?" Sara's request to read the
manuscript died on her lips as she looked at the penciled
sketch in the right-hand corner of the first page. There
were other doodles at the bottom of the page, but it was
the one at the top that made her grow cold.

The drawing had been done hurriedly, but Lowell Kincaid's talent lay in the quick character sketch. Strong,

simple lines defined the figure in only a few brief strokes. It was the head of a wolf.

"No," Sara whispered as she stared at the drawing. "Oh, no."

"Sara? What's wrong?" Adrian tossed aside the sponge he had been holding and came toward her, his expression one of grave concern.

Feeling decidedly unnerved, Sara sank back down into the desk chair and looked up at him. "See that drawing on your manuscript?"

Adrian glanced at the page and then back at her strained face. "What about it? Your uncle is always doodling and sketching. You know that." He leaned down to flip through the rubber-band-bound stack. "Look. There are little drawings on nearly all the pages."

"I know. But this is more than just an idle sketch." She swallowed, struggling to remember details. "There was a real wolf in his past, you see. A renegade killer. Never mind, it's a long story. Uncle Lowell told me about him one night over a few drinks." Dazedly she stared down at the drawing. "Adrian, if this is the 'unfinished business' my uncle is taking care of, he's in real trouble. We've got to do something."

Adrian's mouth tightened. He reached down and picked up the manuscript. "We are going to do something. We're going to stay out of Lowell's way and let him handle his unfinished business."

"Adrian, we have a responsibility!"

"My responsibility is to take care of you. Very clear; very simple. That's what your uncle wants and that's what I'm going to do. Now, if you really want to do something useful for Lowell, come on into the kitchen and help me clean up the mess. If we don't take care of it, some helpful, foraging skunks or worse will take care of it for us."

Chapter Three

She was genuinely scared, Adrian reflected a few hours later. Tense, nervous, restless and scared. He had spent the past three hours alternately trying to reassure her that Lowell Kincaid could handle his own problems and trying to convince her that she was letting her imagination play havoc with her common sense. Neither attempt had been particularly successful. But then, he hadn't had a lot of experience attempting to soothe the fears of others.

It had been late by the time they'd finished cleaning up Lowell's cabin, and when Adrian had suggested they spend the night at a motel instead of driving all the way back to Seattle, Sara hadn't argued. He'd scrupulously booked two rooms at a charmingly rustic little lodge located just off the main highway.

Now, as he studied her across the restaurant table, it occurred to Adrian that he was going to have his hands full trying to carry out the task Kincaid had assigned him in that damned recorded phone message.

Nothing was going the way he had thought it would, and the knowledge irritated him. For the better part of the past year the unknown Sara had been hovering in the back of his mind, her nebulous image planted there by Lowell Kincaid.

"The two of you are going to be great together," Lowell had told him with vast assurance. "But you both need a little time. You've got to get *Phantom* out of your system and she has to reach a few conclusions on her own. I figure in another few months—"

"Lowell, you may be my best friend but I don't want you playing matchmaker. Understand?" Adrian had been very firm even though he'd already downed a great deal of beer before the conversation had gotten around to the subject of Kincaid's niece.

"You're going to love her, pal. Trust me. The two of you have a lot in common."

"That's rather doubtful, isn't it?"

"I know people, Adrian. You should realize that by now. She's perfect for you. She's intelligent and full of life. She's also fundamentally genuine and honest. She'll help you keep your life in balance. You need a dose of enthusiasm and optimism. You're too cautious. Furthermore, she's capable of making a commitment to the right man. Luckily for you, she hasn't found him yet. And she won't as long as she hangs around those wimps she's been dating for the past few years. She's smart enough to play with the dross but wait for the real gold." Lowell had grinned. "She's really very good at playing with life. In college she played at being a pseudo-intellectual. She used to spend hours arguing about philosophical treatises. A lot of people thought she was serious, including her teachers. Got good grades. When she graduated she decided to play at being an artist for a while. Rented a genuine garret, wore her hair long and went around in paint-stained jeans. She actually sold a couple of paintings through a gallery that made the mistake of taking her seriously. Then she went through an activist phase during which she went around protesting against environmental polluters. Eventually she wound up as the epitome of the young, upwardly mobile urban professional. She always did have a good sense of timing. She also has a real flair for management. She enjoys life the way some people enjoy a game.''

"And just what am I going to be offering her in return?" Adrian had asked roughly as he popped the top on another can of beer. The discussion was outrageous, but such conversations were allowable when you were sharing several beers with your only real friend. Besides, there was something about the unknown Sara that intrigued him more than he wanted to admit. He found himself wondering what she would think of him if Lowell ever got around to introductions.

"She needs someone strong, someone who can appreciate what she has to offer. She also needs a counterfoil for her natural enthusiasm and impulsiveness. Someone stable and steady. When she does give her heart for real, it will be completely. She'll need someone who will make the same commitment to her that she'll be making to him. A lot of men aren't capable of that. They might know several fancy names for spaghetti or how to select the right brand of running shorts but that's about the extent of their sensitivity.''

"Been reading those articles on the 'new male,' I see. I warned you about that. You should cancel some of those magazine subscriptions. Bunch of garbage and you know it.''

"Is that so? Well, how many men would you trust with your life or your wallet or your woman these days?" Lowell had countered.

That had struck a chord, Adrian remembered. "Not many. Maybe you. That's about it.''

"And you're about the only one I would trust with anything I value. I value my niece, Adrian. Perhaps because there's something in her that reminds me of myself."

"So you're going to give her to me? I'm not sure that you're taking your responsibilities as her uncle seriously enough."

"I know what I'm doing. You should be thanking me. You need a woman who can give herself completely. You also need someone who has a real understanding of loyalty. You could also use someone who occasionally shakes you up a bit. You're so damned controlled, son, that it worries me at times. It's as though you've built a carefully organized, well-defined little world for yourself and nothing gets in unless you've fully analyzed and comprehended it first."

"I like to be sure of things, Lowell. You know that."

The older man had grinned complacently. "Once you get to know Sara you'll realize you can be sure of her in all the ways that count. There's a lot of love and loyalty in that woman, and the man who taps it is going to be very rich. You'll see."

The conversation, as Adrian recalled, had gone downhill from there. The beer had flowed freely, and mercifully it had inspired Lowell Kincaid to bring up other topics for discussion. Adrian couldn't remember too many of them the next morning, but he definitely recalled the little matter of Kincaid's niece.

Phantom had absorbed most of his time and energy in the ensuing months. He hadn't seen a great deal of anyone, not even Lowell Kincaid, but the older man had known what he was doing. As usual.

The seed had been planted, and as he'd worked steadily, often painfully, on the novel, Adrian had found the presence of the mysterious Sara hovering in the corners of his mind. Sometimes late at night after he'd put in hours on the manuscript he'd dosed himself with brandy and gone to bed thinking about what he would do if he had Sara there. He'd let himself fantasize about having a woman who loved him, a woman who knew what loyalty meant. And then he'd gone to sleep with a body that still ached from the stirrings of an irrational passion.

On the rare occasions when he did talk to Kincaid, Adrian had heard himself ask after the woman with what he hoped was deceptive casualness. Lowell had supplied information readily enough, telling him about her success in her job or the latest "wimp" she was seeing.

When he'd begun to realize he didn't like hearing about the newest males in Sara's life, Adrian had finally acknowledged to himself that he might have a problem. It was ridiculous and quite asinine to start wanting a woman you'd never met, but the sense of anticipation had taken firm root. That anticipation had been followed by a curious sensation of possessiveness that was even more perplexing than the fantasy-induced desire.

Her undefined image had remained on the borders of his mind, always waiting for him. She was there when he took a break during the day from *Phantom*. She emerged to haunt him before he went to sleep at night. And she casually made herself felt when he sat by himself in front of the fire in the evenings sipping a lonely glass of wine.

Lowell had said he'd see about introducing Sara to Adrian when the book was finished. Over a period of months she had begun to seem like the prize at the end of a quest.

Last night when he'd returned from his small celebration of the sale of *Phantom* and walked home to find the lady in his study, Adrian had experienced the disorienting sensation of having met his destiny. The quest had been completed and now his gift was within reach. The fantasy hadn't diminished since the previous evening.

It should have, Adrian thought objectively as he watched Sara prod a sun-dried tomato in her pasta salad. Fantasies were supposed to die quick deaths when reality took over. But reality was proving very interesting in this case, far more gripping than fantasy.

"So what are we going to do?" Across the table Sara finally gave up on her salad and set down her fork. Challengingly she waited for Adrian to say something brilliant.

Adrian realized he couldn't rise to the challenge. "Nothing."

"As an answer, that lacks a certain something," she muttered. "In management training I learned that you're always supposed to sound confident and in charge."

"Maybe I should take the course."

"This is not a joke, Adrian. We can't just sit around and wait."

"Why not? It's what your uncle wants us to do. We'll drive back to Seattle in the morning. You can stay with me on the island until Lowell returns."

She eyed him with abrupt wariness. "I don't think that's such a good idea."

"It sounds perfectly reasonable to me. You're certainly not going to spend the time waiting in Lowell's cottage. If you think I'd leave you there knowing that whoever went through that place once might return, you're out of your little ex-corporate skull."

He hadn't raised his voice, but Sara felt the diamond-hard determination in him more clearly than if he'd shouted the words.

"Don't worry," she said bluntly, "I'm not particularly eager to stay alone at Uncle Lowell's cottage. Not after seeing that sketch of the wolf."

Adrian glared at her and picked up his wineglass. "What the devil is all this nonsense about the wolf, anyway? You've been acting as if you'd seen a ghost ever since you saw Lowell's dumb doodle on my manuscript."

"I did. In a way." Moodily Sara stared at the tablecloth in front of her, remembering. "It's a long story, Adrian."

"We've got a long evening ahead of us," he noted grimly. "You might as well tell me the tale."

"I only know bits and pieces of it." Sara sighed and pushed aside her half-eaten meal. "Uncle Lowell never told me all the details. He probably couldn't because of security reasons, although lately my uncle has begun to demonstrate an amazing disgust for all the bureaucratic paranoia that generally controls matters of security." A brief flicker of amusement lit her eyes for a few seconds as she thought about that. She heartily approved of the trend.

"So what did he tell you about this wolf business that has you so upset tonight?"

"There was a man," she began slowly, recalling the conversation with her uncle that had taken place nearly a year ago. "A man who carried the code name of Wolf. Uncle Lowell said it suited him." Sara gave Adrian a level glance, willing him to understand the importance of what she was trying to say. "Lowell said he was so good at what he did, so dangerous, that when he walked into a room the temperature seemed to drop by twenty degrees."

Adrian considered that in silence for a moment and then murmured very distinctly, "Bull."

Sara scowled at him. "It's true."

"Your uncle's right. You do have an overactive imagination."

"It was Uncle Lowell who told me about the guy. That business of the room going cold was his description, not mine. He meant that the man could literally chill your blood. Even Uncle Lowell's blood, apparently. Now do you want to hear the rest of the story or not?"

Adrian shrugged and buttered a roll. "Go ahead."

"All right. But only if you're going to listen seriously to what I'm saying. This is not a wild tale, Adrian. Uncle Lowell meant every word the night he told me the story. He was...upset."

"Lowell was upset?"

"Yes. You see, he knew the man they called Wolf. The guy was supposed to be his replacement. Uncle Lowell had the job of grooming him to step into his shoes when he retired."

"Lowell officially retired five years ago."

Sara nodded. "But my uncle kept tabs on his replacement, I guess. He must have been very uneasy about him right from the beginning. He said this Wolf was almost frighteningly ruthless. He seemed to have no emotions, no human sensitivity. Sending him on a mission was like aiming a gun and pulling the trigger. From what Uncle Lowell said, the man would probably qualify as a sociopath. You know, someone who doesn't really function in society. No emotional equipment. Sick. Working for the intelligence group Uncle Lowell was in gave him an outlet for his antisocial tendencies and his ruthlessness. If he hadn't gotten that kind of job, he probably would have ended up as a first-class criminal."

"Lowell said all this?" Adrian seemed both skeptical and reluctantly fascinated.

"Some of it I've inferred from his description that night. My uncle was very restless about something that evening. He wanted to talk to someone, I think. I've never seen him in quite that mood. And he'd certainly never made a habit before of talking about his, uh, former business associates. Sometimes he'd tell me stories and tales but they were always deliberately vague on details. I could tell that the story wasn't being embroidered or altered for security reasons this time. Anyhow, he'd come down to spend a weekend with my family in San Diego. We had all gone out to dinner, and when we were finished he drove me over to my apartment. I knew something was bothering him, and when he started talking, I just let him go on until he'd gotten it all out of his system."

"Did he give you any specific details on this character he calls Wolf?" Adrian asked softly.

"You mean like a description or his real name? Of course not." Sara smiled wryly. "Even when Uncle Lowell's in a chatty mood, he knows how to watch his tongue. I guess he spent too many years being cautious. All I know about Wolf is that Lowell was worried. I think he believed his protégé might be slipping over the edge. Wolf was dangerous enough when he could still be aimed by his superiors and fired like a weapon, but if he could no longer be at least minimally controlled... If he decided to go into business for himself, for example..."

"You're saying Lowell thought the guy might have gone renegade?" Adrian demanded.

Sara took a breath. "That's the impression I got that night. I only know that Uncle Lowell was tense and worried about what he had helped create."

Adrian chewed meditatively on another chunk of his roll. "Dr. Frankenstein and his monster."

"I know it sounds melodramatic," Sara admitted, "and if I hadn't seen that little drawing of a wolf's head on your manuscript, I wouldn't have thought twice about that conversation with my uncle. But after hearing the message on the telephone-answering machine and seeing the mess that cottage was in and then finding the drawing—" She broke off, her anxiety clear in her eyes.

"Why do you suppose your uncle happened to make that little doodle on the front page of my manuscript?" Adrian asked reflectively.

Sara lifted one shoulder negligently. "You know him. He's constantly sketching and doodling. He uses whatever's handy. I've seen him make the most intricate little drawings on cocktail napkins or paper towels or the back of his income-tax forms. Your manuscript probably happened to be nearby when he was thinking of this Wolf person. Or..." Sara's eyes widened as a thought caught her attention. Maybe something in your manuscript reminded him of the wolf."

"Not likely. Not from the way you've described the guy," Adrian said flatly.

Sara thought about that. "Then he must have been thinking of the wolf at a time when your manuscript was lying nearby. Which means that something was making him uneasy. He tells us in that recorded message that he's going to take care of unfinished business. I think...I think Uncle Lowell always considered Wolf unfinished business."

"Because he'd trained him and then turned him loose?"

"Something like that. How would you feel if you'd

been assigned to train someone and had him turn into a...a criminal or worse. Perhaps a renegade killer. Wouldn't you feel you had to do something about it?''

"Not a pleasant thought," Adrian said slowly.

"But wouldn't you feel responsible?"

"I might."

"Then maybe—"

Adrian interrupted abruptly. "But, Sara, that doesn't explain Lowell's message completely. Remember, he said he was out to protect our, er, wedding present."

"I know. I can't figure out that part," she admitted morosely.

"Face it. We don't stand a chance in hell of figuring any of this out until your uncle gets back and tells us just what was going on. The only thing we can do is wait." Adrian's rare smile flickered briefly at the corners of his mouth. "At least I got assigned a task to keep my mind off Lowell's problems."

"What task?" She frowned at him across the table.

"Taking care of you. I'm supposed to keep you out of mischief, remember?"

"Oh, that." She waved the entire matter aside. "That was just a casual comment on my uncle's part."

"Nevertheless, I feel obliged to take it seriously. After all, you're worried, and if someone doesn't keep an eye on you, I can envision you getting into all sorts of trouble."

"Don't be ridiculous."

"You might," Adrian concluded without any trace of amusement at all, "even manage to make some trouble for your uncle."

That caught her attention. "What on earth do you mean?"

"I think that, left to your own devices, you'll convince yourself that Lowell really is in trouble. You'll start poking around, perhaps asking questions. There's no telling what small waves you might set in motion that could ripple back to Lowell."

Sara studied him, stricken. "You're serious, aren't you? I wouldn't do anything to jeopardize my uncle."

"I know you wouldn't do anything deliberately, but how could you even begin to guess what might or might not have an effect?"

"Oh, come off it, Adrian, I'm hardly in a position to do anything dramatic one way or the other," she protested.

"No?" He pushed aside his plate and leaned forward, his arms folded on the table in front of him. "What if you go back to talk to that neighbor of his? What if you decide to do a little investigating on your own? Find out if anyone noticed someone hanging around your uncle's cottage recently, for example. And what if someone notices you and takes exception to your involvement? I can see you doing all sorts of little things that could blow up in Lowell's face. Or worse yet, your own face."

"That's ridiculous and you know it. Now you're the one whose imagination is running wild," she scoffed. But deep down she felt a prickle of guilt. It had occurred to her only a few minutes earlier that it might be interesting to talk to her uncle's neighbors. A vague plan to talk to some of them had been formulating in the back of her mind. She knew her flushed cheeks betrayed her.

Adrian gave her a very deliberate look. "Going to deny you were making a few plans?"

"Well, no, but I certainly don't think . . ." She trailed off, flustered.

"Umm. I think my little assignment is going to be the

tough one," Adrian groaned. "I have a hunch Lowell knew exactly what he was doing when he asked me to keep an eye on you. If you're finished playing with your food, let's head back to the rooms. It's getting late." He stood up without bothering to wait for her agreement. The waiter hurried over with the check.

Disgruntled at the abrupt termination of the meal and the conversation, Sara got to her feet more slowly and allowed Adrian to walk her out of the small restaurant. Her head was spinning with worry, speculation and half-formed plans. In fact, her attention was focused so completely on her thoughts that she didn't notice where Adrian was guiding her until she suddenly became aware of flagstone under her strappy little sandals. He was leading her along a path that wound around the motel.

"A little late for a walk, isn't it?" she asked, glancing into the shadows of darkened stands of trees. Behind them the lights of the motel flared in the night.

"I thought a walk before turning in might calm you down a bit." Adrian took a firmer grip on her arm as she stumbled lightly on a cluster of pebbles. "Watch your step."

"That's tough to do since I don't see well in the dark," she complained.

"I'll guide you."

"You can see in the dark?" she asked very politely.

"Umm. I've always had good night vision."

"That must come in handy for this sort of thing," she allowed still more politely.

"What sort of thing?"

"Enforced midnight marches with unsuspecting females," she drawled.

"It's only nine-thirty and believe it or not I can't even

remember the last time I went for an evening walk with a female, unsuspecting or otherwise." He hesitated, mulling that over. "It's very pleasant."

"Even though I'm having trouble walking in a straight line?"

"That's the best part."

"Oh." Her brief amusement vanished as suddenly as it had appeared, and Sara went back to thinking about her missing uncle.

"It won't do any good, you know," Adrian said after a moment.

"What won't do any good?"

"Worrying."

"But I'm so good at it." She sighed.

"What you need is something to take your mind off your problems." Adrian came to an unexpected halt, catching hold of her with both hands as she stumbled into him. "And I think I need the same thing," he added almost under his breath as he stood very close in the darkness and ran his palms down her arms.

Sara felt the strength in his hands as he pulled her close. She looked up, aware of a fierce surge of sudden awareness as she realized he was going to kiss her. For an instant she tried to read his shadowed gaze, seeking answers to questions she couldn't formulate. But in the almost nonexistent light his eyes were colorless and infinitely unintelligible. She was enthralled by her own reaction to that gaze. It lured her, promising something she wasn't sure she wanted. Before she could fathom the strange sensation, Sara felt herself pressed against him, and in the next moment Adrian's mouth was on hers.

What startled her most about his kiss was the urgency in it. It seemed to wash over her, a combination of male curiosity, hunger and carefully restrained desire. The first kiss from a man was usually tentative, polite and as practiced as he could make it. This was something else again. There was nothing tentative or polite about it. Nor was there any element of practiced seduction in the damp heat of his kiss.

Sara was tinglingly aware that it was the most honest kiss she had ever received. She wasn't sure how she knew that with such certainty but there was absolutely no doubt in her mind. It was like finding gold after years of sorting through scrap metal. The vivid realization brought forth a response from her that she'd had no intention of indulging until it flared into life. Then it could hardly be denied.

Slowly, savoring the moment of unexpected awareness, she slid her arms around his neck and found the dark pelt of his hair with questing fingertips. She was thirty years old, she thought, and not given to such episodes of instant attraction. This was something unique and she was wise enough to know it.

"Sara?"

Slowly, reluctantly, Adrian lifted his mouth from hers. He raised one hand to tangle in her hair while with the other he stroked the length of her back. She could feel the intensity in him as he urged her soft thighs against the hard planes of his lower body.

"I believe you said this was supposed to give me something else to think about?" she murmured gently.

"I don't know about you, but I may have given myself a little too much to think about tonight. Forgive me, honey, but I've been wondering what you would taste like for a long time." Once again he lowered his mouth to hers.

Sara felt her lips being parted and then he was deep in her unresisting mouth, exploring her with such intimacy that she trembled. For countless moments time stood still for her there on the narrow path. She gave herself up to the intriguing, captivating touch of a man who qualified as a near-stranger and wondered why he seemed so right to all her senses.

She offered no resistance as Adrian drew her deeper and deeper into the embrace. When his palms slipped down to cup the contours of her derriere, she stood on tiptoe, nestling closer. His leaping desire made itself felt through the fabric of his jeans and her own body struggled to answer the ancient call. Sara had never known such driving urgency. When Adrian freed her mouth to seek out the sensitive place behind her ear, she heard herself murmur a throaty response. His breath was exciting and warm in her hair.

Then, slowly at first but with gathering strength, the night breeze began to make itself felt. Sara became vaguely aware of the gathering chill as it swirled and eddied around her. The warmth of Adrian's body warded off some of it but not all. He seemed to realize what was happening at about the same moment and slowly lifted his head.

"I think it's time to go back," he said huskily.

"Yes." She didn't argue. He was right. It was time to go safely back to her own bed. But she felt unexpectedly weak and she found herself holding on to his arm.

For a moment longer Adrian's palms framed her upturned face. She sensed the hesitation in him and was warmed by it. He was reluctant to break the spell and that pleased her. She didn't want to be the only one caught up in the magic, Sara realized.

"If it weren't getting so cold out here and if you'd had a little more time to get used to the idea. . ." Adrian let the rest of the sentence trail off as he took her hand and started back toward the lights of the motel.

"Get used to what idea?"

"Never mind," he told her laconically. "My imagination is proving to be as vivid as yours, although it seems to be running along different lines."

Sara smiled serenely to herself in the shadows, knowing exactly what was going through his head. He wanted her, and the knowledge sent a primitive thrill through her veins. Adrian wouldn't do anything about it tonight, of course. It was much too soon. They barely knew each other and there were a great many factors that might get in the way of a relationship between them. Still, tonight she would go to sleep with a sense of anticipation that was entirely new to her.

But an hour later as she lay in bed in the room next to Adrian's Sara realized that, anticipation or not, sleep was not going to come easily that night. Adrian had succeeded in distracting her for a while, she decided ruefully, but now that she was alone again, too many jumbled thoughts were swirling in her head. Her mind skipped around from worries about her uncle and his "unfinished business" to memories of Adrian's urgent kiss. She needed something to relax her.

"Like a good book," she decided aloud, pushing back the covers. And she knew just where to get one.

Padding barefoot across the carpet, her long cotton nightgown trailing behind her, Sara went to the suitcase in the corner. Opening it, she reached inside and removed the manuscript of *Phantom* that she had picked up off her uncle's desk. For a moment her gaze rested thoughtfully on the sketch of the wolf in the upper corner, and then she told herself to ignore it. She was after relaxation, not added worry.

A deep curiosity filled her as she climbed back into bed and started *Phantom*. Silently she admitted to herself that it was the desire to learn something more about the man she had spent the day with rather than a wish to see how the story ended that prompted the feeling. How much could you tell about a man by his writing, she wondered.

On the surface, *Phantom* was high adventure. It involved the perilous race to retrieve a cache of gold that had been smuggled out of South Vietnam during the last, chaotic days of the war. The treasure had been hidden near the Cambodian border and had been inaccessible for years because it was simply too dangerous to go after it. Only a handful of men knew the location.

As the story opened, it was learned that more than a treasure had been hidden. Secret documents that could destroy the career of a powerful government official had been buried along with the gold. Suddenly any risk was worth taking to retrieve the cache.

The action was well plotted and moved with the swiftness of an avalanche, but what held Sara's attention until nearly two in the morning was the inner conflict of the protagonist, the man called Phantom.

He was portrayed as a man who had clearly reached the limits of his emotional and physical endurance. Too many years of tension and violence had taken a savage toll. Now he had been assigned one last job by the government agency for which he worked. He was told to retrieve the gold and the documents hidden with it. At any price.

In the end the man called Phantom did the job he had been assigned to do, but it had nearly destroyed him. Then he had accidentally discovered that the incriminating documents buried with the gold constituted a shattering indictment of the man who ran the very agency for which he himself worked. The secret papers pointed at treason at the highest levels. Phantom had learned far too much. He had not been expected to survive his mission, but now that he had, his life was in jeopardy.

By the time Sara finished the harrowing and emotionally gripping tale, she felt exhausted but not at all relaxed. The writing had been lean and stark, which didn't surprise her. Adrian Saville struck her as the kind of man who wouldn't use one more word than necessary to tell his story. But she was left with the same question she'd had when she'd begun reading. How much insight could you gain into a man by reading his fiction?

Restlessly she restacked the manuscript pages and climbed back out of bed. She put *Phantom* back in the suitcase and turned to eye the rumpled sheets. She really didn't feel like climbing back into bed just yet. The book had left her far too keyed up and strangely tense.

On impulse she walked over to the sliding-glass door that opened onto the balcony and unlocked it. Taking a deep breath of the chilled mountain air, she stepped outside.

"You should have been asleep hours ago."

Sara jumped at the sound of Adrian's voice. Whirling, she saw him lounging against the railing of the balcony next to hers. He had one foot propped on the lowest rung and his elbows planted on the top one. The shadows hid the expression on his face, but she was aware of a strange tension in the atmosphere between them.

"I couldn't sleep," Sara whispered. "I've been reading."

"*Phantom?*"

"Yes."

"Learn anything?" he inquired sardonically.

Sara half smiled. "Only that I think you're going to have a very successful career as a writer of suspense novels. I couldn't put it down, Adrian."

"But did you learn anything?" he pressed softly.

She wished she could see his face. "You know I started it out of curiosity, don't you?"

"Umm."

"Well, I finished it because it was a very gripping tale. But I don't think I learned much about you in the process." She paused, thinking. "No, that's not true. I guess I did pick up a few things along the way."

"Such as?"

"You have a set of rather fundamental values, don't you? You believe in integrity and justice. Things like honor and loyalty are important to you. If they weren't you wouldn't have been able to portray the hero's emotional turmoil so well. You tore that poor man apart, Adrian. Halfway through the book I almost hated the writer for doing that to his protagonist. And then in the end, even though you pull together all the strands of the story and see that justice is done, you leave us wondering a little whether or not Phantom will survive emotionally."

Even as she spoke Sara realized the truth of her own words. She had learned something about Adrian Saville by reading his manuscript, and what she had learned was disturbing on some levels. This was not a man who would ever understand games, let alone a lighthearted approach to life. On other levels Sara was aware of a strong feeling of respect. There were so few men who knew what it meant to have a personal code of honor and integrity. Adrian must know or he would never have been able to create Phantom. On still another level of awareness Sara experienced a sensation of compassion. Adrian must have known what it felt like to hold yourself together by sheer willpower. She wondered what he'd gone through in order to comprehend the depths of that kind of struggle.

"You wanted a miracle cure?" Adrian turned his head to look out toward the night-shrouded forest.

"I like happy endings," Sara admitted with a soft smile.

"I'm not sure there are any."

Sara leaned sideways against the rail, the chilly breeze whipping the hem of her nightgown around her ankles. "Adrian, I swear, if you turn into one of those cynical New York-style writers I won't read your next book."

He looked at her then and she saw the flash of a genuine grin. "Maybe the trick is not to write endings. Just cut the story off after the main issues have been resolved and let everyone go their own way. Readers like you can assume it all ends happily."

"You won't be able to fool me," she warned. "I know a real happy ending when I see one."

"I'll work on it," he promised so quietly she could barely hear him.

"Adrian?"

"What is it, Sara?"

"About the basic story line of *Phantom*..."

"What about it?"

"Where did you get the idea of the gold being hidden during the last days of the Vietnam war? It was very ingenious. And you made all the action so realistic."

"I got the idea from your uncle. He told me the tale of the gold."

"Really? It's a true story?"

"It's just a legend, of course. There are always a lot of tales and legends that come out of a situation like the last days of South Vietnam. Lowell told me the story one night about a year ago. Supposedly the gold was used by U.S. intelligence to buy information and finance certain clandestine operations. Your uncle told me privately that it's far more likely the gold was a payoff from some big drug deals that were going on in the south. Vietnam was a hotbed for that kind of thing toward the end of the war. At any rate the last man to actually see the gold was a U.S. agent. He arrived at his rendezvous point minus the treasure. No one really knows what happened." Adrian shrugged. "And thus are legends born."

"You added the bit about the secret incriminating documents?" Sara hazarded.

"It's called literary license. I needed an extra fillip to make the tale more than just a treasure hunt."

"You certainly accomplished that." Sara shuddered. "I really empathized with your hero. I think I fell a little in love with him."

There was a moment of silence from the other balcony and then Adrian said very calmly, "I'd much rather you fell in love with me."

Chapter Four

Perhaps it was the knowledge that she was concealed in the shadows of her balcony and that Adrian was isolated, in turn, on his own little island that made Sara feel safe enough to indulge the dangerous curiosity. Or perhaps she was still wondering just how much she had learned about him from reading his book. Then again, it might have been simply a woman's endless need to probe a man's words, searching for the real meaning. Whatever the cause, she couldn't resist asking the question.

"Why?"

"Because I think it might be very pleasant to have you fall in love with me."

The answer was simple enough, Sara had to admit to herself. Straightforward and honest. Just like the man. The bluntness of it served to wilt the small blossom of excitement within her before she'd even had a chance to fully analyze it. She stifled a small sigh of regret.

"Pleasant," she mused. "That sounds a little insipid."

He seemed surprised at her interpretation. "No. Not at all. I've learned to value the pleasant things in life," he continued slowly. "Pleasant things are civilized.

They bring an element of grace and gentleness and peace into our lives. A glass of wine before dinner or a can of beer on a hot afternoon, a late-night walk on a beach, a friend you can trust with your life, a woman whose love is unshakable even if she knows you've been to hell and back. A wise man values such things.''

"It must be the writer in you that can put the love of a woman in the same category of pleasantness as a glass of wine. Don't expect a woman to be impressed, however. We like to think we're special,'' Sara said with a degree of lightness she wasn't feeling.

"You're not going to take me seriously, are you?''

"Not tonight. It's two o'clock in the morning and we've had a disturbing day. I feel a little strange after reading *Phantom*; restless in some way. And as for you, you're a man whose understanding of life's pleasures seems to be different from the way other men view them. I'm not sure I understand you. All in all, I think there are too many jumbled emotions and unknown factors hanging around tonight for me to risk taking you seriously.'' She said it all very easily but Sara believed every word she was uttering.

"You may be right,'' Adrian agreed. He paused before asking, "Are you always this cautious with a man?''

She laughed in spite of herself. "It's the only area of my life in which I am careful. Or at least that's what my family would tell you. A woman can get burned falling in love with a man who's only interested in the superficial pleasures and pleasantries life has to offer. And there are so many men out there who are only interested in the superficial things. Uncle Lowell is right. But then, he usually is when it comes to judging people.''

"I'm different, Sara,'' Adrian told her as he faced the sea. "I'm not one of your superficial wimps.''

"No, I don't think you are. But I'm a long way from figuring out just exactly what category of male to put you in, Adrian Saville. And until I do..."

"You'll be cautious?"

"I think so. Good night, Adrian." Deliberately breaking the spell, Sara turned and stepped back into her room. Resolutely she closed the sliding-glass door and pulled the curtain. She stopped for a moment, listening to the silence, trying to examine the strange emotions swirling within her. Perhaps she was only feeling the remnants of the passion Adrian had ignited with his kiss.

But that kiss had ended hours ago. Perhaps she was simply disquieted by the tale of Phantom, she thought. No, there was far more to it than the restlessness left by the powerfully told story of a man on the brink. She had to face the fact that her suspicions concerning Adrian's serious approach to life were true. In all probability he really did look upon her as the prize he'd been promised by Lowell Kincaid.

What made her deeply uneasy was that she wasn't resisting the idea of being handed over to Adrian nearly as much as she ought to. Was it because she couldn't bring herself to take the notion seriously? Or was it because she was finding herself attracted to this stranger in a way that she'd never experienced with any other man?

Pleasant! Adrian thought it would be *pleasant* to be loved completely by a woman he could trust. Sara gritted her teeth. The man had a lot to learn emotionally. Either that or he needed a new vocabulary! After having read *Phantom*, though, she couldn't believe he lacked emotions.

But after having read his novel she could believe he was the kind of man who was determined to stay in control of the emotional side of his nature. The story of Phantom told her that on some level Adrian viewed the emotional side of life as full of risk. He would want to be very certain of a woman's love before he could allow himself to trust it, Sara realized.

It was all too complicated to figure out tonight and there were so many other things to worry about. Sara took a deep breath and went back to bed.

It was the kind of conversation that neither of them would want to mention the next morning. She felt certain of that. The late hour and the inherent safety of being on separate balconies with the soft rustle of the wind in the trees as background had combined to create a strange mood that had infected both of them. The mood would be gone by morning, and she had a hunch Adrian was wise enough to let it go.

Besides, she didn't really care to be lumped into the same category as a glass of wine or a can of beer.

Out on his balcony Adrian watched the shadowy sway of a tall pine and decided that, as a writer, he really ought to pay more attention to his choice of words.

Obviously words such as "pleasant" and "pleasure" were not the right ones to use around Sara Frazer. To her they were part of the games one enjoyed in life. Not matters of seriousness. She just didn't realize how much he valued the softer things in this world, or how seriously he took everything. Well, he'd try to watch it in the future.

After all, he sure as hell didn't want to fall into the same category as all those lightweight males Kincaid claimed she dated.

Straightening away from the railing, Adrian paced back into his room and closed the door. He had been unable to sleep earlier, his body far too aware of the fact that Sara was awake next door. The glow from her room while she read had lit her balcony and had been plainly visible from his own room. Now that she'd finally turned out her light perhaps he'd be able to get some rest.

THE NEXT MORNING Sara decided to take the initiative. She would put the mood and the conversation back onto a safe track. Setting an assured, easygoing tone was second nature for her. It was a skill she'd picked up early on in the world of corporate management and perfected even more in the world of casual dating.

"I've been thinking," she said as Adrian held the car door for her the next morning, "that you never really got a chance to properly celebrate the sale of *Phantom*. You had a beer by yourself and a glass of wine with me later, and that was it. Since then, I've had you running around helping me break into a private house, clean up a nasty mess and calm my fears. This evening I think we should celebrate properly."

"How?" Adrian turned the key in the ignition.

"I'll cook dinner for you. How does that sound?" She smiled.

"It sounds very pleasant." His mouth twisted. "I mean it sounds very nice." He cleared his throat and tried again. "It sounds great." He appeared pleased with his final choice of words. "Can you cook?"

"A good yuppie can fix the current gourmet fad food at the drop of a hat," she assured him.

"How about an ex-fad food like pasta?"

"No problem, as long as it's not macaroni and cheese. Imbedded in my brain cells is a recipe for a wonderful pasta and vegetable dish that will knock your socks off."

"No meat?"

"Absolutely not. Meat would ruin the delicate flavor of the dish, anyway. We'll need a nice Chardonnay to go with it."

He nodded. "Sounds like we'd better make a stop at the Pike Place Market before we board the ferry home."

"Terrific. I'd love to see the market. I've heard about it for years. I keep meaning to go whenever I visit Uncle Lowell, but somehow we've never had the time." Her sudden enthusiasm bubbled over.

"It's one of Seattle's main attractions. The only problem is finding a place to park. The place is usually crawling with tourists on a day like this."

They followed the highway down out of the mountains, crossed the bridge that connected Bellevue and Mercer Island to Seattle and then descended the steep streets downtown to First Avenue. Seattle's aggressive new skyline faced Elliott Bay, hugging the western coast of the continent and waiting eagerly for the daily traffic of cargo ships from around the world. The Pike Place Market, an old and honored institution, occupied prime territory a block from the waterfront. But if anyone had dared to suggest that it be razed and replaced by a high rise, he would have been lynched by the local citizens, Adrian told Sara. Seattle loved its market, with its blocks of vegetable stands, craft shops, bakeries and restaurants.

Adrian pulled off the neat coup of finding a parking space not more than a block from the busy outdoor market. He seemed quite proud of himself for being able to avoid one of the expensive parking garages. Men always seemed to see it as a challenge to find street parking, Sara realized with an inner grin. She congratulated him as he reached for her hand and led her up a flight of steps into the bustling atmosphere.

"I got lucky," he acknowledged modestly. "Stay close. I don't want to lose you."

Street musicians, a mime, a puppeteer, craftspeople and various and assorted panhandlers added noise and interest to the basic color of a working public market. Sara was fascinated by the array of intricately arranged vegetables in the produce stalls. The fish vendors hawked their wares in loud voices, waving live lobsters around to attract attention. Meat vendors offered every cut imaginable. Tourists and locals thronged the crowded aisles and spilled out onto the cobbled street that ran down the center of the market. Sara noticed that Adrian did not glance at either the fish or meat stalls.

"There's a shop where we can get the pasta at the far end of the market," Adrian advised as Sara halted to study an artistically arranged pyramid of red peppers. "And there's a wine store across the street."

"Why don't you go select the wine and pick up the pasta while I choose the vegetables?" Sara suggested. "I'll meet you back at the flower stall on the corner. That way we can save a little time. It's getting late."

Adrian hesitated. "Sure you won't get lost?"

"I'll be fine. The flower stall in fifteen minutes." She smiled up at him.

"Well, all right. You said you wanted a Chardonnay?"

"Right." Sara turned to plow through a gaggle of tourists who were trying to photograph the red peppers forming a pyramid. She was intent on finding the perfect broccoli. And she mustn't forget some Parmesan cheese, she reminded herself. There was a cheese vendor up ahead.

Somewhere between selecting the broccoli and choosing the fresh peas Sara began to lose track of time. Fifteen minutes went by very quickly and she was in the process of ordering the grated Parmesan when she happened to glance at her watch and realized she was going to be late meeting Adrian back at the flower stall. But surely he wouldn't hold her to the exact minute, she decided. He'd realize she was bound to be a little late what with all the hustle and bustle and the endless distractions around her. On the other hand, she had a hunch Adrian Saville was a man who valued punctuality. No sense kidding herself, she thought wryly. He would insist that she be where she said she would be when she said she would be there. Demanding punctuality was an element of control one could exert, and Adrian liked exerting control.

She thought about that as she ordered the cheese, realizing she had just had a strong insight into Adrian's personality. He needed to be in control of his environment. He needed to be sure of things. Maybe she'd better hurry.

She handed her money to the cheese vendor and accepted the package of Parmesan. It was as she turned away to plunge back into the stream of foot traffic that a large, male tourist careered into her.

"Excuse me," Sara said hastily, hanging on to her armful of packages. "It's so crowded here, I—" She broke off as the man gripped her arm.

"Your uncle wants to see you," the stranger grated. His fingers tightened, digging into her skin through the fabric of her shirt. He began pushing her deeply into the passing crowd.

Sara nearly dropped her parcels. Her mouth fell open in shock. "My uncle!"

"Come on, lady, we don't have time to waste."

She looked up at him, taking in the narrowed dark eyes, the gray-streaked black hair and the aquiline cast of his features. She was suddenly very scared.

"Who are you?" she managed, aware that she was being pushed toward the far end of the cobbled street. Around her the crowd ebbed and flowed. A string of cars vainly searching for the few parking spaces right next to the market stalls inched through the crowds. The flower stall was in the opposite direction. "What do you know about my uncle? And let go of my arm!"

The man didn't answer, intent on making progress through a cluster of tourists wearing name tags that declared they were all from New York. They seemed to resent his insistence.

"Hey, watch it, buddy," one of the group snapped.

"I thought folks out here were supposed to be laid back, not pushy. I coulda stayed home if I wanted this kinda treatment," muttered a heavyset woman with a huge camera strung around her neck.

The man with the face of an eagle didn't bother to respond. He simply forced his way through the grumbling tourists, pushing Sara ahead of him.

"Wait a minute," Sara gasped, beginning to panic. "I'm not going with you until you tell me who you are and what you know about my uncle! Now, unless you want me to start screaming—"

"Sara!"

She turned her head at the sound of Adrian's voice. "Adrian! Over here."

With a savage oath the man holding her arm released her. Sara spun around, trying to watch him as he melted into the crowd. He disappeared in an instant.

"Sara, what the hell is going on?" Adrian came up

beside her, pushing aside a few more New Yorkers in the process. He paid no attention to their enraged lectures on manners. "When you didn't show up at the flower stall on time, I figured you'd gotten lost. You're just lucky I spotted you when you stepped out into the street a minute ago. Who was that guy?"

"He said my uncle wanted me," she gasped. "He grabbed my arm and started pushing me along as though I were a sack of potatoes or something. Adrian, he knew who I was! How could he possibly know me? I've never seen him before in my life. And how could he know about Uncle Lowell?" She felt a wave of relief as she huddled against Adrian's side. His arm wrapped around her waist, fastening her securely as he began propelling her back toward the car.

"What did he look like? Tell me his exact words, Sara," Adrian ordered.

Sara clutched her packages and tried to think. "He looked very vicious. Sort of like a hawk, and his eyes were mean."

"Sara, that's not exactly a description, that's an emotional reaction, for heaven's sake."

"Well, I can't help it. I didn't have a lot of time," she defended herself. "He—he had dark eyes and dark hair that was turning gray. I'd say he was probably in his mid-forties. He was wearing very nondescript clothes. I can't even remember what color his jacket was. He said my uncle wanted to see me and that we didn't have a lot of time to waste."

"Those were his only words?"

"I think so. He was quite rude. Just ask those New Yorkers."

"He simply walked up to you and said that?" Adrian demanded. "Nothing else?"

She shook her head, trying to think. "No, I don't think so. I asked him who he was and what he knew about Uncle Lowell, but he didn't answer me. I was getting ready to start screaming when you showed up. Adrian, I have to tell you, I was very glad to see you! In fact I was never so happy to see anyone in my life as I was to see you a few minutes ago!" It was the truth, she realized. The sight of Adrian had meant safety.

They reached Adrian's car and he unlocked the door. His eyes narrowed as he took her arm to settle her in the front seat. "You're trembling."

"That man scared me," she said evenly. "There was something very frightening about him."

"Given the fact that it looks like he was trying to abduct you, I imagine he was somewhat scary," Adrian growled as he slipped into the seat beside her and started the car. "The bastard. I should never have left you alone."

"You know, I said he had hawklike features but you could describe them another way," she noted thoughtfully.

He slanted her a sharp glance. "How?"

"You could say that with those dark eyes and those strict features he looked a little like a wolf. Ruthless and potentially violent."

Adrian froze, his hand resting on the steering wheel. "You're letting your imagination get carried away again, Sara."

"I don't think so," she whispered, staring out the window. Behind them an impatient driver who wanted the parking space honked loudly.

With an oath Adrian put the car in gear and pulled away from the curb. He headed down toward the wharf and the ferry docks. "Sara, listen to me. I'm the writer in the crowd, remember? Leave the melodramatic touches to me."

"But I didn't get a really *cold* feeling," Sara went on, remembering her reaction. "I was scared and my palms got damp, but it wasn't like the temperature dropped twenty degrees or anything."

"For pete's sake, it's eighty-three degrees today! The meanest-looking guy in the world is hardly likely to make you feel as though the temperature dropped into the low sixties."

"True," she admitted dryly. "And I suppose Uncle Lowell only used that bit about the temperature drop for effect."

"Your uncle likes to tell a good tale and he's quite happy to embellish it for a willing audience."

Sara's mouth curved upward. "I know. I've been a willing audience since I was five years old." But there had been something different about the way her uncle had described the man called Wolf. Sara hadn't had the impression that her uncle was embroidering a story for her benefit. He had been in an oddly reflective mood the night he'd told her about the man he'd trained. Lowell Kincaid had been uncharacteristically quiet that evening. Almost morose.

"Forget your uncle's descriptive turn of phrase," Adrian said grimly as he guided the car into the line of traffic waiting for the white ferryboat. "We've got more important problems on our hands, thanks to him."

Sara shivered. "You mean the fact that someone knows who I am and managed to find me in that crowd at the market?"

"Exactly. We have to assume someone followed us. Probably from your uncle's cabin. Must have been watching it. The freeway was busy coming into Seattle today. It would have been hard to spot a tail even if I'd had the sense to be looking for one.''

Adrian's self-disgust was plain in his voice and it bothered Sara. "It's certainly not your fault that man found me in the market. For heaven's sake, don't blame yourself, Adrian."

"Well, he's not going to find you alone again."

"What are you talking about?"

"I'm going to start doing my job," he stated resolutely.

She smiled. "You mean keep an eye on me?"

"Umm. You'll stay at my place, not the inn, while we wait for Lowell to get in touch. I don't want you out of my sight again."

Sara absorbed the deep determination in his voice and knew he meant every word. Adrian had decided he had a job to do, so he was going to do it properly. That meant in his mind that he had to be in complete control of the situation. She would be spending the next few days with him. On the whole, she wasn't inclined to object at the moment. The man in the market had scared her. The relief of having Adrian appear at the critical moment was still with her. She wouldn't forget that sensation soon. The instinctive knowledge that he offered safety and protection was one more element to add to her growing list of things that seemed to fascinate her about Adrian Saville.

"What do we do about him?" she asked after a moment.

"The man you think is Wolf?" Adrian shrugged negligently. "Nothing right now. There isn't anything we can do except take care to keep him away from you."

"But we have no idea when Uncle Lowell will get back from wherever it is he's gone. We can't just wait indefinitely," she protested.

"Sara, honey, a long time ago I learned the value of patience. We'll wait."

"I think we ought to do something, Adrian."

"We'll wait," he repeated stonily.

"But that man seemed to know where Uncle Lowell was," she pointed out.

"If that character knew where your uncle was, why would he need you?" Adrian asked simply.

"Good point. Why *would* he need me?"

"Possibly because he intended to use you to lure your uncle out into the open."

Sara swallowed uneasily. "You have a devious turn of mind, Adrian."

"Umm. Probably an occupational hazard of being a writer of thrillers."

"So we wait?"

"It's either that or try the police—and your uncle specifically asked us not to do that."

"I doubt there's much they could do anyway," Sara said unhappily.

"No, I don't think there is."

"I guess we'll have to start locking your front door, won't we?" she offered, trying to keep her tone light.

"Lock the front door?" He glanced at her quizzically. "Oh, you mean the door you walked through so easily the other night."

"No offense, Adrian, but I got the distinct impression you haven't had to be too security conscious on your island," she said gently.

"Don't worry about it. You'll be safe. There's an alarm system installed. Lowell helped me install it a year ago."

"It wasn't on the night I walked in the front door?"

"It was on."

"But I never heard an alarm and no police came," she protested.

"My system works on a slightly different principle from most alarm setups."

"What principle?" She was deeply curious now.

Adrian parked the car inside the ferry and reached for the door handle. "The idea that it's sometimes simpler and more effective to trap an intruder inside the house than attempt to keep him out. I can set it in the reverse mode, however, and keep intruders out just as easily as I can let them in. When I'm inside the house I set it that way. But when I'm gone, I use the first setting."

She blinked, not finding the idea either simple or effective sounding. But what did she know about alarm detection systems, Sara asked herself. "I see," she responded vaguely. "If I had tried to get back out of the house the other night, would I have found myself trapped?"

His mouth picked up at the corners in one of his brief flashes of humor as he helped her out of the car. "Weren't you?"

"Hardly. I mean, you just walked in and happened to find me in your study," she grumbled. He was leading her up to the passenger deck and it was hard to hear him distinctly in the noisy stairwell.

"I knew where you were in the house before I came through my own front door, Sara. I carry an electronic device that warns me when the system's been activated. The device starts working within a mile of the house."

"Really?" She was impressed.

"You never had a chance," he drawled.

She laughed. "Is that supposed to reassure me?"

"If you don't like my alarm system, blame your uncle. He's the one who helped design it."

"It sounds like something he'd come up with," Sara admitted. "It's that sense of humor of his. It would be just like him to design a system that can reverse the general principles of burglar detection. It fits in with some of his other theories, such as hiding something right out in the open where the whole world will see and overlook it. Well, if you're convinced it's safe, I'll trust your judgment."

"I'll take care of you, Sara," he said very seriously.

He meant it, Sara realized. The knowledge touched her on a very deep, perhaps primitive level. She hadn't met a lot of men who would say that sort of thing these days. And if they did say it, a woman couldn't risk believing it completely. Adrian Saville, Sara decided, meant it. And she could trust him.

She thought of something as they took a seat in the passenger section where they could watch the Seattle skyline recede into the distance. "Did you remember the pasta?"

"How could I forget the featured item in my celebration dinner?" he asked whimsically.

In spite of the unnerving scene at the public market, Sara found herself enthusiastically preparing her specialty pasta and vegetable dish later that evening. Adrian poured each of them a glass of wine and lounged in the kitchen, watching as she put the finishing touches on his dinner. He seemed to be fascinated with her every move. The kitchen took on a cozy feeling that made Sara almost forget her fear that afternoon.

"I can see you're going to expand my culinary horizons," Adrian noted as he sat down at the kitchen table he had set while Sara had fixed the Parmesanflavored sauce for the pasta. "This sure beats macaroni and cheese."

"When did you stop eating meat?" she asked casually. Too late she remembered the last time she had asked him a question on the subject he had cut her off rather quickly.

"A little over a year ago," he answered calmly.

Relieved that he didn't seem to be taking offense over the issue, she decided to risk another question. She couldn't seem to stop wondering about every aspect of this man, Sara realized. "You don't miss it?"

"No." He plucked up a spinach leaf from the salad bowl. "Great dressing on the salad."

"Thank you." She hesitated and then tried again, delicately. "Did you just suddenly lose your taste for meat?"

"In a way." He eyed her silently as she sat down. "I was going through my mid-life crisis at the time. When I emerged, a lot of things in my life had changed. I quit my job, moved to a new state, started a book and decided I really preferred being a vegetarian."

"All those changes sound wonderful." She smiled. "I'm in the mood for some massive changes myself. Have you ever married?"

He arched his eyebrows as he forked up a mouthful of pasta.

"Sorry. I didn't mean to pry," Sara mumbled, lowering her eyes to her plate. It was difficult to know just how far she could push with this man.

"It's all right," he surprised her by saying after a moment. "I'm just not used to personal questions. No, I've never married. There's never been time. What about you?"

"No. I always seem to be changing careers and that

tends to keep the available pool of men changing, too. The right one never seemed to come along.''

''You'll know him when you find him?''

''Definitely.'' Sara laughed softly. ''Uncle Lowell has been telling me for two years that the right man never was going to come along in the world in which I was living. He's always been a bad influence on me. Just ask my parents. They think I get my occasional bursts of unpredictability and unconventional behavior from his side of the family.''

Adrian nodded. ''He can be unpredictable and unconventional but he has a way of getting things done. He really did give you to me, Sara. I'm not making that up.''

The camaraderie she had been feeling faded into a new kind of uneasiness. ''It was a joke, Adrian. I'm sure of it. Even Uncle Lowell wouldn't go that far.''

''Then why the matching gifts?''

''The crystal apples? They probably just took his fancy in some shop and he decided to buy a couple.''

''He told me he had them specially made by a craftsman on the coast who works in glass,'' Adrian said.

''Adrian, I really don't know why he would give us a matching set of crystal apples, but I don't see that it matters one way or the other!''

''And what about that message on the tape at his cottage? The bit about protecting our wedding gift?''

''Now that,'' she admitted dryly, ''was fairly bizarre. Your guess is as good as mine. But knowing Uncle Lowell, he was probably referring to something obvious.''

''It would be just like him,'' Adrian agreed thoughtfully.

''When he shows up,'' Sara went on forcefully, ''I'm going to have a few pointed remarks to make to him.''

It was after dinner that Sara began to experience a strange nervousness. She knew the focus of it was the inevitable approach of bedtime and the necessity of making a dignified exit that was neither provocative nor rude. You learned to distinguish such subtle variations of behavior when you'd been through as many different careers as she had, she decided ruefully.

It wasn't that she was expecting a heavy-handed pass from Adrian. He didn't seem to do things heavy-handedly as far as she could tell. Just very deliberately. He certainly wouldn't pressure her into bed. But there was no denying the sensual tension that now existed between them, and if he alluded to it, she would find it difficult to deny.

The graceful approach was to keep things light and casual, she decided. That's the tone she would strive to maintain. After this first night it would be easier. Tonight would set the tone for the rest of her stay under his roof. She sensed it instinctively.

"Ah, a checkerboard," she exclaimed as she followed him into the living room after dinner. It struck her as the perfect answer to the question of how to spend the rest of the evening. "Are you any good?"

"At checkers? Fair, I guess. I'll give you a couple of games." Adrian poured two brandies and carried them across the room to the table where Sara was busily setting up the game. "I've played your uncle a few times."

"He prefers chess."

"So do I, usually."

"I only played it during my college years," she confided cheerfully. "It seemed to fit the academic image. Haven't played it since. I didn't really like it." She lined up the checkers in their little squares. "All that business about strategy and having to think several moves ahead was far too much like work to me. When I play games, I like to *play*."

"I see." He gave her a half-questioning, half-amused glance. "Checkers may be simpler but it's a game of strategy, too."

"You play it your way and I'll play it mine," she ordered, reaching out to make the first move.

Four games later they faced each other across the width of the table. Adrian's expression was one of wry wariness. Sara was feeling quite cheerful.

"That's two wins apiece," she pointed out. "One more game to settle the matter."

"Who the hell taught you to play?" he grumbled as he set out his pieces.

"I'm strictly self-taught," she acknowledged brightly. In truth, she was secretly pleased with her two victories. They had been achieved with wild, haphazard moves that clearly offended her opponent, who had won his two games with careful, precise strategy.

"It shows. You didn't win those two games with hard work. You got lucky on some wild moves. You have an extremely off-the-wall manner of playing, if you don't mind my saying so."

"You're just envious of my inborn talent. The way you play, a person would think the fate of the nation hinged on your next move. You're much too serious about the game, Adrian. You'd have more fun if you'd just loosen up a bit."

He looked at her, light eyes intent. "I'm afraid I tend to be a serious sort of man."

"Not given to fun and games?"

"No."

Sara caught her breath as she realized that they were suddenly, inexplicably discussing more than a game of checkers. For reasons she didn't want to analyze she was afraid of the new direction. Desperately she tried to find a casual way of turning the conversation around before it strayed into the realm of the personal again. "Well, we'll see whose approach works best with this next game. I warn you, I'm going to be at my most off-the-wall!"

"In the long run, strategy and planning always succeed more often than wild luck, Sara."

"Prove it," she challenged rashly.

He shrugged and proceeded to do so. Fifteen minutes later Sara was left staring in vast annoyance at the board. She didn't have one single playing piece left on it. Adrian had beaten her with cool, deliberate ease, never relenting for a moment. Every move from first to last had been plotted and carried out with ruthless intent. Her cheerfully haphazard approach had netted her only a few of his playing pieces. Even those, she was convinced, he had deliberately sacrificed at various points to lure her into traps he had set.

"I demand a replay! You don't play fair. You play exactly like my uncle."

"What's unfair about it?" he asked, tossing the checkers back into the box.

"I don't know, but there must be something sneaky and underhanded about all that strategy," she complained. "It must be quite terrifying when you and Uncle Lowell play together."

"The games tend to last a long time," Adrian said with a faint smile.

"Who wins?"

"We're fairly evenly matched."

"You mean you win frequently?" she asked curiously. "Umm."

"That's interesting. I don't know of anyone who can

consistently beat Uncle Lowell at checkers or any other game. But sometimes I can take him," she added proudly.

"With one of your wild moves?"

"Yes." She grinned. "The thing about people who always use intense strategy is that you can occasionally upset them with my technique."

"Only occasionally. Not consistently," Adrian informed her politely. "You got lucky twice tonight, but that was about the best you could do, playing with your style."

"Something tells me that people who play with your style will never appreciate people who play my way."

And on that note, Sara decided suddenly, she had probably better make her gracious, unprovocative exit to the bedroom he had given her earlier.

Chapter Five

Adrian watched moodily as Sara went off to bed and wondered how he was going to get to sleep himself. When she had disappeared into the bedroom, he sprawled in an armchair and considered having another brandy. He needed something to squelch the restlessness that seemed to be thrumming through his veins.

This sensation was far worse than the disoriented feeling he'd had when he'd finally finished the book and put it in the mail. Then he'd felt suddenly at loose ends, as if everything had ended too quickly. But tonight's uneasiness was multiplied a hundred times by the dull ache of desire.

He could not remember the last time he'd desired a woman as intensely as he wanted Sara.

Adrian stared across the room at the waiting brandy bottle and decided against pouring himself another glass. He needed it, but this was not the night to indulge. Not when he was standing guard over a lady who had no real conception of the kind of trouble that might be waiting outside the door.

"Kincaid, you old devil, you really pulled out all the stops this time, didn't you?" he muttered, leaning his head back against the chair. "Who or what are you hunting?"

Whoever Kincaid's quarry was, Adrian didn't have any doubts about the outcome. Lowell had been out of the business for a long time, but he'd once been the best there was at what he did. He'd get his man. In the meantime, Adrian knew exactly what was required of himself. Kincaid had assigned him the task in that phone message. His responsibility was to take care of Sara.

"We also serve who only sit and wait," he paraphrased, mockingly solemn.

The fact that someone had actually approached Sara that afternoon was eating at him, fueling his unease and gnawing at his mind. His instincts were to run with her, take her as far away as he could, and hide her well. But when he left emotion out of the process and concentrated on logic, he knew she was safest here in the house. The alarm system Kincaid had helped him install was good. The best. The place was a walled fortress. Actually, when he thought about it, most of his life had become a walled fortress. Strong, secure, protected, with everything under control.

Until he'd walked into his den the other evening and found the lady with the crystal apple standing in the filtered gold of a setting sun.

He really should be trying to get some sleep, Adrian thought. He wasn't doing himself any good sitting here fantasizing about a woman with an apple. And there was no need to stay on guard all night in this chair. There would be ample warning if anyone tried to get to Sara while she was here. But somehow the thought of going off to a lonely bed was depressing. It didn't make any sense, because he was used to a lonely bed. But tonight the prospect bothered him.

Forcing his mind away from the tantalizing image of Sara undressing for bed down the hall, Adrian wondered just where Lowell Kincaid was at the moment. The older man had dropped out of sight and would probably stay out of sight until it was all over. Good, logical strategy. In the meantime all Adrian could do was wait and keep watch over the woman in his care.

Patience, he had told her that afternoon, was of great value. He wasn't sure she had believed him. The thought edged his mouth with a wry flicker of amusement. The lady did things with a certain impulsive flair. He could see why she probably wasn't cut out for the corporate world in the long run. She didn't have the patience for elaborate strategy and she didn't show any interest in restraining her impetuousness. In the short time he'd known her she'd enthusiastically broken into two private houses, comprehended and been a little shaken by the gut-level action of *Phantom*, nearly gotten herself abducted, and fixed him a celebration dinner with all the excitement of a woman who genuinely cared about his success. She'd topped that off by serenely taking herself off to bed as though she were simply a visiting relative rather than a woman who'd been subtly tantalizing him all evening.

Yes, he could see why she probably couldn't have gotten too much further in the corporate world. They liked flair in that world, it was true, but they liked it coupled with a certain amount of predictability and internalized respect for the corporate image. Adrian had a strong hunch Sara didn't have any such thing as an internalized respect for that type of image. Just as she probably hadn't had any for the academic image or the artistic image. She would play at maintaining the corporate facade the same way she played at being a yuppie. After a while, upper management would probably have figured out that she wasn't one hundred percent committed to their world. Apparently she had figured it out first and decided to make a graceful exit.

The same kind of exit she'd made tonight, Adrian concluded grimly. Did she know he was sitting here, his body in a state of semiarousal while his mind tried to anticipate the next move the guy outside in the shadows might make? He wished to hell Kincaid would call and provide some clue as to what was happening. In the meantime all he could do was sit tight and practice the virtue of patience. It was a virtue he'd learned well.

Two hours later Sara came drowsily awake and lay still in the wide bed wondering what had brought her up out of a light sleep. It had been hard enough to get to sleep in the first place. She was momentarily annoyed at the intrusion.

Then the reality of where she was and why came back and she sat up, absently rubbing her eyes. She listened for a moment but heard nothing. A wary glance at the curtained window showed no menacing shadows. Why on earth was she awake? Perhaps it was simply nerves. She certainly had a right to a severe bout of nervous tension, she assured herself. Patting a yawn, she thought about getting up for a drink of water or a glass of milk. Then she noticed that light was seeping under her bedroom door from the hall. Adrian must still be up, she realized in concern.

If he wasn't able to sleep, it was because of her. He was sitting out there in the living room, worrying. Sara was certain of it. The man took his responsibilities too much to heart. She didn't want him staying up all night to stand guard over her.

Pushing aside the covers, she climbed out of bed, found her robe and went to the door. The hall outside her room was empty and the light left on in it seemed to be the only light in the house. Perhaps she was wrong. Maybe Adrian had gone to bed after all. She would feel much better if he had.

As long as she was up she might as well see if there was any milk in the refrigerator. Stepping out into the hall, Sara walked toward the living room, intent on reaching the kitchen. It was as she left the lighted hall and moved into the shadows en route to her goal that she saw him.

"Adrian?"

He was standing near a window, his lean frame a dark silhouette amid the various dark shapes of the living room. She knew he was watching her, although the silvered eyes were lost in pools of shadow.

"Do you make a habit of running around a lot at night?" he asked gently. "This is the second evening in a row that I've found you out and about instead of tucked into bed."

She smiled. "The fact that you've been awake to observe my nocturnal habits means yours are a little odd, too. Why aren't you in bed, Adrian?"

"I wasn't sleepy," he said simply.

"I don't believe you." She took a few steps forward, her bare feet silent on the wooden floor. "You're worried, aren't you? I thought you said the house was safe."

"It is."

"Then you should be in bed, not prowling around out here."

"Is that what I was doing?" He seemed vaguely amused. "Prowling?"

Sara moved still closer. She came to a halt a foot away from him and lightly touched his arm. "I don't think I'm going to be able to sleep unless you do. I'm not used to someone fretting over me like this. It makes me feel strange, Adrian. You don't need to assume this kind of responsibility toward me."

"I don't have any choice." His tone was suddenly grim.

"You mean because of that message my uncle left on the tape?" She groaned. Her fingers tightened urgently on his arm. "Adrian, you mustn't take that too seriously. I'm not really your responsibility. There's absolutely no need to feel that you have to play bodyguard."

"After what happened this afternoon?" he asked dryly.

She shook her head resolutely. "When it comes right down to it, Adrian, that was my problem, not yours. I mean, I certainly appreciate your interest in my welfare, but I don't want you to feel you have to get so involved."

"I've already told you; I don't have any choice." He lifted his hand to touch her cheek. "And I think you know it."

Belatedly she remembered that he could see much better in the dark than she could. Sara was very much afraid he might be able to read the uncertainty in her eyes as she looked up at him. "Adrian, please. . ."

"What are you afraid of, Sara? That you might come to rely on me? Your uncle says you move in a world where you can't count on a man when the chips are down."

"Sometimes my uncle exaggerates," she said huskily, acutely conscious of the roughness of his fingertips. She wanted to move away from his touch and couldn't.

"Your uncle knows a lot about human nature. He learned it the hard way."

"But he's prone to sweeping generalizations," she protested. "He met a couple of the men I've dated and decided everyone in my world was like them. I don't think he approves of the 'new male,' " she added, trying for a spark of humor.

Adrian didn't respond. His hand slid down the side of her throat, resting just above the collar of her robe. "I don't think you approve of the 'new male' either, Sara, or you would have been married by now."

"It sounds as though you're prone to sweeping generalizations, too! Actually, there is a lot to be said for the new breed of male. He acts as if he's sensitive, communicates his thoughts and feelings with all the right words; he's into things like art and gourmet cooking and he's able to handle the idea of a woman in the professional world, or says he is. . ."

"And he thinks in terms of relationships instead of commitments. But a woman like you needs commitment, according to your uncle. That says it all, Sara. Your uncle is right. You would never have found what you were looking for in your old world."

"How can you know so much about me?" she whispered, feeling confused and unsure.

"Your uncle has told me a lot about you. For nearly a year he's been feeding me bits and pieces of information about you. Enough to torment me and bait me and tease me. I've remembered everything he said. And now that I've had you with me for a couple of days I've had a chance to learn a few things on my own."

"You're an expert on human nature, too?"

"Umm." The hand on her throat was warm and compelling. He traced the curve of her shoulder as if deeply intrigued by it.

"And did you gain your knowledge the hard way, also?" she demanded, striving to maintain her sense of balance, both emotional and physical.

"There is no easy way."

"Adrian. . ."

"There's nothing else to say, Sara. We're together in

this. I'm going to look after you, whether you think I have the right to do so or not.''

She moved her head in a slow negative. "Because my uncle 'gave' me to you?''

"Perhaps. I haven't had a lot of gifts in my life. I've learned to take care of the ones I do get.''

"Just as you've learned to value life's little pleasures?''

He muttered something under his breath, something that sounded disgusted. "You misinterpreted what I meant last night.''

"Did I?''

"And now you're using that misinterpretation as an excuse to withdraw from me tonight, aren't you?''

"Yes,'' she acknowledged, aware of an ache of pain and regret because of her own defensive behavior. She wanted to toss it aside and give into the promise of the moment. Feeling torn in a way she had never known before, she couldn't bring herself to release her grip on his arm and walk back to the bedroom. It should have been a simple enough action. She knew it would certainly be the wisest thing to do under the circumstances.

"Sara, you don't have to be afraid of me,'' he said so softly she almost didn't hear him. It was the urgent need in his voice that got through to her.

"I know that.'' The bluntly honest words were out before she could halt them, a response to the urgency in him. Hastily she tried to retreat. "It's not that I'm afraid of you, I simply don't want you assuming so much responsibility toward me.''

"I know. Because you're afraid that if you give me that right, you'll come to rely on me and at some point in the future that could be dangerous, couldn't it?''

"Dangerous?''

"You're afraid that one day you'll turn around and I won't be there or I won't be the man you think I am at the moment you need me most."

Sara took a deep breath and tried to control the trembling in her fingers where they rested on his sleeve. "That's quite an analysis."

"I told you; I've been studying you. Between your uncle's observations and my own, I've got a fair amount of data," he murmured.

"So you think you know a great deal about me now, is that it? What about you, Adrian? What do you need?"

"You."

The single word was a monolith between them. Sara knew there was no way around or over the starkness of his answer. She could only retreat or accept it. It was not possible to ignore it.

Intellectually she knew she should retreat. But her intense emotional reaction anchored her to the spot. She could not move. In that moment she knew she wanted him, too. The one element of caution that she had always practiced in an otherwise playful approach to life seemed to be disintegrating. The strange swirl of emotions she experienced around this man was blowing into a full-scale storm. Sara was no longer certain she could resist the impact.

"Adrian," she heard herself whisper, "are you sure?"

"Do you have to ask?"

"No." She looked up at him wonderingly. "No, I don't think I do. I've never met anyone like you."

"I know. I've never met anyone like you, either." The hand on her throat held her very still as he brought his mouth down to hers.

Sara trembled a little beneath the warm onslaught of his kiss, and there was a soft sound far back in her throat that was lost against his lips. She felt the need in him and the leashed hunger and knew that the honesty of his desire was going to be overwhelming.

Slowly her palms lifted to rest against his strong shoulders as her mouth flowered open.

"Sara..."

Her name was a husky groan uttered deep in his chest and then he was tasting the damp warmth behind her lips. The aggressive intimacy of the kiss seemed to swamp her, making her sway against him. Adrian steadied her, holding her with a kind of fierce gentleness that provided all the strength she needed.

Slowly he lifted his head until he could look questioningly down into her face. His eyes gleamed with a silvery brilliance that captivated her, and she knew in that moment that she was lost. Or found. She couldn't be sure which. Nothing seemed normal or totally rational. But one fact seemed to emerge from the shimmering world of her emotions. If Adrian wanted her tonight, she was his.

He must have read the vulnerable response behind her lowered lashes because he let out a long sigh and lifted her into his arms.

"It's all right, Sara." His voice was a dark and passionate stroke along her nerves. "It's all right, honey. I'll take care of you. I'll take care of everything. I've waited and wondered so long. I didn't even realize how much I needed you until you finally walked into my life."

Sara felt the easy power in him and rested her head against his shoulder. Unconsciously she surrendered the last remnants of her caution. She didn't care where he was taking her or what would happen when they arrived. Never had she been so certain that it was safe to abandon the future for the moment. There was no longer a distinction between the two in her mind. In fact, it seemed to her that there could be no real future without this timeless interlude. Adrian needed her and she needed him.

She was vaguely aware that he carried her into his own bedroom, not hers. Carefully he stood her on her feet while he turned back the covers. His eyes never left her face. When he'd finished the small task, he stood in front of her and put his hands at the base of her throat. There was more than passion in his touch, Sara realized. There was that sense of need and urgency she had responded to last night on the balcony of her motel room. Once more it enthralled her and this time there was no barrier to keep her from tumbling into the glittering net.

"Don't think about anything else except us," he whispered as he slowly slid his hands inside the robe and pushed it off her shoulders. "Please, Sara. Just us."

"I don't think I could concentrate on anything else even if I wanted to," she said truthfully. Again she shivered. The light robe fell to the floor at her feet.

"Are you afraid of me?"

Sara shook her head. "No."

"You're trembling." He seemed incredibly concerned over the fact. His fingertips stroked her bare arms and then he touched the rising swell of her breast just above the edge of the nightgown.

"I know, but not because I'm afraid." She smiled a little as she covered one of his hands with her own. "You're trembling a bit, too."

"I'm shaking like a leaf. I want you, Sara. I've been wanting you all evening. No, longer than that. I've been wanting you for months." The words were raw with honesty.

"Adrian, it's probably much too soon—"

"No," he interrupted roughly. "It couldn't possibly be too soon. Not for us."

His hands moved down over her breasts and she felt the tantalizing heat of his palms through the thin material of the nightgown. She knew he must realize that her body was already responding. Sara could feel the tautness of her nipples as they came tinglingly alive. She caught her breath and began to fumble with the buttons of his shirt.

"Please, Sara," he breathed into her hair. "Yes, please."

His need filled her with a longing to satisfy and comfort him. Slowly she made her way down the front of his shirt until it parted, exposing the dark hair on his chest. So entranced with the vivid sensuality of the moment was she that Sara was hardly even aware of her nightgown floating to the floor.

But when Adrian's hands slid down her back to the full curve of her hips, she moaned softly and stumbled a little against him. She glanced up into his face and read the masculine anticipation there.

"You're so soft," he murmured in tones of wonder. His fingers sank luxuriously into the flesh of her derriere and he pulled her tightly against him.

"You're not soft at all," Sara said unthinkingly and then buried her flushed face against his chest as he growled his amused response.

"No, I don't suppose I am. I feel as though I'm made up of angles and rough edges. You, on the other hand, are composed of curves and gentle valleys. Places where a man can lose himself."

He let his fingers trail into the cleft between her but-
tocks and Sara's nails dug lightly into his skin as he followed the path to the dampening juncture of her thighs.

"Adrian..."

"Say my name like that again," he demanded hoarse-
ly as he picked her up and settled her on the bed. "It
sounds different when you say it."

"Does it?" She lay watching as he yanked off his
shirt, stepped out of his shoes and unclasped his jeans.
A moment later he stood nude beside the bed, the light
from the hall emphasizing his lean, hard body. He was
wonderful, she thought dazedly. Everything she could
ever want in a man. It was strange to be so certain of
that, because until now she hadn't been quite sure just
what she had wanted in a man. She had only known that
she hadn't found it.

"Oh, Adrian," she whispered as he came down beside her. "Adrian, I didn't know..."

"Didn't know what?" He flattened his palm on her
stomach and smoothed her skin down to the curling hair
that veiled the heart of her femininity.

"Never mind. I don't think I can explain it just
now." She curled into him, shifting languidly under his
touch. "I can't even think right now."

"There's nothing to think about." He leaned down to
kiss the peak of her breast. His tongue teased the firm
bud of her nipple until she cried out and pulled him
closer. "That's all you have to do right now," he told
her approvingly, the words heavy with desire. "Just give
yourself to me. Let me open my present. I've been waiting so long for you, sweetheart."

She obeyed, wrapping her arms around his neck as he
touched her with growing intimacy. When his prowling
fingers found the hot, damp center of her need, she said

his name again, this time with an urgency that matched his own.

"Sara, my sweet, Sara." He pinned one of her legs with his strong thigh and probed her deeply with a deliciously questing touch. When she shuddered, he muttered hot, dark words of encouragement into her ear.

She lifted herself against his hand, unable to resist the caress. Never had she responded so completely and so readily. Her senses seemed inflamed, thoroughly alive and aware in a way that was new to her. Fascinated by the world of sensation that was beginning to spin around her, she stroked his smoothly muscled frame. Her palms slipped over the sleek contours of his back, down to the hard planes of his thigh. Then, with gentle boldness she moved her fingertips around to find the flat terrain of his stomach. For an instant longer she hesitated. Then her hand went lower.

"Yes," he grated with harsh need when she dared to tease his male hardness. "Take me inside, sweetheart. Let me have all of you. I need you so."

She couldn't find words but he seemed to know she was ready. With passionate aggression Adrian pushed her into the pillows and lowered himself down along the length of her.

"Put your arms around me, Sara, and never let go," he commanded. "Never let go. . . ."

She did as he instructed, pulling him to her until she felt the blunt hardness of him waiting at the gate. The knowledge that he was on the verge of entering her fully and completely brought a brief, startling flicker of alarm. For an instant Sara had a vision of the reality that lay beyond tonight. *This man was unique. After tonight nothing would ever be the same.*

The fleeting glimpse of the future was gone an instant

later as Adrian moved heavily against her. All of Sara's senses returned to the moment, lost once more in the pulsating excitement.

"Oh, *Adrian*..." The words were torn from her as she felt the full impact of his body taking possession of hers.

"Hold me, Sara."

Instinctively she obeyed as she adjusted to his sensual invasion. Then he began to move within her, slow, tantalizing strokes that pushed her senses into tighter and tighter bundles of energy that strove for release.

The end was a revelation to Sara, a new understanding of her body and its responses. She found herself clinging to the man above her with an abandon that she would never have believed if she hadn't experienced it firsthand.

"That's it, honey," he rasped as she cried out his name once more. "Let go. Just let go. I'll take you with me all the way."

Willingly, unable to do anything else, Sara gave herself to him completely and gloried in the knowledge that he was returning the gift in full measure. She heard the sound of her name as it was wrenched from him and then he was pushing deeply into her one last time. His hard body shuddered for a long moment and then collapsed. Outside the window the night breeze briefly stirred a stand of fir and then all was silent.

It was a long while before Sara became aware of the sprawled weight that still trapped her in the depths of the bedding. She opened her eyes to find Adrian lying on top of her, his head on the pillow beside hers. He was watching her from behind half-closed lashes.

"Am I too heavy for you?" he asked lazily.

"Umm."

His mouth flickered in brief amusement as he recognized her deliberate imitation of his characteristic response. "What does 'umm' mean?"

"I don't know. You're the expert. You tell me."

"It means 'uh-huh.' " He sighed regretfully and slowly rolled onto his side. Then he gathered her close. "Too bad. You're very comfortable."

"Am I?"

His head inclined downward once in a short nod. "Incredibly comfortable. I can't recall when I've been this comfortable. Or this relaxed. Or this content."

"Neither can I," she said honestly. It was the truth. Tonight there were no pretenses or games or caution. Her fingertips worked small, idle patterns on his chest. "Adrian, I've never felt quite like this before in my life."

"You don't sound as if you're sure you like feeling this way." He touched her cheek.

Nothing will ever be the same. "It feels strange."

"We'll get used to it," he assured her.

"Will we?"

"You're nervous all of a sudden, aren't you?"

"No," she denied quickly.

"Sara, honey, don't try to fool me now. You can't do it," he told her gently.

"Well, maybe I am a little nervous. It was too soon, Adrian."

"It was inevitable, so the timing doesn't really matter."

"We hardly know each other."

"You were a gift to me, remember? I was bound to open you as soon as I could."

She flushed. "I thought you were a great believer in patience."

"Only when it's the best option."

"You don't think we should have waited awhile

longer? Made certain of our feelings?'' she asked anxiously.

"I am certain of my feelings," he told her roughly.

"I don't want you confusing your feelings of responsibility for me with . . . with your, uh, more personal feelings."

He looked down at her in mocking pity. "Believe me, I'm not mistaking a sense of responsibility for raw passion. From my point of view the two are quite distinct. You're the one who sounds confused."

"You're not?"

"Not at all, Sara. If anything, tonight just makes everything even simpler and more straightforward."

She eyed him curiously. "What does that mean?"

"It means we don't have to have any more arguments about my right to take care of you, for one thing." He brushed her parted lips and then drew back to study her expression. "You belong to me now. That gives me all the rights I need."

"I've never met a man so anxious to assume responsibility," she tried to say lightly. But she was very much afraid her voice cracked a little on the last word.

"I've never been particularly anxious to assume responsibility for anyone else," he told her seriously. "With you, it's different."

"And what do you want from me in return?" she asked carefully.

"I've already told you, remember?" He pushed a strand of hair back behind her ear. "I want you to love me. I like the idea of having you love me. I like it very much."

"You think it would be 'pleasant,' " she couldn't resist saying somewhat tartly.

"You said you fell a little in love with the hero in *Phantom*."

"So?" she challenged softly.

"How do you think he would treat a woman whose love he wanted?"

The question startled her. She frowned. "I think he would take care of her. She could trust him."

"I want you to trust me the same way."

She half smiled. "You're not Phantom."

"I created him. There must be something of me in him and vice versa."

Sara studied his intent features. She had asked herself so many questions about the similarities between Adrian and his hero the previous night when she'd read the manuscript. "Yes, I think there might be."

"Trust me, sweet Sara," he grated, rolling onto his back and pulling her down on top of him. "Trust me with your love. Like your uncle, I know what has value in life. I'll take good care of you."

"Aren't you worried about how well I'll take care of you?" she parried, aware of the renewing tautness in body.

"You won't play games with me."

"What makes you so sure?" she demanded, rather irritated with the certainty in his voice.

"Because it would tear me apart if you did," he said simply. "You wouldn't do that to me, would you, Sara?"

Horrified at the thought, Sara cradled his face between her palms. "No, Adrian. Never that," she vowed.

Unaware of how deeply she had just committed herself, Sara kissed him, translating the verbal promise into a physical one. His hands came up to wrap around her waist and he arched his lower body demandingly into hers.

"Adrian?"

"Umm."

She didn't bother to ask him what he meant. It was becoming very obvious. Sara parted her legs for him and her mouth locked with his as he began the spiraling climb to passion.

THE FIRST HINT OF DAWN was in the sky the next time Sara came awake. There was a moment of lazy curiosity as she opened her eyes and absorbed her surroundings. Adrian's room was a thoroughly masculine affair, with its warm cedar walls and heavy, clean-lined furniture. It was as orderly and controlled-looking as the rest of his house. She was finding it interesting until she became aware of the weight of his arm across her stomach. Then she awoke completely.

Memories of the night filtered back in a haze of lingering passion and midnight promises. She turned to look at Adrian and was grateful to discover he was still sound asleep. What exactly had she agreed to last night, she wondered with a sudden feeling of panic.

There had been talk of love and responsibility and a promise not to play games. But it seemed to her that most of the dangerous, reckless promises had come from her. The only thing he had vowed in return was to take care of her.

It was crazy, Sara chided herself as she cautiously slipped out from under his arm. She hadn't intended to let things go so far. She had never meant to wind up in bed with him, at least not so soon. She had barely met the man. This was exactly the sort of behavior she had instinctively avoided in the world she had just left. What on earth was the matter with her?

Adrian stirred restlessly when she slid off the bed but he didn't awaken. On silent feet Sara fled down the hall to her own room and scrambled about for her jeans and a shirt. She badly needed to get out of the house for a while. She needed time to think and reevaluate the whole situation. Her family had often warned her that her periodic bouts of impulsiveness would land her in real trouble someday. Even Uncle Lowell had felt obliged to point out that there were some risks involved in playing games with life.

But last night had been no game. Last night had been for real. Twenty-four-karat real.

Shoving her feet into a pair of sandals, Sara yanked a lightweight Windbreaker out of her suitcase and hurried down the hall to the living room. She let herself out the front door and stood on the porch, inhaling deeply of the sea-sharpened morning air.

For a moment she hesitated, unable to think clearly enough to decide on a destination. Then she remembered the car she had left parked in the inn parking lot. With a small sigh of relief at having provided herself with a focus for the morning walk, she hurried down the steps and out to the road. She would walk back toward town and pick up her car. Wonderful. It would give her something useful to do while she tried to sort out her future, she thought. Sara patted her jeans pocket to make certain she had the keys.

Behind her she was unaware of the house purring to life with news of the unauthorized exit. Adrian came instantly awake as the nearly silent vibration in the headboard jolted him. The alarm-clock radio beside the bed was blinking in a fashion that had nothing to do with its normal function. The message was quiet but clear.

The house was doing its duty. Faithfully it undertook to warn its owner that Sara was gone.

With an oath that was half rage and half pain, Adrian threw off the covers and reached for his clothes.

Chapter Six

The flash of rage and pain gave way to another emotion even as Adrian slipped out the front door. Fear began to claw at his insides, and in that moment he could not have said whether it was fear for Sara's safety or fear that she was leaving him. The two seemed to combine in the bottom of his stomach, forming a knot of tension that increased as he realized she was already out of sight. He was at a loss to explain how he could have been so sound asleep that he hadn't even felt her leave the bed. Normally he never slept that deeply. Last night had altered something as fundamental as his sleeping patterns and that was unnerving in some ways.

The truth was he hadn't handled last night all that well. He'd practically pushed her into bed, Adrian berated himself. He should have waited. He'd known it was much too soon. She hadn't spent nearly a year with a fantasy nibbling at the edge of her mind the way he had. She couldn't know what it was like to have a fantasy become reality. As far as Sara was concerned she'd only known him a couple of days. She must have awakened this morning with a head full of doubts and anger aimed at him.

So she'd taken off without bothering to say good-bye.

Damn it, he thought furiously, where the hell could she have gone? There had been no sound of a car. She must be on foot and that meant she couldn't have gone far.

The car. Hers was still at the inn and it probably represented escape to her. The road would seem the fastest way into town to her, Adrian decided. Without hesitating a second longer, he loped down the steps and started up the drive toward the winding road that led into the Winslow.

He saw her just as he reached the pavement. She was walking briskly along, her light-brown hair catching a sheen of gold from the dawn light. It complemented the faint gleam of gold from the little chain on her wrist. He remembered the way the tiny little bracelet had glittered last night against her skin. She had told him that her uncle had given it to her a long time ago. Her slender, soft body moved with an ease that seemed to emphasize the intriguing roundness of her hips and the subtle, feminine strength he recalled so vividly that morning. Adrian watched her in silence, remembering the sweet passion he had tapped during the night.

The year's wait had been worth it, he acknowledged to himself as he began to pace silently a few yards behind her. He had not set himself up for disappointment by allowing Lowell to build an image in his head. In his wildest imaginings, though, he could not have envisioned that she would wrap her arms around him with such abandoned demand. Nor could he have dreamed up the clean, womanly scent of the real Sara Frazer. It was unique to her and he would never forget it. There was no way his fantasies could have created the exact feel of her soft thighs as she opened herself to him and there was nothing in fantasy that approached the real-life sensation of sinking himself deep into her soft, clinging warmth.

But it was the words he remembered with such stark clarity that morning. Her soft words of need and the promises he had coaxed from her lips. He had thought the words would hold her even if the lovemaking could not. She had told him she would not play games with him and she had said she wanted him.

But this morning she was running from him.

It would be easy enough to catch her. She wasn't even aware of him prowling along behind her on the empty road. Her mind seemed focused on her destination, whatever that was. Was she planning to take the car and head back to San Diego? Or would she go to Kincaid's house and wait there for her uncle?

Not that it mattered, Adrian thought grimly. His hand curled and uncurled briefly in a subtle act of tension. He couldn't let her leave.

He ought to just catch up with her and explain very succinctly why he couldn't let her off the island. Perhaps she would be rational about the matter. Or he could simply overtake her, scoop her up and carry her back to the house. She'd probably start screaming. Then again maybe it would be simplest if he caught her and swore never to touch her again as long as she did as she was told. And just how would he manage to keep a promise like that?

None of the alternatives seemed viable. With a savagely stifled oath, Adrian continued to trail her along the narrow road. It was ridiculous following her like this, unable to make up his mind about how to handle her. Kincaid would collapse in laughter if he could see him now. The Adrian Saville he knew had never been prone to indecision or uncertainty.

Several yards ahead Sara walked toward town with an energy that was fueled by a sense of impending fate. She couldn't explain the feeling of being caught in a trap, but the sensation was strong in her mind. A part of her could not regret last night no matter how hard she tried. But another side of her warned that everything had happened much too quickly. It was so completely alien for her to catapult herself into a situation like that. She shook her head morosely, unable to comprehend her own emotions. Throwing herself into bed with a virtual stranger was one game she had never played.

There was no denying that the unfamiliar blend of emotions she had experienced around Adrian had taken her by surprise. In a way, it seemed almost logical, almost inevitable that they had culminated in last night's sensual conclusion. That sense of inevitability, however, was new and disturbing. What irony that Adrian had been worried about her playing games with him! Nothing had ever seemed less like a game than her own fierce response in his arms. Perhaps if it had seemed more like a game, she would be feeling far more comfortable this morning.

Of course, Sara decided caustically, she could always reassure herself that Adrian wasn't exactly a stranger. Hadn't Uncle Lowell apparently chosen him for her? Dear outrageous, unpredictable and not infrequently brilliant Uncle Lowell. The man should be dangled over hot coals for creating this mess.

Uncle Lowell.

Her uncle's name brought a dose of common sense. This whole mess had been precipitated by Lowell Kincaid. Where was he and when would he return?

Sara's brows were shaping a thoughtful line above her hazel eyes when she finally reached the inn on the outskirts of the small town. Her car was still waiting patiently for her in the parking lot. She hoped the inn management wasn't upset about her tardiness in picking up the vehicle. Digging into her pockets for the keys, Sara started forward.

She had her hand on the door handle, absently trying to identify the slip of paper she noticed resting on the front seat when the shock of Adrian's voice behind her spun her around.

"You can't just disappear into the mists, you know. Only fantasies can evaporate like that and you're not a fantasy any longer." The remark was made in a cool, conversational tone that completely belied the shimmering intensity of his gaze. He stood a few steps behind her, his hands thrust into the back pockets of his jeans. The familiar canvas shoes were on his feet and Sara dimly realized that he must have followed her for nearly a mile without making a sound in those shoes.

For an instant the unlikely combination of the easy tone and the fierce demand of the silver eyes caused Sara to feel as though she had somehow lost her balance. Her hand closed tightly around the door handle behind her as she steadied herself.

"I didn't realize you were behind me," she finally managed, pulling herself together quickly. It was ridiculous to let him throw her like this. "You should have said something."

"If you'd wanted company, you probably would have mentioned it before you decided to sneak out of the house."

She was taken back by the tightly reined emotion she sensed in his voice. Was it anger or pain? In that moment she couldn't be certain. But she knew she'd prefer that it was anger. Even in her uncertain state of mind this morning she realized that the last thing she wanted to do was hurt Adrian Saville. On the other hand there was such a thing as self-preservation. Sara acknowledged that she felt more than a little on the defensive.

"I didn't sneak out of the house. I simply went for a walk and decided to pick up my car while I was out. You're the one who was sneaking around! You and those sneaky shoes you wear!"

"The last time I let you go off by yourself you nearly disappeared, remember? It's my job to keep you out of trouble until your uncle gets back."

"Is that what you were doing last night?" she challenged, goaded by the accusing tone of his voice. "Keeping me out of trouble?"

"If we're going to talk about last night, let's do it somewhere else besides this damn parking lot," he growled. He stepped forward and closed his fingers around her upper àrm. "We can get a cup of coffee down at the wharf."

"Adrian," she began firmly, and then decided against an argument. Uneasily Sara acknowledged that she couldn't tell what he was thinking this morning. Nor could she be sure of the state of his emotions. Given the uncertainty in his mood and her own odd feelings, it seemed wisest to avoid an outright confrontation.

He led her down the hill from the inn to a pier that thrust out into the beautiful, sheltered cove that was called Eagle Harbor. A marina full of peacefully tethered boats of all shapes and sizes extended out from the pier. On the other side of the cove Sara could see private homes tucked away above the water's edge. At this early hour there were several people lounging on the rail, or working on their boats. Fishing rods and tackle were in evidence as folks came and went from the marina to the small wharf buildings. Near the entrance to the short pier a small shop featured coffee and fresh pastries. Adrian bought two containers of coffee to go and wordlessly handed one to Sara.

"Thank you," she murmured with exaggerated politeness.

He didn't bother to respond to her comment. Instead he seemed to be deep in thought as though he were struggling to find the right words. The idea that he was having trouble made Sara relax a bit. She had the impression Adrian was not accustomed to dealing with this morning's sort of situation. She was glad.

"I wasn't exactly going to disappear into the mists," she tried tentatively.

"No?" He sounded skeptical.

She shook her head, sipping at her coffee as they walked out onto the pier. "No. I only intended to pick up my car and drive it back to the house. If I'd been planning to duck out, I would have taken my suitcase. Or at the very least, my purse."

"Umm."

She slanted him a glance. "What is that supposed to mean?"

"That you've got a point," he said grudgingly. "I should have thought of it. I just figured you were so upset about last night that you raced out of the house without bothering to pack or say good-bye."

Sara focused on the far end of the pier. "I was upset about last night." She felt him examine her profile but she didn't turn her head to look at him.

"I rushed you into bed," he said finally.

"*We* rushed into bed," she corrected firmly.

"You're not going to let me take all the blame?"

"Do you want all the blame?"

Adrian took another sip of coffee. "No. I'd like to think you had a hand in the final decision. I don't have much interest in playing the role of seducer of unwilling females.''

The response that came to Sara's lips was cut off abruptly as a fisherman who had been unloading his morning's catch walked past with a bucket of water in which two fish swam lethargically. The man turned to wave to a comrade who hailed him from a nearby yacht. Quite suddenly he stumbled over a fishing-tackle box that someone had left on the pier. In the next instant the bucket of fish tilted precariously and one of the silvery, wriggling creatures fell out. It landed right in front of Adrian's foot and lay shuddering as it began to die.

''Whoooeee, look at that sucker!'' a young boy exclaimed excitedly.

''Must be six pounds if it's an ounce,'' another man said approvingly. ''Nice catch, Fred.''

The man named Fred grinned proudly as he caught his balance. ''Thanks, Sam. Thought I'd do 'er over a mesquite fire tonight. The wife's having the neighbors in for cards.''

Sara was aware of a familiar pang of regret at the sight of life going out of the fish. She understood about the food chain and that humans were inclined to be carnivores but she preferred her fish neatly filleted and packaged in plastic in a supermarket.

She glanced away from the fish before realizing that Adrian had come to a halt and was staring down at the creature that lay dying at his feet. There was no expression on his face. He simply stood silently watching the wriggling, flopping fish. The man who had caught it leaned forward to retrieve it.

Without stopping to think, Sara reached out and grabbed Adrian's wrist. He glanced up as she pulled him firmly around and led him toward the pier entrance. He followed her lead, not saying anything as they walked away from the sight of the now-dead fish.

"That sort of thing is hard enough on us supermarket carnivores," Sara heard herself say casually. "I imagine it's rather sickening for a vegetarian."

"Don't worry, I'm not going to be sick out here in public," he said dryly.

She cast him a quick, assessing glance. "No, you're not, are you?"

"I'm a realist, Sara. I don't eat meat but I understand how the world works," he said quietly.

"Yes, I suppose you do." She dropped his hand, feeling foolish at having made the vain effort to protect him.

"That doesn't mean I don't appreciate the thought," he told her softly.

"What thought?"

His mouth was edged with quiet amusement and a hint of satisfaction. "You were trying to shield me from a bit of reality back there. It was very—" he hesitated, hunting the word "—very compassionate of you."

"Forget it," she said sturdily. "Now about our plans for the immediate future..."

"Does this mean we've finished our discussion of the immediate past?" he inquired politely.

"There's nothing to talk about. We've both agreed that we were equally to blame for rushing into the situation." She straightened her shoulders. "We're adults and we should be able to analyze our actions and learn from our mistakes. We are stuck here together until my crazy uncle sees fit to get in touch, so we will have to conduct ourselves in an intelligent manner. Now, I suggest we both put last night behind us instead of trying to rehash it."

Adrian shrugged. "Suits me."

"I'm so glad," she muttered too sweetly.

"You weren't running away this morning?" he confirmed quietly.

"No, I was not running away. I just wanted a little time by myself. I felt as if I needed some fresh air."

He nodded and then said calmly. "I think I can understand that."

"Kind of you," she drawled.

"Just make damn sure you don't do it again."

A faint trickle of unease went through her at the cool way he spoke. "I beg your pardon?"

"I said, don't do it again."

They were back in the inn parking lot, approaching Sara's car. She had the keys in her hand but her mind was on his quiet command. "Adrian, one of the reasons I decided to get out of the corporate world is that I don't take orders well. We'll get along much better if you don't get carried away with your sense of responsibility."

"I hear you," he said agreeably.

"Good." She reached down to open the car door and slid into the front seat.

"Just don't go running off again without me," he concluded as he settled smoothly on the seat beside her. He held out his hand for the keys.

Sara felt goaded. "The next time I try it I'll be sure to look back over my shoulder to see if I'm being followed."

He lounged into the corner of the seat, never taking his eyes from her stormy gaze. "I thought we were going to act like adults about this."

She drew a deep breath, aware of feeling extremely childish. "Sorry," she mumbled. "You're right, of course. I should never have left the house alone this morning. I wasn't thinking. I was feeling rather, er, emotional. I assume you don't have that problem frequently yourself?"

He didn't smile at her sarcasm. "Wasn't I emotional enough for you last night?"

Sara felt a flush suffuse her face. "What you appeared to be feeling last night is often referred to by an entirely different name."

"Passion?"

"Try lust," she bit out.

"I thought we just got through agreeing that we're adults. If that's the case, then I think it's safe to say both of us know the difference between lust and..." He hesitated. "And other feelings."

She stared at him in silence for a long, troubled moment. She knew the difference, she thought. She just wasn't quite ready to admit that what she had felt last night went by a very dangerous name of its own. It was called love.

Instinctively Sara moved a bit farther over in her seat, seeking to put some distance between herself and Adrian. The car seemed filled with him, she thought. As she slid across the upholstery something crackled beneath her thigh. Belatedly she remembered the slip of paper she had noticed earlier on the car seat. Grateful for the minor distraction, she reached for it.

"You'll give me your word you won't take off alone again?" Adrian asked in a neutral tone as he switched on the ignition. He glanced at the paper in her hand as she unfolded it.

"Oh, I'm nothing if not cooperative."

"I appreciate it. What's that?" He put the car in gear, ignoring her sharp tone.

"I don't know. Just a piece of paper that was lying on the seat. I don't remember..." Sara's voice trailed off in stunned amazement as she read the short message she held.

Adrian frowned at her, his foot on the brake. "I said, what is it, Sara?"

"A problem. A very big problem." Mutely she held the typed message out to him.

Adrian stared at her wide eyes for a second longer before switching off the ignition again and reaching out to take the note from her hand.

It wasn't a long note. Sara had it memorized after reading it through twice.

The one-fifteen ferry to Seattle. Come alone.
You'll be safe.

"Well, hell," Adrian said thoughtfully.

TWO HOURS LATER he was still acting and sounding very thoughtful. It infuriated Sara because she had argued herself hoarse in the meantime. She no longer felt in the least thoughtful. She felt quite desperate in fact. For the hundredth time she paced to the far end of the living room and whipped around to glare at Adrian, who was lounging quietly on the sofa. He had one foot on the coffee table in front of him and was flipping through a magazine with absent attention.

"Listen to me, damn it!" Sara was sure her voice would give out at any moment. It seemed to her she had been yelling at him for hours. "I haven't got any choice! I have to be on board that ferry at one."

"You don't have to be anywhere at one." Adrian's responses had been quiet and reasonable for two solid hours. They were driving Sara up a wall. How could anyone remain quiet and reasonable and totally inflexible for two solid hours?

"How else are we going to discover what this is all about?"

"People who leave notes in cars are no doubt creative enough to think of alternatives when Plan A doesn't work." Adrian turned the page of his magazine. "Under the circumstances I think it would be better to make them resort to whatever it is they didn't want to do first. No sense letting them have the easiest option. Gives them an advantage."

"Adrian, I don't want to wait around for Plan B!"

"That's what the guy is probably counting on. Be patient, Sara."

Sara swung away, striding restlessly back to the other end of the room. Anger and nervous dread alternated relentlessly in her head. She was furious at Adrian's refusal to even consider letting her go alone on board the one-fifteen ferry. The nervousness was a growing fear that whatever her uncle was involved in was proving to be more than he would be able to handle. She braced a hand against the window frame and stared out at the stand of trees that guarded the drive.

"Uncle Lowell must be in very big trouble," she forced herself to say carefully.

"Or someone wants you to think he is."

"Since when are you the expert on how people such as that man Wolf think and operate?" she snapped. "You've only written one thriller, for heaven's sake. That hardly qualifies you as an authority on the real thing."

Adrian put down the magazine. "Sara, I'm only doing what your uncle asked me to do."

"I understand," she said, trying to be patient. "But you're taking his instructions much too literally. The situation calls for a little improvising. Something's gone wrong, don't you see?"

"No."

Her fingers closed into a futile fist and she leaned her forehead against the window. She was rigid with exasperation. "Adrian, please listen to me."

He came up behind her, moving soundlessly across the floor to rest his hands on her shoulders. "Honey, if I let you go on board that ferry by yourself, we wouldn't be exactly improvising. We'd be following someone else's plan. Surely you spent enough time playing corporate manager to know that following the opposition's game plan is usually not to your advantage."

"We've got to find out what he wants!"

"What he wants," Adrian said distinctly, "is to use you."

"We don't know that. Maybe he has news. Maybe he wants to give us some information. For heaven's sake, Adrian, whoever left that note might not even be what you call the 'opposition.' He might be a friend of my uncle's trying to get a message to me."

"Sara, your uncle has a strange sense of humor but I don't see him pulling a stunt like this."

"Whoever is going to be on that ferry is someone who knows something about Uncle Lowell. I'm going to find out who it is and what he knows." Sara lifted her head away from the window, aware of Adrian's fingers sinking heavily into her shoulders.

"Sara..."

She shook her head, tired of arguing, her mind made up. "No, Adrian. I'm through discussing the matter. I'm going to be on the ferry. Be reasonable. What can happen to me on the boat? It will be full of people commuting to Seattle. Whoever is going to meet me will be trapped on there, just as I will be until the ferry docks. He can hardly pull a gun and shoot me, can he? After all, he'd be stuck with the body until he gets to Seattle."

He turned her around beneath his hands, his face drawn and grim. "Sara, this isn't a game like corporate management or checkers. You can't handle it with your casual off-the-wall style. You don't know what you're getting into."

"I'm already into it," she pointed out stiffly. "And I can't stand the waiting, Adrian."

He searched her face. "I can force you to stay here."

"Not unless you tie me up and throw me in a closet," she retorted.

"That's a possibility."

"Don't be ridiculous!"

He dropped his hands to his sides and turned to walk back toward the sofa. "You can't go alone," he finally said flatly.

She frowned, trying to decide if she'd just won part of the battle. "But the note said—"

"Damn the note!" He glanced at her over his shoulder. "You can't go alone."

"Are you saying you're going to come with me?"

"If you're refusing to listen to my advice, then I don't have much choice, do I?" he asked, sounding bleakly resigned.

"Not unless you really do tie me up and throw me in a closet." Sara tried for a tremulous smile, hoping to lighten his mood now that she appeared to have won the confrontation.

Adrian just looked at her. "The temptation is almost overwhelming."

Sara let the smile fade abruptly. "You're not a good loser, Adrian."

"No. I never was."

She'd won half of the concessions she needed, Sara realized. It shouldn't be tough to get him to agree to the rest. The note had specified that she be on the ferry alone.

"I'm glad you've decided to be logical about this, Adrian," she began cautiously.

"I generally am logical and reasonable."

"Then you can understand why I have to go alone today."

"Forget it, Sara. I'm not that logical and reasonable. Try to get out of this house alone and you'll find me standing in the way. Think you can walk over me?"

At ten minutes to one, Sara was sitting beside Adrian as he drove down the ramp onto the ferry. The crowd was a small one for the afternoon crossing and they easily found seats in the main lounge. Scanning every face that went past her, Sara suddenly realized that her palms had grown damp around the strap of her shoulder bag. She wasn't accustomed to this kind of tension, she decided unhappily. Her body felt unnaturally alert, poised for the unknown. There had been no sign of the wolf-faced man in the ferry terminal.

"It's very stressful, isn't it?" she muttered to Adrian, who was sitting across from her in the booth they had chosen by a wide window.

"Very," he agreed wryly.

"You can jot down your feelings and put them in your next book," she suggested with false lightness. "It'll add a note of realism."

"I'll do that."

Sara twisted the shoulder strap. "What if he doesn't show because you're with me?"

"Frankly, I'll be relieved."

She glowered at him. "Are you going to drag this little incident out every time we quarrel in the future? Throw it at me and use it to illustrate how headstrong and foolish I am?"

"I doubt I'll need any additional evidence. You seem to provide enough on a day-to-day basis." He paused, thinking, and then asked interestedly, "Will we be doing it a lot?"

"Doing what?" she grumbled, watching people as they filed past to the snack counter.

"Quarreling."

"I hope not," she said feelingly. "It's wearing. I feel as though I've been through the wringer today and the main event hasn't even taken place."

"Umm."

The ferry moved out of its slip, beginning its crossing to Seattle. In the distance a giant freighter loaded with containers of cargo headed toward the bustling port of Seattle. Sea gulls hoping for tidbits kept pace with the ferry, wheeling and gliding alongside.

"You know, Adrian, there's something to be said for living in this area,'' Sara remarked wistfully. "It's beautiful country."

"Umm."

Sara was about to demand an explanation of his monosyllabic response when she caught sight of the man who was walking into the lounge from the outside deck. She went very still as she recognized the grimly handsome aquiline features. He looked at her down the length of the passenger lounge.

"Adrian," Sara whispered tightly, "it's him. The man who tried to grab me in the market."

With a casual movement that Sara couldn't help but

admire, Adrian turned calmly to stare at the hawk-faced man. He examined him in silence for a moment and then swung his gaze back to Sara. "Looks like he's going to go ahead with Plan A, even though some of the details have been changed."

"You mean the fact that you're with me?" She watched the stranger make his decision and walk firmly down the aisle of window seats. "If you want to know the truth, Adrian, I've changed my mind. I'm glad you're here. Very glad."

"It's always nice to be appreciated," he muttered just as the other man came to a halt beside Sara.

"Miss Frazer?" His voice was quiet and unruffled.

Sara swallowed, trying to keep her face unemotional. "Yes."

"I'm Brady Vaughn. I'd like to talk to you."

"We assumed that from the rather melodramatic note you left in her car," Adrian said before Sara could respond. "Why don't you sit down and tell us what this is all about."

Brady Vaughn coolly examined Adrian and then appeared to dismiss him. He returned his attention to Sara. "This concerns your uncle, Miss Frazer. It's a very private matter."

Sara stared up into the darkest eyes she had ever seen. The man was towering over her, and if Adrian hadn't been sitting quietly across from her, she would have felt terribly vulnerable. As it was she instinctively took her cue from Adrian and gestured at the seat beside her. "Whatever you have to say can be said in front of my friend. He is as concerned about my uncle as I am. Please sit down, Mr. Vaughn."

"For your own sake, Miss Frazer, I think the fewer people involved in this, the better."

"I'm already involved," Adrian growled softly. "Sit down, Vaughn, or leave us alone."

Sara held her breath as the tall man flicked another assessing glance at Adrian, who returned the look expressionlessly. Then the aquiline-faced Vaughn shrugged and sat down beside Sara. When he spoke he ignored Adrian.

"This is rather a long story, Miss Frazer."

"Perhaps you could summarize?" Adrian suggested easily. "We've got short attention spans."

Sara saw the flare of impatience in Vaughn's eyes. "Please, Mr. Vaughn. Tell us what's going on."

Vaughn rubbed the side of his jaw with an air of contemplation. Then he nodded slowly. "To put it simply, Lowell Kincaid is in trouble."

Sara caught her breath. "Do you know where my uncle is at the moment?"

"We think he's in Southeast Asia."

"Southeast Asia!" Sara glanced in astonishment at Adrian, who kept his gaze on Brady Vaughn. "What on earth would he be doing there?"

Vaughn sighed. "I told you this was a long story. The truth is it goes all the way back to the last days of the Vietnam war."

Sara went still. "Go on."

"Your uncle was working for the government in those days, Miss Frazer. He was assigned to the embassy in Saigon but he spent a lot of time in the countryside. He knew his way around South Vietnam as very few Americans did. He had friends in the oddest places." Vaughn looked a little pained. "If you remember the news reports, you'll recall that things were very chaotic toward the end. Panicked crowds from the city tried to overrun the embassy walls in Saigon. Everyone wanted a seat on one of the evacuation helicopters. Things were in turmoil. A lot of men such as your uncle had to play it by ear when some of the normal chains of command broke down.''

With a disturbing sense of déjà vu, Sara listened to the tale. She never once looked at Adrian to see how he was reacting. Something told her she should respond to Brady Vaughn as though she were hearing the story for the first time. Not as if she had read the nucleus of it in a manuscript called *Phantom*.

''There was a lot of valuable material that had to be salvaged during the U.S. evacuation of the country,'' Vaughn was saying quietly. ''Some of it was taken out by helicopter but some of it was sent out through less obvious routes. Your uncle was in charge of handling a particularly valuable shipment. He was to take it across a border. To be blunt, Kincaid reached his rendezvous point in Cambodia but the shipment he was assigned to safeguard never made it.''

''I see.'' Sara's throat felt constricted.

Vaughn looked at her with a cold, even glance. ''We think he's decided to go back and bring out the shipment he left behind, Miss Frazer.''

''Who's 'we'?'' Adrian inquired politely.

Vaughn frowned. ''The people for whom Kincaid used to work.''

''The government?'' Sara pressed.

Vaughn inhaled slowly. ''Yes and no.''

''That's a little vague, isn't it?'' Sara asked tartly.

Vaughn's handsome features twisted ruefully. ''I should make it clear, Miss Frazer, that while I have ties to the same agency for which your uncle worked, this is something of a personal matter for me. I am not representing the government in this.''

"You want that shipment for yourself?" Adrian drawled.

Vaughn shook his head tiredly. "There's no chance of getting that shipment out of Southeast Asia. Kincaid will only get himself killed trying. I'd like to prevent that. Your uncle and I go back a long way together, Miss Frazer. I owe him. He was my friend."

"Who would kill him if he went back?" Sara whispered.

"The story of that lost shipment of, uh, material, is not exactly a secret, Miss Frazer. There have been rumors and speculation for years. A couple of very dangerous people are aware of its existence and of the fact that only your uncle knows where it is. They've dropped out of sight since Lowell Kincaid did. I have reason to believe they've gone after him. I want to get to Kincaid before those others do."

"And just where do I fit into all this?" Sara demanded urgently.

"Your uncle is a very independent man. Especially now when he no longer has any ties to his former employers. He probably won't listen to me but I think he might listen to you. I want you to come with me, Miss Frazer."

"Come with you where?" she asked dazedly.

Vaughn slid a speculative glance at Adrian and then refocused intently on Sara. "I'd rather not say our destination. But it will be in Southeast Asia. There are ways of getting a message to your uncle once we're in contact with certain local people."

"I don't have a passport," she heard herself say.

"That detail can be handled. Leave it to me."

Adrian stepped in, his voice remote and restrained. "She needs time to think it over, Vaughn."

"How much time?" Vaughn kept his gaze on Sara. "We haven't got a lot to spare."

"Forty-eight hours," Adrian answered for her.

Sara glanced at him and once again instinct made her follow his lead. "Forty-eight hours, Mr. Vaughn. Please. I have to think about this."

Brady Vaughn got to his feet. The Seattle waterfront was rapidly filling the horizon. He touched Sara lightly on the shoulder. "Forty-eight hours, Miss Frazer. For Kincaid's sake, please don't take any longer." He turned and walked away.

Sara sat staring at Adrian as the ferry bumped gently into the dock. She ran her damp palm over her shoulder where Brady Vaughn had touched her. "Does it feel as if it's gotten colder in here?" she asked vaguely.

Chapter Seven

Sara concentrated on another bite of the chocolate-chip ice cream she was eating as she strolled along the Seattle waterfront. Beside her Adrian neatly devoured the pecan-flavored cone he had chosen. The ferry wouldn't be leaving for another half hour. It had been Adrian who had suggested they take a walk on the picturesque wharf before they caught the boat. Neither had said much until after they bought the ice cream at one of the many fast-food stalls that dotted the wharf.

Sara knew the reason for her silence was probably the same as Adrian's. They were both lost in contemplation of the scene on the ferry with the man who called himself Brady Vaughn. Finally Sara polished off the last of her cone and flipped the napkin into a trash container outside the entrance to the aquarium.

"You know what I think?" she announced, thrusting her hands into her pockets.

"What?" Adrian seemed fascinated with his disappearing ice cream.

"I think that legend Uncle Lowell told you about the gold is not pure fiction."

"Brilliant deduction."

She slanted him a disgusted glance. "Either it's for real or else—"

"Or else other people such as Brady Vaughn believe it's for real, which amounts to the same thing," he concluded grimly.

"Know what else I think?" Sara went on determinedly.

"Let me guess. Your uncle's idea of the perfect wedding gift is a cache of gold buried somewhere in Southeast Asia." Adrian swore softly.

Sara sighed. "He always did like gold. Said it was the only real hedge against an uncertain world. I can imagine him thinking gold would be the perfect present for me. Whenever he's given me a gift, it's usually been made out of gold." She extended her wrist briefly, displaying the thin gold chain. "And he did say something about going off to protect our, uh, wedding gift."

"Does chronic idiocy run in your family?"

"My uncle is not an idiot!"

"I know," Adrian agreed derisively. "He just has a bizarre sense of humor. You'd think I'd realize that by now."

Aware of Adrian's irritation, Sara felt obliged to turn the conversation away from a defense of Lowell Kincaid's odd actions. There would be time enough to defend her uncle later. With any luck he would return to take up his own defense. Heaven knew it had always been a little tricky making excuses for him. Sara decided to go on the offensive.

"Are you quite certain that Uncle Lowell didn't say anything about that legend being for real when he told you the story?" she demanded.

"He told me it was only a tale. There are others like it that came out of the war, you know. I turned up a lot of them while doing research for *Phantom*. It certainly isn't unique."

"Really?" Momentarily distracted, Sara stared up at him, her eyes widening. "Tell me some of them."

Adrian lifted one shoulder in a heedless shrug and tossed away the end of his cone. A trolley car designed to carry tourists from one end of the waterfront to the other clanged past along tracks that paralleled the street. Adrian didn't speak until the sound of the whistle had faded. "Well, there's a story about the CIA agent assigned to destroy vital documents in the hours before the embassy was overrun."

"And?" Sara prompted.

"According to the legend he kept some of the more interesting ones, such as a list of agents and their covers operating in Asia. Then he tried to hold an auction."

"He was going to sell the list to the highest bidder?"

"That was the plan, I gather."

"Did he?" she demanded interestedly. "Hold the auction, I mean?"

"Sara, it's just a legend. How should I know what happened?"

"Oh." Disappointed, Sara pushed for more information. "What other tales did you hear?"

"Leftover legends from that particular war?" Adrian's heavy brows came together in thought. "I think there was a story or two about businessmen who were supposedly hired by the U.S. government to supervise construction projects in Saigon and the surrounding area. Apparently they used their visits to South Vietnam to establish heroin connections that continued long after the war ended, making them very rich men. Then there are the tales of gold deals made in the north. The list of such stories is endless, Sara. Wars breed them. Just think of all the stories and legends that came out of World War II. People still write novels based on them."

"I see what you mean. So when Uncle Lowell told you the story of the gold, you assumed it was just that: a story."

"Umm." Adrian appeared lost in thought. "It still might be just that."

"I don't know," Sara mused. "I can see Uncle Lowell doing something like this—hiding a cache of gold in a bizarre location and then telling me it's supposed to be my wedding gift."

"*Our* wedding gift," Adrian corrected. "Don't forget he gave me the story first."

Sara ignored that. "What I can't see is him stealing the gold in the first place."

"We don't know that he did. At this point all we've got is Vaughn's version of things."

Sara shivered. "Creepy guy, isn't he?"

Adrian looked at her with a wry expression. "That's one way of putting it."

Sara came to a halt and leaned over the railing to stare out across Elliott Bay. Several long piers on either side of her, many full of import shops and souvenir stands, poked fingerlike out into the water. Around her, children ate popcorn and other assorted goodies while their parents browsed around the shops and enjoyed the sun. Another large ship was making its way into port flanked by tugs. Its deck was stacked high with containerized cargo. The ship carried a strange name and a foreign flag. A sailing yacht skirted the tip of a pier, seeking a place to tie up so that its passengers could come ashore for a meal at one of the many restaurants featuring fish. The sight of all the seagoing traffic made Sara think of places she had never been to and which, under normal circumstances, she would probably never go to, places that had bloody histories stretching back a thousand years.

"Have you ever been to Southeast Asia, Adrian?"

There was silence for a moment and then Adrian moved to lounge against the rail beside her, his eyes following her gaze. "Why do you ask?"

"Just curious. I was wondering what it's like."

"You're not going to find out in the company of Brady Vaughn," he told her roughly.

Her head came around, her face mirroring her serious mood. "I may not have a choice, Adrian."

His fingers tightened on the railing. "You think I'm going to let you get on a plane with him forty-eight hours from now?"

Sara moved restlessly, not quite certain how to handle the harshness in him. "That reminds me," she said, not answering his question. "What made you think of asking for a couple of days' leeway?"

"I didn't ask."

"That's right." She nodded, remembering. "You just told him that we were going to take that much time, didn't you? That was very quick thinking, Adrian."

"I try," he murmured sardonically.

She frowned. "Maybe writing thrillers helps you think fast on your feet in situations such as this."

"I was sitting down at the time."

She peered suspiciously at his profile, wondering if he'd actually attempted a small joke. "Well, I'm just glad you were there. I'm not sure that he wouldn't have been able to pressure me into going with him if I'd been alone."

"You're not accustomed to dealing with people like him. They can be very convincing, especially when they're using the fate of someone you love as bait."

"You really think Vaughn is lying?"

"There's a hell of a lot we don't know about this mess, Sara."

She was silent for another moment or two as she turned things over in her mind. "He must be who he says he is, Adrian."

"Who? Vaughn? What makes you think he's telling the truth?"

"Well, there was that business about being able to get me a passport on two days' notice, for one thing. I mean, no one but a real government agent could accomplish that."

"Money and the right connections can buy just about anything in this world."

"Oh, yeah?" She was beginning to resent his calm, cynical superiority. "And just where would someone like Vaughn go to buy a fake passport?"

There was a slight pause and then Adrian said quietly, "He might try Mexico City."

"Mexico City!"

"Umm. It's huge, Sara. One of the largest metropolitan areas in the world. Here in the western hemisphere it's one of the places frequented by a certain kind of 'in crowd.' A man can shop for anything, including a fake passport. He can also get lost there and reappear on the other side of the globe without bothering to answer a lot of inconvenient questions."

She stared at him. "More lore you've picked up from writing thrillers?"

Adrian watched the sailing yacht make another pass along the piers. "Legends and tales, honey. A writer of thrillers collects them."

"Which is probably why Uncle Lowell couldn't resist feeding you that story of the gold."

"Probably. Lowell knows a sucker when he sees one."

"Well, we'll deal with him later," Sara vowed. "In the meantime, we have to deal with Vaughn."

"Sara, we can't trust that guy one quarter of an inch," Adrian said evenly. "You said yourself he's a, uh, creep."

"But he knows where Uncle Lowell is," she protested.

"He *says* he knows where he is. But if we go on the assumption that we can't trust Vaughn, we have to assume we can't trust anything he tells us, right?"

"It's very confusing, isn't it?" she groaned. "And in the meantime Uncle Lowell could be in real trouble."

"I think we're the ones in real trouble, thanks to good old Uncle Lowell," Adrian said, pushing himself away from the rail. "Come on, honey. The ferry will be leaving soon. We'd better get going."

"Forty-eight hours isn't a very long time, Adrian."

"I know."

"What if my uncle doesn't get in touch before the deadline?"

"I didn't set the deadline because I hoped Lowell would have sense enough to contact us. I set it to give myself some time."

Sara glanced at him in astonishment. "Time to do what?"

Adrian wasn't looking at her. He appeared to be concentrating on the brightly dressed crowds of casual strollers who were ambling along the waterfront. "Sara, I'm going to leave you alone for a while tomorrow." He spoke slowly, as though measuring each word.

"Why?" she demanded, utterly startled.

He hesitated. "There's something I want to check out. A man I want to see."

"Are you going to try contacting that government agency my uncle used to work for?" she demanded.

"No. I'm not sure we could trust any answers we got from that source," he told her honestly. "Look who we're dealing with from that department now."

She wrinkled her nose. "Vaughn. I see what you mean. So who are you going to contact?"

"Somebody who may know for certain whether or not Lowell really is in Southeast Asia."

"But if we don't know it for certain, who would?"

"Sara..." Adrian reached out and threaded his fingers through hers. His tone was low and urgent. "Sara, would you please not ask any more questions? Your uncle and I have talked a great deal during the past year. He's told me things I don't think he's told anyone else."

"But, Adrian..."

"Please, Sara. Just trust me, okay?"

She wanted to scream that no, it was not okay. She wanted to tell him it had nothing to do with trust, that she simply deserved some explanations. Sara was infuriated and frightened and she felt like lashing out but she realized with an instinct that went to the bone that it wouldn't do any good. Her uncle had apparently shared some confidence with Adrian that neither of them had seen fit to share with her. Adrian would not tell her anything else at this point. She was certain of it.

"If you've known someone we could contact all along, why haven't you already done it?" she asked in a carefully controlled voice.

"Because your uncle wouldn't want me doing it unless I thought we had a full-fledged crisis on our hands. Up until now I've been going by what he said in that taped message."

"You've been assuming he could handle his 'old business.'"

"Yes."

Sara pulled her hand free from his, putting a small distance between them. "All right. There's not much I can say if you won't tell me what's going on. Go ahead and contact whoever it is you think can give us some information."

"You're angry, aren't you?"

"I'm feeling a little annoyed at the moment, yes," she bit out. "I don't like being kept in the dark."

"I'm sorry, Sara," he began but she cut him off.

"Forget it. Just don't ever again accuse me of playing games. You're turning out to be a real pro at the art."

That stilled him for a moment. He said nothing until they were back at the ferry terminal and walking on board the boat. Then Adrian told her the rest of his decision. "It will take me most of tomorrow to do what I have to do. You'll be alone at the house."

Sara threw herself down on a seat, her arms folded across her breasts in cool disgust. "Why? Or is that part of the game?"

He sat down beside her, his hands clasped loosely in front of him. He studied his linked fingers. "I'm not playing games, Sara. I have to leave you alone because I wouldn't dare risk using the phone to contact your uncle's friend, even if I thought I could get through to him."

She watched his profile through suddenly narrowed eyes. "You think the phone's tapped?"

"After meeting Vaughn, I'd say we have to assume the worst, wouldn't you?"

"Probably. What do you mean, you aren't sure you could reach this man on the phone even if you did dare use it?"

"From what your uncle says, this guy isn't the sort who trusts people over the phone. I'll have to see him in person."

"Where is he?"

"Not far," Adrian answered evasively. "I can catch a plane and reach him in a few hours. I'll leave as soon as I can book a flight in the morning. I should be home by late tomorrow afternoon."

"And in the meantime I just sit patiently waiting, is that it?" Sara muttered.

"Sara, you'll be safe in the house," he told her quietly.

"I'd rather go with you."

He shook his head, staring down at his clasped hands.

"Can't you at least tell me why I can't accompany you?"

"Sara, please—"

She interrupted whatever it was he intended to say with an exclamation of impatience. "Forget I asked."

They were politely remote with each other for the rest of the day. They walked up the street from the ferry docks and into Winslow so that Adrian could make his plane reservations at a pay phone. Sara was too proud even to attempt to overhear his conversation with the airline clerk. Later she berated herself for not having tried to eavesdrop. At least she could have found out where he was going. When he rejoined her to walk back to the cottage, she asked only if everything was settled.

"I can't get a flight out until nearly seven tomorrow morning."

"I see."

"That means I'll have to take the first morning ferry to Seattle."

"Yes."

His mouth thinned as he listened to her aloof responses. "Sara, there's one thing I want to make very clear."

"That would be a change."

He ignored that. "You're not to leave the house for any reason after I've gone."

"I understand." She didn't look at him, her gaze fixed stonily ahead.

"Good. You're safe in the house after I've set the alarms. No one can get in unless he decides to use explosives."

"What a pleasant thought."

"Don't worry about it," Adrian said dryly. "Just give me your word of honor you won't leave the house until I get back."

"Or until Uncle Lowell gets back," she amended smoothly.

He nodded. "Promise?"

She wondered briefly what would happen if she didn't promise and decided not to push the matter. "All right. Word of honor."

"I swear I'll return within a few hours, Sara. I'll be back on the five-fifty-five ferry."

"I believe you."

"Then can't you stop giving me the ice treatment for a while?" he asked gently.

"Speaking of cold," she drawled slowly.

He gave her a sharp glance as they walked down the drive and opened the door of the house. "Is that your imagination I hear cranking up again?"

"I think Vaughn might really be the one they called Wolf," Sara told him in a low voice. "It would make sense, wouldn't it? He was once very close to my uncle, so he might know about the gold."

"There's no sense speculating about it, Sara."

"Why not? Maybe if we speculate long enough and hard enough, we'll come up with some answers."

"Not on that subject." He stood in the hall for a moment, listening. Then he ushered her inside.

"Just think, Adrian. That creep is probably the renegade. Uncle Lowell might have gone to Southeast Asia thinking he could hunt him down and remove him before he got the gold."

"Sara, all we've got at the moment are a lot of questions. Not answers."

"But why would Vaughn be hanging around here if he was after Uncle Lowell's gold?"

"How the hell should I know?" Adrian stalked into the kitchen and put a kettle of water on the stove.

Sara trailed after him. "Adrian, I think we're missing something. Something crucial."

"Like your uncle?" he suggested bluntly.

"I mean a clue!" she gritted. "Listen to me, Adrian. Let's assume Uncle Lowell really does have some connection with that gold and that he had some fantastic notion of giving it to us as a . . . a wedding gift."

Adrian leaned against the stove waiting for the water to boil. He crossed his arms on his chest and eyed Sara deliberately. "All right, for the sake of argument, let's assume it. Now what?"

Sara tried to construct her thoughts into a logical sequence. Frowning intently, she began to pace the kitchen. "Okay, he knows where that gold is but he hasn't made any attempt to date to retrieve it. At least no attempt that we know of. In that taped message he didn't say he was going to *fetch* our wedding gift. He only said he was going to *protect* it."

"True." Adrian watched her closely.

"Now if he suddenly decided he had to protect it for

us, it must be because he got word that someone was out to steal it. We have to assume that very few people would even know for certain that the tale was anything more than a legend. The most logical person my uncle might have confided in besides you or me is his ex-protégé."

"We're back to Wolfie?"

"This is not a joke!" she hissed.

Adrian exhaled heavily and turned around to pour the boiling water into two cups. "I know. Go on."

She glared at his broad shoulders. "Not only is Wolf or Vaughn or whoever he is the one man who might know about that gold and might even know its approximate location but we have the evidence that Uncle Lowell was definitely thinking about him before he left for parts unknown."

"You mean that sketch on my manuscript. Sara, that's pretty damn slim evidence."

She shook her head. "I don't think so. I think it means that the man called Wolf was on Uncle Lowell's mind recently and that could easily be because he had reason to fear the guy was going to make a move on the gold. Something or someone we don't even know might have tipped him off. Who knows how many mysterious contacts my uncle has left around the world? You yourself are going to try to find one of them tomorrow!" She flung her hands outward in a sweeping gesture. "Don't you see? Uncle Lowell is trying to protect our so-called wedding gift from the one man who might be able to steal it."

"Then what's Vaughn doing hanging around the Northwest?" Adrian asked logically. "Why isn't he in Southeast Asia?"

"Because he doesn't know where exactly in Southeast

Asia the gold is hidden. No one knows except Uncle
Lowell. Vaughn is probably looking for my uncle. Maybe he thinks he can use me somehow." Sara nibbled on
her lower lip while she considered that. "My uncle has
dropped out of sight. He told the neighbor he'd gone
hunting. Guess who the quarry is?"

"Wolfman?" Adrian asked mockingly.

"Go ahead and laugh if you want, but I think I'm getting a handle on this."

"I'm not laughing at you, Sara." Adrian handed her
a cup of tea. "You may be right for all I know. But I
think the first thing to establish is whether or not your
uncle is where Vaughn says he is. And I only know one
way to do that."

"Find that man whom Uncle Lowell mentioned. I
know. I'm not going to argue with you any more on that
score, Adrian. I can see your mind is made up," she said
wearily.

It was over a rather strained dinner a couple of hours
later that Adrian brought up the subject again. Sara was
poking idly at the roasted red pepper salad she had
made when, after a long silence, Adrian spoke.

"There's one other thing," he began thoughtfully.

She glanced up. "What's that?"

"Lowell told me the story of the gold for a reason. He
knows it forms the kernel of the plot in *Phantom*."

"That's right." Sara set down her fork.

"If you're right about the wedding gift being that
cache of gold, then what he was really doing was—"

"Giving you the first clues about what your wedding
gift actually was and where it was located," Sara finished on a note of excitement. "I can see him doing
something like that."

"So can I. Damn it, I may pound the man into the

ground if and when he finally does show up," Adrian growled. "He knows I don't like games."

THE SPARSE CONVERSATION AT DINNER faded into a very long silence by mid-evening. The strain in the atmosphere grew stronger as bedtime approached. Adrian watched the clock move slowly toward ten and knew from the remote expression in Sara's eyes that he would be sleeping alone tonight.

He'd been expecting to find himself in a cold bed, of course, ever since he'd awakened that morning and realized that for Sara everything was happening much too quickly. She had a right to some time to adjust to the idea of having him as a lover. After all, she didn't have all those months of fleshing out a fantasy that he'd had. He was too much of a stranger yet, too much of an unknown quantity.

Adrian inclined his head politely when she excused herself and disappeared down the hall to her own room shortly after ten. He sat in his chair, legs stretched out in front of him, and repeated the admonitions he'd been giving himself all evening.

Not enough time.

Too much of a stranger.

Too many other problems at the moment. Big problems.

And she was mad as hell because he wouldn't take her with him tomorrow.

All in all, a formidable list, he thought wryly. But the logic and the rationalizations didn't seem to be making much of an impact on the pulsing desire that was going to keep him awake tonight.

He thought about what he had to do in the morning and told himself that he needed sleep, not a night spent brooding in an armchair. He'd already had enough of those during the past year.

No doubt about it. He needed sleep; he could do without the brooding and he had no right at all to go to Sara's room. All three things were perfectly clear and logical in his head. But, as he'd learned the hard way, clear logic didn't always chase away the shadows of emotions. Adrian wondered briefly at that. Emotions were odd things. There had been a time when others had sworn he didn't have any. Adrian knew better.

Slowly he got to his feet and began a silent tour of the house. Sara would be safe here. The house could keep out intruders. And he would be back for her as soon as possible. Quietly he checked and double-checked the hidden alarms and the exotic barriers Kincaid had helped him install. Lowell, with his skillful hands and his crafty, convoluted mind. *Where are you tonight, my friend?*

His soft-soled shoes making no sound on the hardwood floor, Adrian walked from one checkpoint to another, reassuring himself that the gift from Lowell Kincaid would be safe. Keeping Sara secure was the most important priority in his world, Adrian realized. It was a strange feeling to accept such total responsibility for another human being. Almost primitive in a way. He considered just how completely she had infiltrated his thoughts and then he headed down the hall toward his bedroom.

He would not pause in front of Sara's door. He would not listen for a moment to see if she was restless in her bed. He would not stand in the hall and let himself think about what she would do if he opened her door. He was a disciplined man and he could deal with his body's hungers.

It was the hunger in his mind he wasn't sure about, Adrian admitted as he approached Sara's closed door. How did you discipline the need for another person? Especially when you'd spent a lifetime not really needing anyone?

His steps slowed in spite of all the logic and discipline, and Adrian was vaguely aware of his hand curling tightly against his thigh. She would be asleep by now.

Sara lay very still in the wide bed, her hair fanned out on the pillow, and watched the shifting light under her door. She couldn't hear him but she knew he was standing there. She sensed the tension in her body and realized she was waiting for the door to open. She'd been lying there waiting for it since the moment she'd turned out the light and climbed into bed.

Because, Sara thought grimly, there was no way she could allow him to leave in the morning without letting him know that he had a right to be in her bed tonight.

The knowledge was sure and complete in her mind. She couldn't account for the certainty, but it was there.

Sara threw back the covers and sat up on the edge of the bed. She was reaching for her robe when the door of her room opened soundlessly. Adrian stood framed in the doorway, his face in deep shadow. Sara's fingers froze around the fabric of the robe as she looked up at him.

"You're not asleep." His voice was low and gritty; the words a statement, not a question.

"Neither are you." Sara let the robe drop from her hand. The wave of longing that swept through her was startling in its intensity. She was afraid that if she tried to stand up she wouldn't have the strength.

"You should have been asleep," he told her very seriously.

"Should I?"

"It would have made things...easier." He didn't move in the doorway.

"Easier for whom?"

"For me."

Sara drew a deep breath. "But not for me," she whispered, and held out her hand in an ancient gesture of feminine invitation.

"Sara?" Adrian's voice was raw with the question.

"Come to bed, Adrian. Please."

He hesitated for a timeless moment. Then he moved forward in a dark, silent glide that swept her up and bore her back onto the bed.

"Adrian..."

"Hush, Sara. There's no way on earth I could let you change your mind now." He was sprawling heavily on top of her, his hands pinning her passionately against the pillows as he sought her mouth with his own.

She wanted to tell him that she had no intention of changing her mind, that she wanted him, needed him, that she had never felt like this about a man before in her life. But the words seemed to be locked in her throat as he began to make love to her.

Adrian pushed the canvas shoes off his feet without even bothering to sit up on the bed. Sara heard them thud softly to the floor. She felt him fumble with the fastening of his jeans and then the buttons of his shirt. And all the while he kept her achingly close to him, deliciously trapped under his strength.

"I told myself I shouldn't stop at your door," he grated as he kicked his clothing to the floor.

Sara's head moved from one side to the other on the pillow. "No, this is where you belong." She circled his neck with her arms, pulling him close.

"Sara, my sweet Sara." He tugged at the nightgown, pushing it off her shoulders and down to her waist. Flattening the palms of his hands across her breasts, he grazed her nipples with a rasping, tantalizing touch that brought them to taut peaks.

Sara uttered a soft sigh into his mouth and dared him with the tip of her tongue. He responded instantly, thrusting deeply behind her teeth. She traced the contours of his sleek back with her fingertips until he groaned heavily.

Lifting himself for an instant, Adrian pulled the nightgown down over her hips and let the garment fall to the floor beside his jeans. Then he came back down beside her and Sara felt the demanding hardness of him against her thigh. She could feel the almost violently taut need in him and her own body reacted to it with fierce awareness.

Slowly, with deliberately provocative strokes, Adrian caressed her. His fingers played an enticing game on the inside of her leg until Sara thought she would go out of her mind with excitement. When he moved his hand upward, she cried out against his mouth.

Then she was struggling passionately to return the heady thrill and the throbbing anticipation. She slid her hand down his back to the slope of his thigh, feeling the crisp curling hair. Then she explored him more and more intimately until she cupped the heavy evidence of his desire.

"Sara, you're driving me wild," he groaned out.

"Yes, please," she whispered breathlessly.

"Sara, are you sure?"

"I've never been more certain of anything in my life." She used her nails with excruciating delicacy, and he muttered something soft and savage against her throat.

"Adrian?"

"I couldn't stop now if all the forces in hell got in the way," he said, and then he was parting her legs with his own, sliding toward her warmth until he was only a pulse beat away from possessing her completely.

Sara whispered his name again and again, lifting herself with undisguised longing.

"That's it, sweetheart. Give yourself to me. Just give yourself to me. I need you so."

She gasped as he entered her, the shock of his passionate invasion ricocheting through her whole system. Then she tightened her arms and legs around him, wrapping him as close as possible.

Lost in the embrace, Adrian knew only that he wanted Sara to cling to him forever. There was nothing else besides this shattering moment and Adrian seized it with all of his strength. There would be time enough tomorrow to wonder at the intensity of her need, time enough to worry that she was only reacting to the drama of the situation, time enough to reconsider the wisdom of letting himself be swept up in her hot, damp warmth. There was always time enough to regret the past. But he was living for the moment tonight, he told himself, and for this hour he would revel in it. He would allow himself to believe it was all for real.

When he felt the telltale tightening of her body, it precipitated an echo in his own. For an instant he forced himself to raise his head so that he could watch her face during the fiery release. He had a few seconds to wonder at the compelling possessiveness he felt for the woman in his arms and then he was trapped in the vortex of their combined desire. It swept them both to a violent, throbbing climax, left them hanging for a sweet moment and then slowly, slowly ebbed.

The moment in which he had been living was already

becoming the past, Adrian thought distantly as he lay be-side Sara. Soon the morning would arrive and with it another slice of the past. Perhaps there was some sense of balance in nature. Perhaps one piece of the past could offset another. He would have the memory of Sara's warmth tonight to carry with him as a talisman against the chill of tomorrow.

She stirred in his arms. "Adrian?"

"I'm here, Sara."

"Good," she murmured drowsily. "See that you're here tomorrow night, too."

When tomorrow night comes will you really want me here, my darling Sara, he wondered silently.

HE LEFT AT DAWN and Sara was at the door to watch him go. She had awakened the instant he did, her senses aware of his every movement. He'd lain quietly for a long moment looking down into her face and then he'd brushed his lips lightly against hers. Words flooded his head but he couldn't find a way to say them aloud. There wasn't time now to say the things that should be said. Perhaps it was better this way.

Pushing aside the covers, he'd climbed out of bed and headed for the bath. Without a word she'd fixed coffee for him while he dressed and then she'd stood on tiptoe to kiss him good-bye.

"Be careful, Adrian. Please be careful."

"Hey, I'm only going to talk to a friend of your un-cle's," he protested gently. He was afraid of the intensity he saw in her gaze. He liked it better when she was laughing up at him with her eyes or watching him with passion. Adrian realized just how much he had come to value the impulsive warmth that was so much a part of Sara. Life would be very cold without it. "I'll be home by sundown."

"Yes." She didn't argue.

"You won't leave the house," he said again, making it an order.

She shook her head. "Not unless you or Uncle Lowell tell me to leave the house," she answered obediently.

"Sara..." He hesitated on the porch, turning back to her one last time.

"Just hurry, Adrian. I'll be here when you return."

He looked at her, nodded once and left without glancing back again.

Chapter Eight

The house seemed incredibly lonely after Adrian left. Sara wandered around from room to room, wondering if doing a little housecleaning might help her deal with the strange mood in which she found herself. The thought brought to mind the question of who actually did Adrian's housecleaning. Something told her he probably took care of the chores himself. Certainly no one had been in during the few days she had known him to sweep the hardwood floors or dust. But everything seemed orderly and reasonably clean. Keeping his environment neat and precise was undoubtedly a part of his nature. It fit with what she knew of his preference for being in control of his world.

Sara wondered if Adrian had ever felt out of control. When had the need to be in command of everything around him come into existence? Perhaps he had been born that way. Or perhaps something in his past had made him so cautious and controlled. Surely the average person didn't install the kind of sophisticated electronic gadgetry that protected this house unless some event had instilled a raging desire for security. Adrian was definitely not the type of man to let his imagination make him paranoid. He must have his reasons for his self-control and the controls he had imposed on his surroundings. The only time she sensed that he slipped his own leash was when he made love to her.

The images engraved on her mind from the previous night rose to warm her now. She remembered the passion and intensity of the man who had held her. And she recalled her own ungoverned responses.

She drifted into the library and drew a finger along the top shelf of the bookcase. There was a smudge on her hand afterward but nothing really terrible. Just a normal amount of dust. The kind she herself collected on the top shelf of her bookcase. The kind people living alone tended to collect. She wondered how long Adrian had lived alone. Most of his life, apparently.

Finding the thought depressing, she turned away from the bookcase and walked over to his desk. Having been through it once, she felt there was no point amusing herself by browsing through it again. She sat down in the swivel chair and remembered the way Adrian had caught her here a few nights ago. She hadn't heard his approach, she recalled. You hardly ever heard the man. He moved very quietly in those well-worn sneakers.

A shaft of morning light caught the crystal-and-gold apple, making the trapped bubbles come alive for a moment. Sara leaned forward and studied the shimmering effect. She liked the notion of Adrian having sat here at his desk for months, the apple in front of him, while he worked. How many times had he glanced up idly and found himself studying the apple? Perhaps as many times as she had.

But she hadn't known there was a duplicate crystal apple in existence, Sara reminded herself. While Adrian had known all along that there was another apple and that someday he would encounter its owner. She wondered what he had expected her to be like. What picture had her uncle sketched for him? It was suddenly very important to Sara that Adrian had found his gift satisfactory. She wanted to be sure he would return to collect it this evening.

"Adrian," she whispered aloud, "remember what I said about taking care of yourself. I don't think I should have let you go alone." As if she'd had a choice.

Uneasily Sara stood up and walked slowly back out of the study. She'd make herself another cup of coffee and see if she couldn't find something to read. It was going to be a very long day.

She was pouring the coffee when she realized that what she wanted to read was *Phantom*. Perhaps if she went through it a second time, this time knowing her uncle had deliberately been planting information, she might pick up something useful. Digging the manuscript out of her suitcase, she carried it back to Adrian's study and sat down to read it with the cup of coffee at her elbow.

She wrinkled her nose at the sketch of the wolf on the first page and then deliberately set herself to go through the manuscript with an alert eye. There must be something in it. Didn't Lowell believe in hiding things in plain view? He certainly had doodled a great deal on the pages. But then, that was standard operating procedure for Lowell Kincaid whenever he found himself with a pencil in hand and a sheet of paper nearby. The man should have been an artist instead of a secret agent.

Just as had happened the first time through *Phantom*, Sara once again found herself caught up not in the intricacies of the plot but in the hero's pain and savage determination to survive. The feelings of protectiveness she had experienced the first time she read it returned anew. She longed to comfort the hero even as she told herself that only he could endure his own survival both emotionally and physically. In the end she knew she would again be left wanting to know for certain that there really was going to be a happy ending. And once more the question of how much of Adrian existed in the guise of *Phantom* returned to haunt her. This was a first novel. Somewhere she had read that they tended to be the most autobiographical.

Sara was into chapter three when the phone on the desk rang shrilly. The unexpected sound startled her. In the time she had been staying at Adrian's home, the thing had never rung. She hesitated a few seconds before reaching out to pick up the receiver. Then the thought that it might be Adrian calling for some reason made her fumble with the instrument.

"Hello?"

"Sara."

"Uncle Lowell!" Sara sat stunned as she heard her uncle's distinctive growl of a voice. "Uncle Lowell, where are you? I've been absolutely frantic. This whole thing is—"

"Sara, don't talk, just listen to me," Lowell Kincaid said quickly. "Come back to my place as soon as you can."

"But Uncle Lowell—"

"As soon as you can, Sara. I can't explain. I'll be waiting."

He hung the phone up in her ear before she could get in another question.

Her first instinct, Sara realized, was to panic. She had no way to reach Adrian to tell him what was happening, no way to find out if her uncle needed immediate help such as an ambulance, no way even to begin to figure out what might be wrong. All she could do was obey Lowell Kincaid's summons as swiftly as possible. Desperately she tried to reassure herself with Adrian's words about her uncle's competence. *He can take care of himself.*

Whatever else was happening, at least she knew he wasn't in Southeast Asia! If only she could get in touch with Adrian to call him off that wild-goose chase. Frantically Sara tried to think. It took her a moment to break through the paralysis engendered by her uncle's phone call. Then she was on her feet and running toward the bedroom. Her purse was where she had left it, slung on the bed. She grabbed it and scrabbled around inside for her car keys.

Sara was almost to the front door when she remembered the elaborate warning devices built into Adrian's house. Forcing herself to slow down and concentrate, she went into Adrian's bedroom and programmed the alarms as he had taught her so that she could leave without causing a disturbance. Almost as an afterthought she pushed the reset button so that the house would be able to detect intruders. Adrian wouldn't thank her for leaving the exotic alarm system completely turned off. She was afraid to set it to keep out intruders because Adrian hadn't told her how to bypass the alarms if she were to leave and then try to reenter. There was always the chance that she might be coming back here this evening with her uncle. This way the house would recognize that it had been entered, but she would be able to get back inside if she wished. When she was finished, the alarms were set just as they had been the night she'd walked so easily into Adrian's study to search it. She'd better leave a note, too, just in case Adrian returned before she got back.

She dashed back down the hall to the study and found

a pen and a piece of paper. Hastily she jotted down the facts about the phone call and Lowell's summons. Then she glanced around for a means of anchoring the slip of paper. The crystal apple caught her eye. She picked it up and a shaft of morning light broke into a rainbow as it passed through the apple and touched the frozen bubbles inside. Sara found herself staring into the depths of the crystal for a split second. The apple had been the start of this whole mess, she realized. And it had provided the first link between herself and Adrian.

Shaking off the momentary sense of distraction, she plunked the crystal apple down on top of her note. Time enough later to figure out whether the apple was more significant than it seemed.

Finished with the task, she flung herself out the door and down the steps to where her car was parked in the drive. She was furious with her own nervous tension and her anger just served to make her more nervous. It seemed an incredible chore to get the key into the ignition. The wait at the ferry dock was interminable. The Interstate was jammed through the heart of Seattle and over the bridge to Mercer Island. Everything seemed to be conspiring to keep her from making good time out of town.

When at last she was free of the city's congestion, she found it difficult to keep within shouting distance of the speed limit. Every instinct was to hurry. Uncle Lowell's words had sounded extremely urgent. But there had been an oddly flat quality to his voice, she thought as she drove. She'd never heard him sound quite that way.

On the other hand, she had never been around him when he was "working." For her he had always been the laughing, witty man who had seemed to understand her even when the rest of the family hadn't. There had been an affinity between her and her uncle since she was a small girl. Her parents tolerated it good-naturedly most of the time. But there had been occasions when she had been warned that it wasn't right to play games with life. The black sheep of the family might be a lot of fun but he didn't set a responsible example for a young person.

With every passing mile Sara wondered what had gone wrong with Lowell Kincaid's latest game.

It wasn't until nearly two hours later when she was turning off onto the narrow road that led toward the cottage that Sara remembered to wonder why her uncle hadn't mentioned Adrian. If there was anything really wrong, would Lowell have asked her to come alone?

Impatiently she slowed to take the twists and turns of the old road. Quite suddenly she was furious with both her uncle and Adrian. Men and their little macho schemes. And they had the nerve to say she played games! When this was all over, Sara decided as she braked for a sharp curve, she would give them both a piece of her mind. More than that. She'd tear a wide strip off each of them.

The car that blocked the road on the far side of the curve came as a distinct shock. It was sitting across both lanes, making it utterly impossible to get past. Sara, who had her foot on the accelerator again as she came out of the curve, hurriedly slammed on the brakes.

"Damn it to hell!" It was the last straw, Sara told herself as she came to a halt. Well, at least she could walk to the cottage from here. Angrily, her mood fueled by a firestorm of mounting concern, she pulled over to the side of the road, pushed open the door and climbed out. There was no one in the other car as far as she could tell. Who on earth would be stupid enough to leave a vehicle in the middle of the road? Probably some drunk driver who hadn't made it home from a local tavern.

Leaning down, Sara reached inside her own car to yank her purse off the front seat and remove the keys from the ignition. It couldn't be more than a mile now to her uncle's house. Luckily she'd worn comfortable sandals. She straightened up, stepped back to slam the car door, spun around and found herself staring straight into Brady Vaughn's hawklike face.

"Congratulations, Miss Frazer. You made excellent time." He motioned almost negligently with the compact, snub-nosed gun he held in his right hand. "I just put the car across the road fifteen minutes ago. Thought you'd take a little longer to get here."

"I shouldn't have hurried, apparently," Sara managed in a tight little voice. She couldn't take her eyes off the gun. The casually efficient way Vaughn held it seemed as frightening as anything else that was happening. A man who held a gun that coolly must have had plenty of practice. "Who are you, Mr. Vaughn?"

"Let's just say I'm an old acquaintance of your uncle's." He nodded toward his vehicle as he spoke. "Now I think we'd better get these cars off the road. This isn't a well-traveled area but I wouldn't want some stranger coming along and starting to ask silly questions."

"Such as why you're holding a gun on a woman?" Sara didn't move. She wasn't certain she could.

Vaughn's smile was an odd travesty of humor. "Take it as a compliment, Miss Frazer. I learned long ago that the female of the species can be just as dangerous as the male. I don't take chances. Get in the car. You'll drive."

When he stepped toward her, Sara discovered that she

could, indeed, move. She edged back toward the nondescript compact that was lodged across the road. "Drive where?"

"To your uncle's cabin, of course. That's as good a place to wait for him as any."

"I thought you said he was in Southeast Asia!"

"I lied. I do that quite well. You should start getting used to it. A lot of men in your life lie to you. Now move, Miss Frazer. And please, for both our sakes, don't try anything too tricky, okay?"

There was no opportunity to try anything clever even if she had been able to think of something truly brilliant, Sara discovered. At the point of the gun she slid into the driver's seat. Her fingers trembled as she took the wheel. Her red shirt was turning dark under her arms from nervous perspiration. Vaughn got in beside her, his eyes never leaving her for an instant.

The drive to Lowell Kincaid's cabin was a short one. Sara fantasized briefly about stomping down on the accelerator and trying some wild maneuver that might dislodge the weapon from Vaughn's hand but common sense warned her it wouldn't work. There was no way she could get the car up to a fast rate of speed before he could put a bullet in her. There would be plenty of time for him to kill her and grab the wheel.

The cottage appeared exactly as she and Adrian had left it. When Sara obediently switched off the ignition, Vaughn ordered her out of the car.

"Now we'll walk back and get the other one." He stood aside and waited for her to start back down the road ahead of him.

"Why the stunt with the car across the road? Why didn't you simply wait for me in the cabin?"

"I was afraid you might be suspicious about entering

the house when you noticed the strange car in the drive. And there wasn't any convenient place to hide it and still have it readily available." He indicated the cleared area that extended from the drive to the front of the house. "I also didn't know if you and your uncle might have some particular signal."

"You're giving me a lot more credit for caution and observation than I deserve," Sara told him dryly. "I doubt that I would have thought twice about the car. I would have assumed it was my uncle's. And we don't have any special greeting signal! Good grief, I'm his niece, not a secret agent."

"Oh, I'm aware of who you are, Sara Frazer. Very much aware. I'm counting on your identity to lure your uncle out into the open, you see."

She turned to glance back at him over her shoulder. The gun was still pointed unwaveringly at her back. "But that was my uncle's voice on the phone. I don't understand. Where is he?"

Vaughn arched an eyebrow. "It was your uncle's voice, all right. Right off the tape on his answering machine."

"His answering machine! But he didn't say those things on the machine," Sara gasped, startled.

"Sure he did," Vaughn told her with a soft chuckle. "He just didn't say them in quite that order."

"You mixed his words from the tape into different sentences?"

"And recorded them onto another tape. It takes a little work and the right equipment, but it can be done. I had both his recorded message to callers and the message to your friend Adrian with which to work. Plenty of material from which to get a few simple sentences."

Sara stared unseeingly at her car as she rounded the bend. "You appear to be very professional at this sort of thing, Mr. Vaughn," she whispered dully.

"Very," he assured her. "It would be best if you didn't forget it."

She drove the second car back to the cottage under the same circumstances as she had driven the first. When she finally parked it beside Vaughn's compact, he motioned her into the house.

"What now?" she asked quietly as she stepped inside.

"Now we wait. Make some coffee if you like. It's probably going to take a while." Vaughn appeared unconcerned.

"But what exactly are we going to wait for?"

"Your uncle should be contacting us in the near future."

"But why would he do that? How would he even know where I am or that I'm with you?" The shock of the situation was affecting her mind, Sara thought vaguely. She couldn't seem to think properly. Perhaps she ought to take Vaughn's advice and make some coffee. At least it would give her something to do. She was very much afraid that if she sat down or stood still she would begin to tremble uncontrollably.

"Your uncle is looking for me. It's only a matter of time before he figures out I'm waiting patiently right here on his home stomping grounds. And when he does, he'll discover I have you with me."

Sara turned on the tap in the kitchen sink, aware of Vaughn watching her from the doorway. "You're going to use me?"

"I'm going to trade you to your uncle for the information I want," Vaughn confirmed. "I see it all as a business deal."

"And what information is it that you want, Mr. Vaughn?" she demanded softly.

"Don't you think you should start calling me Brady?"

"I don't see us ever getting together on a social basis," she gritted out as she set the pot into place in the drip machine.

"But we are together, Sara," he drawled smoothly. "Perhaps for some time. You made it very easy, really. I was a little worried about how to get rid of the boy-friend. I wasn't sure until yesterday where he fit into the scene. I had a couple of plans I thought would work but he simplified matters considerably when he obligingly left on the morning plane to Mexico City. His leaving for Mexico also confirmed his part in all this."

"Mexico City!"

"I got the clerk at the airline counter to verify that he bought a one-way ticket to Mexico. What's the matter, Sara? Didn't he tell you where he was going?"

"Yes, but I . . . I just don't see how you could find out that sort of information." Sara was surprised that she could get the lie fairly glibly past her lips. Mexico City! It didn't make any sense. You didn't pop down to Mexico City for the day and return by early evening. And just yesterday Adrian had been telling her tales of how a man could disappear into Mexico City and reappear on the other side of the world.

"You can get all sorts of information out of people if you flash the right badges at them," Vaughn informed her. "Poor little Sara. You still don't realize what he's done, do you? You've been had, lady. In more ways than one."

"He's a writer," she explained, struggling for something logical to say. "He does a lot of research and he's had this trip planned for some time. My showing up got in the way of his schedule, I'm afraid. He's setting the next book in Mexico." Did that sound reasonable? "I didn't have the time to go with him."

"Is that a fact?" Vaughn said musingly. "So he just left you up here all by yourself to worry about your uncle? After asking for forty-eight hours to think over your problem?"

"I...yes." It was probably better not to weave any more strands into the story. She wouldn't be able to keep it straight in her own head.

"Not terribly gallant of him, was it?"

Sara said nothing. She focused on the pot filling with coffee.

"You're a fool, Sara," Vaughn finally said calmly. "You've been dumped. As long as Saville figured you were the easiest way to get at the gold, he was willing to play lover. But yesterday when I let him know that others were getting close to the prize, he panicked and decided you were no longer the quickest or safest means to an end. I know better. I know that you still are the best means to this particular end. I'm a patient man, Sara."

She cast him a quick, frightened glance. He smiled again. "Want me to tell you the real reason he's gone south?"

"What's your explanation, Mr. Vaughn?"

"Oh, it's simple enough. Mexico City is a wide-open town. It has a certain reputation in the industry. Among other things it's a jumping-off point for people who want to head for such places as Cambodia without letting the U.S. government know where they're going. You can buy anything in Mexico City, including alterations on your passport. Your boyfriend has skipped out on you. He's probably heading for Southeast Asia."

"I thought," she said weakly, "that the stories about Mexico City were just the product of espionage fiction. Legends and tales."

"Fact, I'm afraid. Your lover has skipped." Vaughn seemed amused.

Sara lowered her lashes. "Why would he do that?"

"Because he's decided to risk going after the gold on his own instead of waiting for your uncle to return. As I said, he got nervous yesterday when he realized others were closing in on it. He's obviously a friend of your uncle's and Kincaid made the mistake of trusting him, both with his niece and with the information about the gold. Kincaid never used to make mistakes like that, but he's getting old. He's trusted the wrong man with the details of what was probably intended to be your dowry. The race is on, Sara, but I'm the one with the inside track. I've got you. I'm not worried that Saville tried to buy himself forty-eight hours for a head start. It won't do him any good because he's obviously an amateur. A greedy amateur, but an amateur nonetheless."

"Why do you say he's an amateur?"

"Because a professional would have realized that you're the most useful key around. And that I'm the biggest threat. A professional would have made a try for me before leaving town, if for no other reason than to find out just how much I know. Southeast Asia is a big and dangerous place to go hunting without specific directions and a few contacts. Saville will probably just succeed in getting himself killed trying for your uncle's gold. And it does nothing to change my plans. One way or another I wound up with you, and ever since you appeared on the scene so conveniently, that's been my goal. I'm a highly adaptable man. Before you came along I was using a different approach. I'd been

through this cabin with a fine-tooth comb. I was just realizing how useless that method was going to be when
you showed up out of the blue. Couldn't figure out who
you were at first, but after you'd left the first time I remembered seeing the phone-answering machine. I
played it back to see if I could pick up any information
about Kincaid's unexpected female guest, and sure
enough, all the news I needed was on that tape. That's
how I found out you're Kincaid's niece.''

"You want that gold, don't you?'' Sara reached for a
cup and poured coffee with exaggerated care. She was
afraid that if she wasn't extremely cautious she would
spill the hot liquid all over her feet. "The gold you said
my uncle left behind in Southeast Asia.''

"Yes, Sara. I want the gold. Pour me a cup, too. Just
set it on the counter. I'll get it. Wouldn't want you trying to throw it in my face with a grand, heroic gesture.''

"So you're going to use me to force my uncle to tell
you exactly where he hid the stuff?'' Sara persisted,
standing back so that Vaughn could pick up his coffee.

"Precisely.''

"You said Uncle Lowell thinks you're in Hawaii,''
she began with a frown as she tried frantically to put the
pieces of the puzzle together.

"I made certain he got information to that effect.
Rumors are very effective in our crowd, even among
the, uh, golden-agers. I wanted him sidetracked for a
while so that I could try getting the data I needed the
easy way.''

"You searched this place,'' she whispered, remembering the chaos she and Adrian had discovered.

"Unfortunately, as I said, my search didn't turn up
anything so convenient as a map or a set of coordinates
that would have made my task a straightforward one. I

really thought I'd have a chance of finding what I wanted because I knew your uncle rather well at one time, Sara. I know his theories on hiding important data, for example. He always got a kick out of concealing things right in front of someone's nose. Kincaid had a sense of humor, you can say that for the man. When I didn't turn up anything, I realized matters were going to get complicated. I made the search look like the work of punks and decided to keep watch on the cabin for a while. It paid off. You happened along and greatly simplified my life.''

Sara leaned back against the counter, her hands braced against the cool tiles. ''Why would my uncle go tearing off to Hawaii just because he thought you were there, Mr. Vaughn?''

''He thinks that after all these years I've decided to go after the gold. He's got a couple of other reasons for following my trail, too. He and a few others, I believe, have some private suspicions about me.'' Vaughn sipped tentatively at his coffee. ''Not bad,'' he declared. ''I enjoy good coffee.''

Sara took a deep breath before plunging in with the next question. ''My uncle has other reasons for hunting you down?''

'' 'Hunting' sounds a bit melodramatic, don't you think? Let's just say he couldn't resist the hint that I might have surfaced and that he might be able to find me.''

Sara met his gaze unflinchingly. ''Do you by any chance go under the code name of . . . of Wolf?''

Vaughn went still, the coffee halfway to his mouth. Slowly he lowered the cup, his dark eyes narrowing speculatively. ''Now what would you know about the man called Wolf?''

Her fingers tightened around the counter's edge. Sara

was beginning to wish she hadn't brought up the subject. "Not much. My uncle mentioned him once. That's all."

"And you've been assuming I might be... Wolf?"

She didn't like the cold amusement that was suddenly in his eyes. "The thought occurred to me."

"Fascinating."

"Well?" she challenged bravely.

Vaughn's mouth drew back in a humorless smile. "Your uncle always could tell a good story."

"Is that all Wolf is? A Lowell Kincaid tale?" she breathed. It was getting difficult to tell legends from reality, she realized.

Vaughn chuckled, shaking his head. "No. As usual with your uncle, there's a germ of truth in the story. There really was a man called Wolf. I never met him. Few people did and survived to tell about it. His cover was very deep and he protected it. They said he had a thing about maintaining his cover."

A man who liked to be in total control of his surroundings. Sara shivered. "What do you mean his cover *was* deep?"

"He's a legend, Sara. Just like the gold that never made it out of Vietnam. But he was real like the gold, too. Lethally real, from what I understand. In my business legends can be real." His mouth twisted ironically.

"But you're not him?"

"Hell, no." Vaughn grimaced. "Give me some credit. The guy cracked up completely, according to the old gossip. Went bonkers on his last mission. He never returned."

Sara was very still. "What do you mean, he cracked up?"

"Just what I said. The story goes that he broke like a

fine-tuned violin string. Came apart. Went crazy. Cracked. Couldn't handle what he was paid to handle. Got himself killed on his last assignment. Why the interest? Because you've been assuming I'm him?''

"The thought had crossed my mind," she admitted softly.

"I'm not especially flattered. The guy may once have been good, the best there was, in fact, but I sure as hell don't intend to lose my nerve the way he did."

"What are you going to do with the gold if you get it?" she pressed, desperate to keep the conversation moving. She had no particular wish to chat the afternoon away with Brady Vaughn, but she somehow felt safer when he was talking.

"I'm going to retire, Sara. Somewhere far, far away. Some nice island, perhaps where a lot of gold will buy a lot of silence and a lot of what I want out of life. I've been living under a great deal of tension for the past couple of years. And you know what they say about the dangers of too much tension. I've done well financially, but as the magazines say, stress takes its toll."

"Like it did on the man called Wolf?" she flung back.

Vaughn shook his head. "That was an entirely different sort of situation. According to the story, he simply broke. With me, dropping out is more of a reasonable, strictly pragmatic business decision. You see, I've been working very hard lately. And I'm a little tired. Holding down two jobs will do that to a man."

"Two jobs?" she questioned, confused.

"Never mind." Vaughn shifted his position in the doorway. "I really don't feel like discussing it any further at the moment. Let's go into the living room and sit down. We might have a long wait ahead of us. But have no fear. Sooner or later your uncle will figure out that he's been sent on a wild-goose chase. When he does he'll rush back here. We'll be waiting for him. I bought some food. Enough to last us a couple of days, if necessary. But I doubt we'll have to put up with each other's company for that long. Your uncle is a smart man."

What did you talk about when you found yourself whiling away the hours with a man who kept a gun in his hand when he conversed with you?

Sara was still asking herself that sometime later as she sat almost immobile on the sofa in front of the cold fireplace. She hadn't moved in so long that she was afraid her foot might have grown numb. When she did move it cautiously, Vaughn glanced at her sharply.

"Going somewhere, Sara?"

"The bathroom, unless you have any objections," she muttered, rising slowly to her feet. There was a tingling sensation in her left foot but it wasn't completely numb.

Vaughn eyed her thoughtfully. "None. There's no way out of that room. I've checked. Try to resist the temptation to forage for a pair of scissors or a razor blade. You'd only wind up cutting yourself."

Sara didn't respond. She turned away and went down the hall to the bathroom. When the door closed behind her, she sagged against the sink and stared at her drawn face in the mirror.

She had to do something. She couldn't bear this endless waiting. What was it Adrian had said about the value of patience? In her case it bought nothing but anxiety. It didn't seem to bother Vaughn particularly, she reflected. He was very professional about the whole thing. Or at least he seemed professional. Hard to judge, given her limited experience in this kind of business. Sara winced.

Vaughn had the ability to wait but would he bother with that route if he thought there might be a shortcut to his goal, she asked herself as she splashed her face with cold water. He'd tried a shortcut once before when he created the diversion that had sent her uncle off to Hawaii. If she could make him think there was an alternative to this interminable waiting, perhaps he would go for it. She dried her flushed face and thought of Adrian's promise to return by early evening.

There was no way he could make it back tonight if he'd actually gone to Mexico and Vaughn seemed convinced he'd gone.

But Adrian had promised her he'd be back. And the house was set on its alarm status. If she were inside the house with Vaughn, Adrian would know as soon as he returned that there was trouble. His small signaling device would warn him there had been an unauthorized intrusion when he came within a couple of blocks of his home.

That scenario would only work if Adrian really was planning to return tonight. If he was even now en route to Mexico City, she was in very bad trouble. Heaven only knew where her uncle was.

Sara wrenched herself away from the mirror. It was an incredible disaster, and if she didn't act, it was going to get worse. She didn't have any illusions about the man in the next room. He was quite capable of casually raping her tonight and killing her later after he had what he wanted from her uncle.

Her only real chance was to bank on the fact that Adrian had told her the truth about returning this evening.

Legends and reality. How could a woman be sure of the difference, she asked herself.

A few minutes later Sara opened the bathroom door and went down the hall to the living room. She saw the fleeting spark of interest in Vaughn's eyes as she resumed her seat on the couch. No, the last thing she wanted to risk was spending the night here with him.

"In another couple of hours we'll have to discuss the sleeping arrangements, Sara," Vaughn mused, tossing a magazine into the bin beside the chair. "I think that could be interesting."

"Really? Do you sleep with your gun in your hand, Mr. Vaughn?"

He chuckled. "I think I can dispense with the gun once I've tied you up for the night. You'd look interesting spread-eagled on a bed."

Sara shuddered and nerved herself for the next bit. "I'm not interested in sharing a bed with you."

"Perhaps I will find it a challenge to see if I can create a little interest," he suggested coolly.

"I doubt it. I'm going to be married soon."

"Are you?" he murmured blandly. "To the boyfriend who just skipped town? You'll have to catch him first, won't you?"

Sara chose her next words carefully. "That gold you're after is supposed to be my wedding gift from my uncle."

Vaughn's eyes narrowed thoughtfully. "Just how much do you know about your uncle's little social-security cache?"

She tried for a mild shrug, her arms wrapped around her drawn-up knees as she sat on the couch. "About as much as you do. You know my uncle. He's fond of dropping little, uh, hints."

"Kincaid never does anything without a reason. And in spite of that easygoing facade, I worked with him long enough to know he's a shrewd and careful man. If he was dropping hints to you about the gold, then he must have truly believed it was safe for you to know about it. No reason he shouldn't think it was safe after all these years, I suppose.''

"In addition to being shrewd and careful, my uncle also likes to plan for the future,'' she added deliberately. "He wanted Adrian and me to know enough about the gold to be able to find it someday in the event something happened to him.''

Vaughn leaned forward on his chair, the gun cradled loosely in his fist. "That's very interesting, Sara. Very interesting. It puts a whole new light on the situation. Up until now I've assumed that no one except Kincaid knew the truth about that gold. It's a fact that your uncle tries not to leave much to chance, though. Tell me more, little Sara. Tell me what made Saville think he's got a shot at the gold. I've been wondering who he plans to contact after Mexico City.''

She caught her lower lip between her teeth, watching him the way a small mouse probably watched a hovering eagle. *Adrian, where are you?* "Mr. Vaughn, I'll make a deal with you.''

He smiled and she could almost hear the way he must be laughing inwardly at her naiveté. The knowledge made her grit her teeth.

"I'm listening, little Sara.''

"If I. . .if I show you where I think the information is hidden, will you take it and go away?''

"I'd have no reason to hang around any longer if I had a map showing the location of the gold,'' he murmured.

Sara wanted to cringe, but she managed to project a hopeful expression. "It's at Adrian's.''

"Your boyfriend's house?"

"He's the man I'm going to marry. Uncle Lowell gave us each a copy of the map. If what you say is true about Adrian being in Mexico, then he must have taken his copy with him. But I have my own. Or at least I have information that will lead me to the gold. I'm not sure that it's exactly a map."

"I can't quite decide whether or not to believe you, little Sara," Vaughn finally said.

She clenched her fingers tightly together. "I can show you."

"But first we have to drive all the way back to that damn island? I don't like islands, Sara. A man can get trapped on islands. So few ways off, you see."

"I thought you were going to retire to an island," she shot back.

"Ah, but that will be different. Much different. There I will have my own means of transportation."

She let out her breath. "Then you're not interested in getting your hands on the information my uncle gave to me?"

Vaughn was quiet for a long while and then he suddenly seemed to come to a decision. "It would make things much simpler if it turned out that you're telling the truth, although I have a few doubts. Still, your boyfriend is several thousand miles away by now following some lead. I'd give a lot to know exactly what kind of lead he thinks he has. Who knows when your uncle will show up." He drummed his fingers on the arm of the chair, his eyes hooded and speculative. "I suppose there's no harm in checking out your story. We could be into the city and over to that damn island within a couple of hours."

"Yes." She could hardly breathe as she waited for the

final decision. Was greed finally going to swamp this man's patience?

He nodded once. "All right, Sara. We'll go. But I warn you that if you've lied to me, I will make things most unpleasant for both you and your uncle. And probably your boyfriend, too."

"I'm not lying," she said with great conviction. "I know where my copy of the information is hidden. I had finally realized it just before you made that fake phone call this morning."

"I do believe you're telling the truth," Vaughn mused as he studied the certainty in her expression. "Fascinating. Remind me to thank you later."

Sure, thought Sara as she got to her feet. *I'll remind you. Just before you pull that trigger.*

Chapter Nine

The drive back into Seattle was the longest and most exhausting traveling Sara had ever done in her life. She decided that the normal stresses and strains of rush-hour traffic are not enhanced by the fact that your passenger is casually holding a gun in his lap.

Brady Vaughn didn't say much during the drive. He was undoubtedly contemplating his imminent retirement, Sara thought as she navigated the off ramp from the interstate and found the street that led down to the ferry docks. He kept the gun discreetly shielded under a jacket but he kept it aimed in her direction. She had a hunch that once she had parked her car on the ferry Vaughn wouldn't allow her to go up onto the passenger decks. The thought of sitting on the car deck for the entire length of the ferry ride was depressing.

She was right, of course. Vaughn simply lounged in his corner of the car and watched her speculatively. Unobtrusively Sara glanced at her watch. Her timing, at least, was good. If Adrian had told the truth this morning, he would be catching the ferry that would be leaving Seattle forty minutes from now. She would have forty minutes to entertain Brady Vaughn. Her fingers flexed uneasily on the wheel.

The whole exercise would be extremely pointless if Adrian didn't show up on the right ferry. Halfway across the bay Sara had a wild thought or two about flinging herself from the car and making a dash to the passenger decks. It would be a futile move and she knew it. Even if he chose not to use the gun, Vaughn could probably run her down easily in the close confines of the parked cars. Besides, she reminded herself, that wasn't the plan. She had a much better one in mind.

If it worked. *Legends and reality.* Where did the truth stop and the legend begin? Perhaps in some cases there was no difference. Perhaps a woman just had to make the leap to faith.

"You look nervous, Sara," Vaughn observed politely. "I trust you're not wasting my time with this little chase? It won't do any good, if you are. I know what I'm doing."

She shook her head. "All I want is for you to take the information about the gold and leave."

"Sounds simple enough. I do like simple plans; don't you?"

"Yes." How simple was hers?

"Will you dream about the gold you could have had, Sara? Will you think about it occasionally in the future? Wonder what it might have been like to have your hands on your uncle's cache?"

Again she shook her head. "Even if the gold is still there, I don't see how I could get it out. How are you going to accomplish that little feat, Vaughn? Just walk into that part of the world and tell the current government officials you'd like to do a little digging on their borders?"

He chuckled. She was learning to hate that poor excuse of a laugh. "Nothing that obvious. I prefer quieter techniques. I have contacts and I'll have cash with which to grease the way. I'll be going in through Cambodia. That gold must be somewhere near the Cambodia-Vietnam border.''

"Gold is heavy. You won't be able to simply hoist it over your shoulder and hike out of the country with it. Not if there's as much there as you seem to think."

"I'll have help," he explained absently.

Sara slanted him a curious glance. "Help?"

"There are men who will undertake a great many risks for a promise of a split of the profits." He shrugged.

"You'll find some mercenaries to help you get the gold out?''

"They undoubtedly think of themselves as entrepreneurs," Vaughn murmured.

Sara closed her eyes and willed the ferry to a faster speed. She couldn't take much more of this unremitting tension. Whether her scheme worked or not, all she wanted to do at the moment was get it over and done with. She didn't see how anyone could live constantly under the stress of genuine danger. It was easy to see how a man or a woman might crack.

The ferry docked eventually and Sara turned the key in the ignition with a sense of fatalism. Forty minutes from now, if she was very, very lucky, Adrian would be driving off a similar ferry. If she was not so fortunate... Sara pushed the thought aside. There wasn't much point dwelling on that possibility. She would deal with it when the time came.

She drove slowly along the narrow road that wound around the island's perimeter, more slowly than was really necessary. Any time she could eat up this way was that much less that had to be used up at the house waiting for Adrian.

For the first time since she had arrived in the Seattle area the weather was finally beginning to live up to its reputation. The day was rapidly turning gray and overcast. A light mist began to fall.

"Come on, let's get going." With one of his first hints of impatience, Vaughn moved the gun in an ugly gesture.

Sara tried to think of something calming to say. "You don't have to use the ferry to get back off the island, you know. You can drive across a bridge on the far side. It's the long way around if you're trying to get back to the airport or Seattle, but—"

"Just shut up. I know my way around."

Of course he did. He was, after all, a *professional*. He wouldn't trap himself on an island. Sara pulled into the driveway in front of Adrian's house. The windows were still dark, so that removed the possibility that by some miracle Adrian had actually arrived home ahead of her. *Forty minutes.*

"Is it true?" she began tentatively as she slowly opened her car door.

"Is what true?" Vaughn reached out and snapped the keys from her hand. He pocketed them.

"That you really have a chance of getting that gold out of Southeast Asia?"

"Believe me, I wouldn't be going to all this trouble if I didn't think it was possible." Vaughn made a careful outside inspection of the house, reassuring himself that no one was around. Then he cast an amused glance at Sara. "What's the matter, honey? Having second thoughts about giving me that map?"

She stopped at the top of the steps and looked back at him. "I admit that until now I assumed the gold was completely inaccessible."

He chuckled. "For years I believed it probably didn't

exist at all! Kincaid hid the truth well behind the legend. He made everyone think it really was just one more wild tale set in the last days of the war. There were a hundred other similar stories and there was no reason to think this one was for real. But a year ago I came across an old file that had been sealed since shortly after Saigon fell. The one thing that damned war generated was paperwork. Files and memos and reports will probably still be turning up twenty years from now. At any rate this one contained some notes by a journalist who claimed he'd interviewed some villagers in the south. He said they told him a story about an American agent who had worked with them toward the end of the war. They described him as a man who knew how to laugh and how to hold his whiskey. A man who was always telling stories. A man who could sketch your face before you even realized he was holding a pencil.''

Sara caught her breath.

"Exactly." Vaughn nodded grimly. "A perfect description of Lowell Kincaid. The reporter's notes went on to tell a fascinating story. It culminated in Kincaid's departure for the Cambodian border with a jeep full of gold. The villagers didn't actually see the gold in Kincaid's jeep but they did see the share of it he left for them. He apparently stashed it in the village well and told the elders to wait until the North Vietnamese had passed through before digging it back out. Just like Kincaid to make a grand gesture like that. He was a brilliant agent, but he had some definite weaknesses. When I put that report together with the legend I'd first heard back in 1972, I began to believe I might be dealing with more than just another war tale. It's taken me months to piece together some idea of what might have happened and where. The file with the journalist's notes led to other files. Eventually I knew I was onto the real thing.''

"What happened to the journalist?" Sara heard herself ask.

"He died," Vaughn said carelessly. "An accident down in South America earlier this year, I believe."

"I see." She wondered how much Vaughn had had to do with the "accident."

His mouth twisted wryly. "I do believe I recognize that look in your eyes, little Sara."

"What look?"

"Greed, love. Pure unadulterated greed. I saw it in your boyfriend's eyes yesterday and it's in yours today."

She feigned a nonchalant movement of her shoulders and turned to open the front door. There was no sound from within. The house was as quiet and innocent-looking as it had been that first night when she'd arrived and searched Adrian's study.

"Doesn't your boyfriend believe in locking his front door?" Vaughn drawled as he followed Sara into the house. He held the gun at the ready while he verified that the place was empty.

"He says there's virtually no crime around here."

"A trusting soul." Vaughn smirked. He took in his surroundings with a quick, professional eye. "I take it back. It goes beyond trusting. I think we can safely say your friend Saville is probably a fool."

"And what about me?" She slung her purse down on the sofa and turned to face him.

"Oh, you're very smart, Sara. Very smart indeed, if you're telling the truth." Vaughn's eyes hardened. "Where's the map?"

She grabbed for her courage, using all of her willpower to keep her expression cool. "I've tried to tell you, it's not exactly a map," she began carefully.

"What the hell are you talking about?" The violence in Vaughn was very close to the surface.

"My uncle has his own unique way of doing things. You know that. He made sure I'd have the information I needed but he hid it in an unique manner. I don't know how he gave Adrian his information, but I think I know where my copy is." Her fingernails dug into her palms. She wondered if Vaughn realized just how scared she was.

"Sara, let's not play any games. You'll lose, believe me. Where's the map?"

"It's not a map. I'm trying to explain. It's a sort of. . .of code."

Vaughn stared at her. "A code? You told me you and your uncle didn't go in for codes."

"I said we didn't have any prearranged greeting signals."

"Then what are you saying?"

"I'll show you." Moving cautiously so as not to alarm him, Sara turned and started down the hall toward the study. This business of trying to think two steps ahead of a man with a gun was tricky. Frighteningly tricky. She glanced at the hall clock. The ferry that might or might not be bringing Adrian to the rescue had left Seattle by now. Her fate was in the hands of the Washington state ferry system. They claimed to have an excellent safety record.

Vaughn was close behind her as she stepped into the study. The crystal apple gleamed on Adrian's desk, still pinning her note. Beyond it the manuscript of *Phantom* waited.

"There," she whispered, indicating the pile of typed

pages. "Everything you want to know about that gold is in that manuscript. My uncle has jotted down little doodles and notes all over the margins, you see."

Vaughn stared first at the stack of papers and then gestured viciously at her with the nose of the gun. "You little bitch. What kind of game do you think you're playing?"

She hugged herself, trying to master the faint trembling that threatened to weaken her limbs. Her head bent forward and a sweep of her hair hid her expression. "It's there. I promise you. And I know how to get at the information you want. It's in code and my uncle once taught me the code. It will take a while, but I can do it."

"Why you little fool!" he snarled. "Stalling isn't going to get you anywhere. There's no one around to come to your rescue. If there was any likelihood of that, I'd never have agreed to let you drag me here."

"No." She shook her head and lifted her chin defiantly. "I'm not trying to stall. I'm...I'm trying to make a deal. You said you were going to be hiring professional help to assist you in getting the gold out of Southeast Asia. Well, I want you to consider me as hired help, too. I can decode Uncle Lowell's doodles on that manuscript. I can do it here and now, in fact, and prove that what I'm saying is true. In return, I want you to cut me in for a piece of the action."

He studied her derisively. "You've got your uncle's nerve, little Sara, I'll say that for you. Decode the manuscript. What a crock of—"

"It's true," she insisted. "You know Uncle Lowell. It would be just like him to hide the information so I would be sitting right on top of it all the time. That manuscript was waiting for me at his cabin the other day. It was right out in the open. You'd overlooked it, naturally. He says people always overlook the obvious. But I recognized the doodles on the margins. It's the code he taught me when I was a little girl. It was a game we used to play together. Give me half an hour and I'll have the information you need to find that gold."

Vaughn was clearly and dangerously undecided. His eyes slid from the manuscript to her face and back again. "Half an hour?"

She nodded quickly. "Is it a deal?"

"I can afford half an hour's wait. I was prepared to wait for much longer than that for Kincaid to return. And your boyfriend is no doubt getting ready to land in Mexico City so there's plenty of time on that end. All right, my greedy little Sara. You've got yourself a deal."

"You'll cut me in for a slice of the profit?" She had to make it sound real, Sara told herself. She tried to inject just the right note of hopeful greed.

"Sure. Why not?" He threw himself down into a chair in the corner. "Half an hour. And if it turns out that you're lying, little Sara—"

"I'm not lying." She sat down slowly behind the desk. From there she was looking through the study door and into the hall beyond. Brady Vaughn would be able to see anyone who came through the door but from his seat in the corner he could not see into the hall as she could. Sara figured she would have a couple of seconds' advance notice if and when Adrian arrived. Nervously she reached out and pulled the manuscript toward her.

She found herself staring down at the sketch of the wolf. For an instant it almost paralyzed her. Then, with excessive care, she turned over the first page of *Phantom* and picked up a pencil.

Time ticked past with a slowness that made Sara think

she was waiting for eternity to end. She would have no way of knowing until the last moment whether or not Adrian would arrive. He would have the warning about the invasion of his house shortly after he drove off the ferry. He would probably leave the car down the road and walk the final few yards, she decided. Neither she nor Vaughn would have the sound of a vehicle to alert them.

Carefully she went through the manuscript, occasionally stopping to jot down a meaningless number or word on the notepad beside her. It would be particularly ironic if there really was a code imbedded in her uncle's margin doodles, Sara decided at one point. A real joke on her. As far as she knew she was looking at nothing more than meaningless notes and drawings.

Time crept past. Outside the window the mist turned to rain. Sara turned on the desk lamp. Vaughn's eyes never left her as she went page by page through the manuscript. His patience was as amazing to her as Adrian's had been. Where did they learn that kind of skill? Perhaps some people were just born with it. It was a cinch she wasn't one of those lucky souls. She shuddered and turned over another page. She would force herself not to sneak another glance at the clock or her watch for at least ten minutes, Sara decided resolutely at one point. The last thing she wanted to do was give Vaughn the idea that she was waiting for someone. She kept her head bent over the manuscript for what she estimated must surely be at least ten minutes if not more and then, unable to resist, she slid her gaze upward to the clock on the wall near the door.

She almost didn't see Adrian standing in the shadows of the hall. When she did, she thought her breath had stopped permanently. He was simply waiting there, watching her in absolute silence. It was as if a ghost had materialized out of thin air and in her odd, light-headed state of mind she might have believed just that if it hadn't been for the rain-dampened Windbreaker he wore. It took her another instant to see the gun in his hand.

"Something wrong, Sara?" Vaughn asked conversationally from the corner. He lifted his gun in an easy threat. "You seem a little tense."

Sara swallowed and dropped her eyes from Adrian's still, shadowed figure to the crystal apple in front of her. "I've just realized that I made a mistake."

"Did you?" Vaughn seemed only politely interested. "Just what kind of mistake would that be, little Sara?"

She picked up the apple and held it so that it caught the light from the desk lamp. "The information you want isn't in the manuscript."

"Then you have a problem, don't you, Sara," he said with brutal emphasis.

She shook her head. "No. I don't think so. Not anymore." She tossed the apple up in the air and caught it again. "Here's what you want, Mr. Vaughn." She tossed the crystal object once more and caught it easily. Beyond the door Adrian did not move. He was as still as midnight waiting to descend. She couldn't see his eyes but she knew they would be quite colorless.

"I think," Vaughn said abruptly, "that I've had enough of your games, bitch."

"Ah, but I'm so good at them," she protested gently. "What you want is right out here in front of your very eyes, Mr. Vaughn. As clear as crystal. Just the sort of trick my uncle would pull, don't you think?" With sudden decision she hurled the apple toward the window.

"What the hell. . . I've had it with you, lady. I'm going to kill you for this!" Without warning, Vaughn's patience snapped. He surged out of the chair, his gun trained on Sara but his eyes following the apple as it crashed against the tempered glass.

The sound of the crystal striking the window and falling to the floor was lost beneath Brady Vaughn's scream of pain and rage as Adrian floated through the doorway and brought the base of the gun down in the direction of the other man's skull. In the split second before the butt of the gun would have made contact with his head, however, some instinct must have warned Vaughn. He threw himself to one side, tumbling across the desk. Adrian's gun struck him violently on the shoulder but it didn't stun him. The weapon Vaughn had been holding, however, fell to the floor and skidded along the hardwood surface until it struck the edge of a rug.

On the other side of the desk, Sara screamed. She was trapped against the wall as the momentum of Vaughn's panicked, sliding rush across the desk threw him toward her. An instant later he seized her even as he stumbled wildly to his feet. Sharp steel blossomed in his hand. He held the knife to Sara's throat, his arm locking her against his body.

"Hold it right there, Saville. Come one step closer and I swear I'll kill her."

Sara couldn't take her eyes off Adrian. The temperature in the study seemed to have suddenly dropped by about twenty degrees.

His face was utterly without emotion. It reminded her of the way he had watched the fish dying at his feet the other morning on the pier but it was a thousand times more remote. He didn't look at Sara. His whole attention was on the heavily breathing man who was holding the knife to her throat.

"Let her go, Vaughn."

"You think I'm crazy? She's my ticket out of here. Drop the gun." He jerked his arm more tightly around Sara's neck. "I said, drop it, damn you! Think I'm playing games?"

"No, I don't think you're playing games." Moving slowly and deliberately, Adrian took a step forward and set his handgun down on the floor at his feet. The blue steel gleamed savagely in the light of the desk lamp.

"Come on, you bitch." Vaughn tugged Sara around the edge of the desk, clearly heading toward the spot where his own weapon had landed when it had been jolted from his hand. "Move, damn you!"

Sara tried to make her body as limp and heavy as possible but the feel of the steel at the base of her throat kept her from refusing to cooperate entirely. Vaughn would use that knife, she knew. Just as he would use the gun when he got his hands on it.

Across the room Adrian stood balanced a step away from his own weapon. If push came to shove, Sara didn't doubt but that he'd make a grab for it. He watched Vaughn the way a wolf might watch a circling hyena.

"Your best bet is to make a run for it, Vaughn. Hanging on to Sara will only slow you down."

Sara felt the tension in her captor's body as he pulled her toward his gun. "I've come too far in search of that gold, Saville. I'm not leaving without getting what I want."

"Sara doesn't know where it is."

"Maybe. Maybe not. I can't quite figure sweet Sara. But Kincaid knows where it is, and when he finds out I've got his niece, he'll bargain."

"You think so? I've never known Kincaid to bargain for anything without coming out on top," Adrian said thoughtfully.

"You don't know him as well as I do," Vaughn assured the other man. He stopped beside the gun on the floor and his fingers bit abruptly into Sara's shoulder. "Bend down very slowly, Sara, and pick up the gun, muzzle first. And keep in mind that I'll have this knife at the nape of your neck."

Sara realized that it would be dangerously awkward for him to try scooping up the gun while still retaining a stranglehold on her. The action might give Adrian the opening for which he was clearly waiting. So Vaughn was going to make her pick up the lethal chunk of steel and hand it over politely to replace the knife.

Sara glanced down at the gun and then up at Adrian's still, unreadable face. If she gave the gun to Vaughn, he would surely use it against the one thing that stood between him and the door: Adrian.

"Do as I say!"

Slowly Sara knelt, aware of the tip of the knife following her nape. Adrian didn't move, his eyes never leaving Vaughn's face. She went all the way down on her knees and reached out reluctantly for the muzzle of the gun.

"Hurry up," Vaughn snarled, forced to bend over slightly in order to keep the knife within striking distance of her neck. "Pick it up and give it to me!"

She wasn't going to get a better opportunity, Sara realized. It was now or never. Handing the gun to Vaughn was the equivalent of signing Adrian's death warrant. She took a deep breath.

Then she threw herself full-length on the floor and rolled to one side, straight into Vaughn's legs. Her falling body covered the gun.

"Damn you!"

The knife flashed as Vaughn was forced to step backward in order to regain his balance. The blade arced downward, scoring Sara's shoulder. She felt the icy sting of the steel even as she struck his left leg. The pain brought a startled cry to her lips.

"Sara!"

Her name was the only sound Adrian made. In the next instant he launched himself across the room in a deadly rush.

But Vaughn was already moving. He hurled the blade straight at Adrian, who must have guessed what was going to happen next. Sara opened her eyes in time to see Adrian throw himself to one side. The blade whipped harmlessly past and imbedded itself deep into the far wall. The rushing assault had served to draw the snake's fangs.

In the small space of time he had bought for himself, Vaughn glanced down and seemed to realize he didn't stand a chance if he took another moment to push Sara off his gun. He raced for the door even as Adrian dived for his own gun.

Sara gasped in pain, her fingers going to the wound on her shoulder just as Adrian leaped for the door. Her cry of anguish stopped him as effectively as a steel cable. He whirled and came back to her even as the sound of Vaughn's running footsteps disappeared down the hall.

"My God, Sara." Adrian went down on his knees beside her. "How bad is it? Let me see." Carefully he guided her to a sitting position, pulling her face into his shoulder as he pushed aside her shirt.

"I...I don't think it's all that bad," she managed, inhaling sharply as she leaned into him. She was trembling. "It just hurts."

"I know, Sara," he soothed in a soft growl as he examined the shoulder. "I know. But you're right. It isn't very deep. Do you think you can handle it yourself?"

"Myself?" She lifted her head in astonishment and then realized what he meant. "Adrian, you're not going after him!"

"I've got to, Sara. You know that."

"No, I do *not* know that," she retorted. "Let the police worry about him. It's not your job—"

"Sara, it is my job." Adrian's face was a cold mask, his light eyes frozen, crystal pools. "After what he's done to you, I don't have any choice."

"No, damn it!" she raged, grabbing at him as he rose to his feet. "You'll never catch him, anyway. He'll take my car. He's got the keys." But even as she argued she realized there was no sound of a car leaving the drive.

"I took care of the car before I came into the house. A precaution." Adrian moved away from her, scooping up the gun and starting for the door. "He'll be on foot and unarmed. This is easy hunting, Sara. Don't worry about it."

"I don't want you going hunting! Please, Adrian, wait...."

But she was calling to no one. Adrian had already disappeared down the hall after his quarry.

Easy hunting. Sara's eyes filled with tears. She didn't want Adrian going hunting. In that moment she would have given her soul to keep him from pursuing Vaughn.

Once again she remembered the way Adrian had watched the fish dying on the pier.

Outside the house Adrian paused briefly on the porch, listening. He shoved the gun back into the leather holster he wore at the base of his spine. The rain was coming down heavily now, obscuring visibility. Sara's car stood silently in the drive, unable to function since he'd clipped two strategic wires.

He'd really made a mess of this, Adrian told himself grimly as he started down the porch steps at a long, loping run. Everything was coming apart in his hands, and to top it all off, he'd nearly gotten Sara killed. The fury and fear he had felt when he'd realized what was happening inside the study were unlike anything he'd ever experienced in his life. The combination of the two had risen up to choke him, causing him to mishandle the situation badly.

But Sara was safe now. The knife had drawn blood but it hadn't gone deep. She had been too close to the floor, depriving Vaughn of an easy target.

Vaughn. Adrian shook his head as his sense of logic returned. There were only two ways off the island, the ferry from Winslow and the bridge at the far end of Bainbridge. Vaughn would head for the highway and try to commandeer a car to go for the bridge. The ferry was already pulling out of its slip on the return run to Seattle. There would be no chance for Vaughn to catch it.

His hunting instincts told Adrian that Vaughn would stick as much as possible to the wooded terrain until he spotted a car that could be hailed. And he would want to keep moving in the general direction of his goal, the bridge. Panicked quarry didn't think to backtrack or race off along a route that would seem to be in the opposite direction. When you were trying to escape, the sense of urgency effectively destroyed a good portion of natural logic.

With grave certainty, Adrian started toward the woods that bounded the road. He moved silently on the wet ground, oblivious to the rain that was soaking his hair and clothing. He knew he was heading in the right direction when he found the scrap of cloth Vaughn had apparently lost when he'd blundered into a thick cluster of blackberry bushes. After that, the trail became increasingly easy to follow.

Just like old times, Adrian thought with a chill that did not come from the rain. Maybe you could never really leave the past behind. Maybe it stayed with you forever.

He had told himself a year ago that a good, solid, iron-tight cover was the answer. A good cover had saved his life often enough in the past. Logically it should be able to provide him with a new life in the future. He'd had it all worked out, every detail in place, every aspect of his new world under control. He was a writer now, a slightly eccentric vegetarian, a man who could fall in love and marry just as other men did. If asked, he could have supplied a complete life history that would have satisfied any inquiring reporter.

The cover had been letter perfect until this afternoon when he'd walked into his study and seen the truth in Sara's eyes. That's when Adrian had learned that there was no such thing as a perfect cover.

She knew who he was. He'd blown it all when he'd stood in the hall with a gun in his hand.

A good cover, it seemed, couldn't quite cover up the past.

Vaughn was moving with increasing carelessness. Probably because there hadn't been any traffic on the quiet road. Maybe he was beginning to realize that making his way to the other end of the island was going to be very difficult.

Not difficult, Adrian thought savagely. Impossible. Vaughn wasn't going to drive, walk or fly off Bainbridge Island. At least not under his own power. Adrian quickened his pace, gliding silently through the rain-wet trees, skirting the berry bushes and listening with every nerve in his body.

In another couple of minutes he heard the first faint sounds of his quarry. Vaughn might be good but he obviously didn't know much about this kind of fieldwork. He was probably more accustomed to the streets of foreign cities. Most likely he'd never done a lot of real fieldwork in Vietnam or South America. An office spy. A man who worked embassies and cocktail parties.

Easy hunting.

Adrian could hear him clearly now. Vaughn wasn't far ahead of him. What lead he'd had had been chewed into by berry bushes, a driving rain and a woodsy terrain with which he wasn't familiar.

Adrian, on the other hand, knew every inch of the woods around his house. He'd walked them often enough, head bent against a cold drizzle, hands stuffed into his jacket. He'd thought about *Phantom* during those long walks. And he'd thought about the mysterious Sara.

Sara. My passionate, impulsive, loving Sara. Sara, from whom he would have done anything to keep the truth. Too late now. The cover was blown.

A rough, hastily bitten-off oath from the man ahead blended with the steady beat of the rain but Adrian heard it. He slipped forward, starting to reach for the gun in the holster at his back. And then he caught sight of the muted, striped shirt Vaughn was wearing. Vaughn was having to swerve in order to go around another thicket of blackberry bushes. Adrian changed his mind about the gun. *Easy hunting. Easy prey.*

You should never have touched her, Vaughn. You should never have gone near Sara. It's going to cost you everything.

Vaughn trotted to the left, searching for a way around the thorny bushes. He heard nothing as Adrian made his silent rush through the trees. In the last second, though, Vaughn felt the movement behind him. He whirled, clawing at his pocket to withdraw a switch-blade.

But he was too late. Adrian's body catapulted into his quarry's, bearing both men to the soggy ground. Adrian had his hands locked around the fist that held the knife. He crushed with all his strength, hearing something snap. Vaughn yelled. The knife fell into a pile of leaves.

It was all over in less than a minute. Adrian had the advantage and he used it. With brutal efficiency he used his hands to stun his opponent. In a startlingly short period of time Vaughn lay limp and dazed beneath his attacker.

Chapter Ten

Sara adjusted the bandage on her shoulder for the twentieth time, using the bathroom mirror to guide her. It had been exceedingly awkward trying to bandage the wound without help but at last she'd gotten the bleeding stopped. She had been right. It hurt like hell, but the slicing cut wasn't all that deep. Her gaze went to the watch on her wrist. It had been over two hours since Adrian had left the house in pursuit of Vaughn.

Too much time. She was growing increasingly frightened as the minutes ticked past. But she felt incredibly helpless. Not because she thought for a moment that Vaughn would succeed in ambushing Adrian, though. Her mouth twisted in response to another stab of pain from her shoulder. No, Adrian would get his man. The wolf was on the hunt and he always did what had to be done.

Just as Phantom always did what must be done.

What truly frightened her was the thought of Adrian being thrown back into the life he had left behind. She would have given anything to keep him from having to resurrect the past. Because now she knew just how hard he had worked to put it behind him. But there was nothing she could do.

Adrian was the man they had once called Wolf, the legend who had been only too real. She had been coming slowly to that conclusion all day as bits and pieces of evidence came together in her mind.

When she had realized that her only hope of escaping Vaughn lay with Adrian, Sara had acknowledged the truth. Her life had depended on the man code-named Wolf, the man she had once imagined was a renegade killer.

And she had known on some instinctive level that Adrian would save her. That was why she had lured Vaughn back to the island house.

It was her love for Adrian that had enabled her to view the evidence of his past with different eyes. That love had begun from almost the first moment she had turned to find him watching her going through his study. She had known in that first glimpse that this man was different. He was her uncle's friend. The kind of man you could count on when the chips were down.

She had known for certain she was in love last night when she'd lain in Adrian's arms and prayed he wouldn't leave in the morning.

It was all so clear now. Crystal-clear, in fact. She probably should have been suspicious from the start about his identity. He was a man who needed to control his environment, to maintain a cover. It was the way he had built a new life.

Sara shuddered and tears filmed her eyes as she wondered how Adrian had felt when he'd realized his carefully structured world was crumbling around him. She ached to be able to comfort him but she was terribly afraid he wouldn't want the comfort. He had depended on no one but himself for too long.

The knock on the door shocked her into dropping the

roll of tape she had been using. Sara frowned into the mirror. Adrian wouldn't knock on his own door, surely. Nervously she held a square of gauze to her shoulder and adjusted her shirt as best she could. Then she went cautiously down the hall to the front door. Standing on tiptoe, she peered through the tiny viewing port.

A man dressed in a wildly patterned aloha shirt and holding a festive striped umbrella stood on the porch.

"Uncle Lowell!" Sara flung open the door and rushed into his arms. "My God, Uncle Lowell, are you all right? We've been so worried. Adrian's gone after Vaughn and it's been over two hours! I've been going out of my mind. How did you get here? Where have you been?"

"Easy, Sara," Kincaid said, smiling down at her. "One question at a time. Where did you say Adrian was?"

Sara stepped back into the house and held the door. "He's gone after Vaughn." She shook her head, trying to sort it all out for him. "Vaughn was holding me prisoner. He was going to trade me to you for information about that damned gold. Adrian rescued me but in the process Vaughn got away."

Kincaid arched shaggy eyebrows. "He did?" He followed his niece through the door, shaking out the umbrella as he did so. "That doesn't sound like Adrian."

"Well, it was all very chaotic, believe me." Sara sighed. "Vaughn was holding a knife at my throat and he'd made Adrian throw down his gun. Oh, it's a long story. But the end result is that Vaughn got clear and Adrian went after him. I've been worrying myself sick, Uncle Lowell."

"What's wrong with your shoulder?" Kincaid leaned forward, thick brows drawing into a solid line.

"Vaughn scratched it with the knife." She turned her

head, trying to look at the gauze-covered wound. "It's not really that bad but it hurts so."

"Knife wounds generally feel like fire. Here, let me see if you've got it properly bandaged."

"The wound is all right, Uncle Lowell. It's Adrian I'm getting frantic about." But she stood still while Lowell glanced at the slice in her shoulder and then taped down the gauze.

"Adrian can take care of himself."

"You two keep saying that about each other but, personally, I'm having severe doubts! And I didn't want Adrian having to...to go back to his old business!"

Lowell tilted his head to one side, studying her speculatively. "So you've figured out what the old business was?"

Sara nodded grimly. "And I mean to have a heart-to-heart chat with you about that. But we can do it later. I've got other things on my mind just now."

"So have I. Got any coffee? After a few days in sunny Hawaii, it's a bit of a shock to come back to Seattle." Lowell started in the direction of the kitchen.

"But what about Adrian?" Helplessly Sara followed in her uncle's wake.

Lowell Kincaid was the same as ever, she decided. You'd never know that behind the laughing blue eyes was a brain that could function in the most convoluted patterns. He was nearing seventy now and had gone quite bald except for a fringe of well-trimmed gray hair. Kincaid had never gone to fat; his body was still whipcord lean. In addition to the aloha shirt, he was wearing sandals and a pair of white cotton slacks that were spotted with rain. On his wrist was a gold watch. It went nicely with the thin gold chain around his neck. Sara knew the gold was real. Her uncle never wore fake gold.

"Adrian will be back when he's taken care of things."
With the familiarity of a man who has frequently been a
guest in the house, Lowell began making coffee. "Damn
sorry he had to clean up my mess, though."

"Uncle Lowell," Sara said with forced patience.
"Why don't you tell me what the hell has been happening?"

Lowell stretched and lifted a hand to rub the point between his shoulder blades. "Well, to put it in simple
terms, I've just spent the last few days following a false
trail in Hawaii. Came back today when I realized it was a
dead end. Vaughn really had me running around the
countryside," he added ruefully. "I feel like an idiot."

"Who is Vaughn, anyway?"

"Old business."

"Oh, yes." She nodded, remembering the taped message. "You said something about taking care of old business."

"Look, when Adrian gets back, he's going to want
some explanations, too. Why don't we wait until we're
all sitting cozily around a nice warm fire. And what about
dinner?"

"Dinner," Sara said vengefully, "is the last thing on
my mind at the moment. What are we going to do about
Adrian?"

"Absolutely nothing. Never was much anyone could
do about Adrian," her uncle said reflectively as he
poured boiling water over instant coffee. "Just aim him
and pull the trigger."

Sara felt sick to her stomach.

SARA KNEW who he was. *She knew who he was.* Adrian
couldn't forget the memory of her description of the man
she knew as Wolf. Her words still rang in his head. A

renegade killer or something equally picturesque. A man who, when he walked into a room, chilled everything and everyone. He'd seen the expression in her eyes when he'd stood in the hall just outside the study early this evening. She had looked up from the manuscript and he'd known that for her the room had grown very cold.

It was all over.

He drove back to the cabin with a sense of deep foreboding. There was a good chance she wouldn't even be there. Then what? When he pulled into the drive and saw the familiar green Toyota, he felt some sense of relief. Lowell was back. And that meant Sara was probably still around. Her car was still there but that didn't mean much since he'd disabled it earlier.

It was nice that Kincaid was home safe and sound, of course, Adrian told himself as he opened the car door. But the real benefit to his return was that it meant Adrian wouldn't have to face Sara alone. He still hadn't figured out what to say to her and he was beginning to accept the fact that he might never figure it out. He'd never been very good with words around Sara. In any event, she would probably be gone from his life soon, anyway.

She wouldn't want to hang around a wolf.

He walked slowly up the porch steps. The wet night had descended completely now and the warm lights of the house beckoned. But Adrian wasn't fooled. He knew the warmth was an illusion. Without Sara, there could be no real warmth in his life. He tried to dredge up some polite greetings, the sort of thing a man might say in this situation. He should be a gentleman about it. Give her an out. But deep inside he wasn't sure he could do it. He wanted her so and he'd begun to believe lately that he could have her. The thought of letting her walk out now filled him with a tight, gnawing tension.

There were a lot of things a man could take in this world but a woman's love was not among them. It had to be given willingly and it had to be for real. He had spent the last few days realizing the truth of that. The wonder of having Sara for himself couldn't be pushed back into the corners of his mind where he now kept other things that were better forgotten. He couldn't give her up.

But she hated and feared the man called Wolf.

The mechanical-sounding words Adrian had been practicing as he climbed the steps were wiped out of his head as the front door was thrown open.

"It's about time you got back!" Sara cried as she flew across the porch. "Adrian, it's been hours!"

He felt the soft impact as she hurled herself against him. Automatically his arms went around her. He was dazed by the greeting.

"Sara?"

"You said you'd be back on the five-fifty-five ferry," she whispered into his wet shirt. "I knew you'd get back on time. I knew all I had to do was have Vaughn here and you'd take care of everything."

He held her fiercely, absorbing the warmth of her. "Yes." He stroked her hair wonderingly. "I got the readout from the house alarm system right after I drove off the ferry." His fingers tightened abruptly in her hair. "I've never been so scared in my life, Sara."

"Hi, Adrian, sorry about all this. Everything okay?"

Adrian gazed over Sara's head, his eyes meeting those of his friend. "Everything's taken care of." He felt Sara shiver in his arms.

Kincaid nodded. "Figured it would be."

"You may have a few questions to answer from your old pals at the agency in the morning, though."

Kincaid's eyes gleamed. "How's that?"

"I left Vaughn tied up in a neat package a few yards off I-90. Then I called the West Coast agency office and left a message telling them where they could find him. When the guy who took the call demanded to know who was leaving the message—"

"You gave him my name." Kincaid grinned ruefully. "Thanks a lot, pal. Well, I guess I can't complain. I deserved it. Lord knows I owe you for taking care of Sara. Besides, maybe Gilkirk and his boys will be so delighted to have their hands on Vaughn they won't want to ask too many questions."

Sara lifted her head, her hands moving upward to frame Adrian's face. "You didn't kill him."

"No."

She smiled. "Of course not. Supper's ready. Go and take a hot shower. I'll pour you a glass of wine." She pulled free and disappeared back into the house.

Adrian stared after her, aware of a gnawing uncertainty. The uncertainty was painful but it was better than the cold, dead certainty of loss he'd been feeling earlier. Uncertainty contained hope. He followed Lowell into the house and headed for the bathroom, stripping off the wet Windbreaker as he moved.

ADRIAN HAD BEEN WATCHING Sara since he'd emerged from the shower, trying to second-guess her thoughts. She'd chattered about the gold while she'd prepared a hearty rice and vegetable salad, making a joke out of her uncle's idea of a wedding gift. She'd poured him and Lowell a glass of wine and put the sourdough rolls in the oven while discussing Lowell's unplanned vaca-

tion in Hawaii. Then she'd kept up a running mono-
logue on Kincaid's new aloha shirt and how typical it
was of him to bring something like that back from
Hawaii.

Lowell had talked easily, too, leaning against the
kitchen counter while responding to her teasing about
his new shirt.

"Glad you like it. Got three more in the suitcase.
Picked 'em up while I waited for the flight back this
morning." He'd glanced down at the front of the
splashy shirt with obvious pleasure.

Adrian had felt left out of the conversation but he
hadn't known how to get into it. Sara and her uncle kept
up a bright dialogue that covered everything under the
sun except the subject of the man called Wolf. Adrian
told himself morosely that it was probably because they
were both too polite to talk about someone when the object of the conversation was within hearing distance
brooding over a glass of wine.

During dinner Sara finally pounced on her uncle, demanding answers. Adrian surreptitiously kept an eye on
her lively hazel eyes while she quizzed Lowell Kincaid.
He searched for signs of disgust or fear or rejection in
her expressive features. The strange inner anxiety was
eating him alive, demanding assurances and explanations and at the same time preparing him for the worst.
Surely, after everything she had believed about the man
named Wolf, she couldn't possibly be this warm and
nonchalant now.

Adrian's fingers crumpled the napkin in his lap and
he glanced down, vaguely astonished at the outward
show of tension.

"All right, Uncle Lowell, let's have it," Sara demanded as the meal came to a close. She leaned back in

her chair, her fingertips steepled beneath her chin as she regarded Kincaid with a gleaming gaze.

"Well," Lowell began with an easy grin, "I had to go to about three shops before I found just the right selection of shirts but when I saw this one with the pineapples on it, I knew—"

"Lowell Kincaid, I am not talking about the aloha shirts and you know it. I want to know about the gold."

"Ah, the gold," he echoed softly. "I figure that you may not be able to get at it until sometime around your twenty-fifth wedding anniversary, or you may have to let your children inherit the treasure map, but either way it makes an interesting wedding present, don't you think? Even if you never actually see the gold itself, you'll have it to talk about and laugh about and tell stories about. I can just hear the tales you'll be telling your kids."

"I think," Sara interrupted firmly, "that we're getting a little ahead of ourselves. I'm not interested in what I may be telling my kids, especially since I don't have any."

"Yet," Lowell interjected wisely.

Sara raised her eyebrows but Adrian noticed she didn't look at him. She kept her attention on Kincaid. "I'm more concerned with the past at the moment. Did you or did you not steal CIA gold and stash it near the Cambodian border?"

Kincaid grinned at Adrian. "She's rather aggressively direct when she wants an answer."

"Umm." Adrian sipped the last of his wine and wondered why Sara hadn't been aggressively direct in pinning him down about Wolf. Maybe she didn't want to know the full truth. He set down the wineglass with grim care.

"Okay, Sara, here's the story," Kincaid began. "For starters, it wasn't CIA gold. It wasn't U.S. gold in any sense of the word, really. It belonged to some very astute gentlemen who were doing an active drug business under the guise of working in a civilian capacity for the U.S. government. I accidentally stumbled across them while working with some friends of mine."

"Friends?"

Lowell nodded. "I had spent a lot of time with the people of a particular village. They had been very useful during the war, supplying information and some very brave young men and women. At any rate, I was in the village when rumors came of the two drug runners being killed. The business career of a drug runner is precarious, to say the least. I was near the scene of the killing and, through a series of, uh, arranged coincidences, managed to get my hands on the gold."

"Uh-huh." Sara sounded distinctly skeptical. " 'Arranged' being the operative word, I imagine."

"I then had myself a problem. I knew things were deteriorating rapidly. Saigon was about to go under, and everyone who had any sense was aware of it. I was several miles away and there was no way I could make it back to the embassy with the gold. I would have been lucky to make it back with my life. So I decided on another route out of the situation."

"A route that would allow you to take some of the gold with you?"

Kincaid chuckled. "You know me and gold, Sara. I couldn't bring myself to just toss it away."

"Vaughn said he uncovered a file that indicated you left some of it behind with your friends in that village."

Kincaid's shaggy brows lifted. "A file, hmm? I wondered how he got curious enough about the gold after all

these years to make a try for it. Well, Sara, let me tell
you a fact of life. There's nothing quite as useful as gold
when you're trying to survive in a country that's recently been overrun by a conquering army. And I owed
those villagers. As for myself, I'd been making some
friends near the Cambodian border and decided to call
in a few favors. I loaded my share of the gold on a jeep
and drove to the border. There was no way I could get it
out of the country, so I buried it, made a map and then
rendezvoused with my contacts. They got me out of the
country.''

"Where does Brady Vaughn fit into all this?'' Sara
demanded.

"Vaughn has been a thorn in the agency's side for
some time. We all knew he was working both sides of
the street.''

"He said something about working two jobs,'' Sara
said dryly. "Was that what he meant? He was selling information to the other side?''

"Information we wanted him to sell, although he
didn't know it. We used him after we learned he'd been
turned.'' Lowell smiled. "But his usefulness was becoming limited from what my former associates have
told me. Apparently the other side felt the same.
Vaughn was smart enough to sense that something was
going wrong and wisely decided to disappear. Apparently he wanted a little nest egg to cushion his sudden
retirement.''

"And he chose your cache of gold.''

"He'd been assigned to Saigon during that last six
months. We'd worked together on a couple of jobs. But
I never did fully trust the man. I tried to plant my own
rumors about the gold whenever I heard it mentioned
after the war. I knew it would be almost impossible to

keep the whole thing absolutely secret. There were all those villagers who knew about it, for one thing. And Lord knows who the drug dealers knew. But I made sure most of the gossip about the missing gold implied the stuff was government material kept at the embassy and used for clandestine operations. I sort of left the impression that the two drug dealers were really agents. And of course I kept my own name out of it. You never know. I didn't want to implicate myself. If someone knew the drug story or got too friendly with the villagers, he might be able to track down more of the tale."

"Apparently some journalist did get friendly with the villagers," Sara said. "And his notes somehow ended up in an old file that Vaughn came across."

Lowell sighed. "I thought after all these years the story of the gold really had become nothing more than a legend."

"Vaughn said he deliberately planted a rumor about him being in Hawaii recruiting mercenaries to help him get your treasure," Sara said.

Kincaid shook his head. "I'm embarrassed to admit it worked. I got wind of the plan and did exactly as he anticipated. I took off for Hawaii." He glanced at Adrian. "I honestly thought I'd have everything taken care of within forty-eight hours or so. Didn't think you'd be bothered with cleaning up the mess."

Adrian couldn't think of anything to say. He just nodded austerely and continued to watch Sara's face through narrowed eyes. Why didn't she say something about what had happened that afternoon. The suspense was going to shred him. A part of him wanted to get the confrontation over and done with. Another part wanted to pretend nothing devastating had occurred. Abruptly he pushed his chair away from the table and went over to where he kept the brandy.

"Can I pour you some, Lowell?" His voice felt thick and scratchy in his throat.

"Sounds great." The older man beamed.

Sara focused on her uncle again. "Vaughn is definitely out of the way? He won't be bothering us again?"

Lowell Kincaid smiled. "You don't have to worry about him. I'll talk to Gilkirk in the morning. But from what I hear the agency's tired of using him, anyway. Even if he got turned loose tomorrow, he realizes everyone knows who he is and what he's been doing. He'd disappear in a hurry."

"He had plans, you know," Sara mused.

Adrian could feel her watching him as he poured the brandy. "What plans?" he managed to ask, although he couldn't have cared less. Vaughn, as Kincaid had just said, was no longer an issue. He'd made sure of that when he'd left the sullen man bound and gagged in the rain beside the freeway. Vaughn was smart enough to know that everything had fallen apart. Vaughn, too, knew what it meant to have his cover completely blown.

"He thought that, given the map and a few carefully selected mercenaries, he could get into Cambodia and get at the gold. He told me all about his scheme," she finished blithely. "Aren't you going to pour me some brandy, too?"

Adrian turned back to the counter and poured another glass. "Sorry," he muttered shortly. When he handed it to her, she raised it cheerfully.

"Here's to finally getting some answers." She downed a healthy swallow.

Lowell grinned. "Haven't I always told you that answers are always crystal-clear once you know where to look?''

With a snap, Sara set down the brandy snifter. "Speaking of crystal-clear answers," she began. And then she was on her feet, hurrying down the hall toward the study.

Kincaid traded glances with Adrian. It was the first time they'd been alone together without Sara in the room. "Everything's under control?"

Adrian nodded. "Yeah. The agency will handle it. I really did lead them to believe you were the one who'd wrapped Vaughn up for Christmas. I guess if Vaughn says too much, though, Gilkirk may figure out I'm still around."

Kincaid chuckled. "Even if he does, you'll be all right. You're old news now, I'm afraid. The last time I talked to Gilkirk I casually brought up your name just to see what he'd say. He wasn't terribly interested, frankly. You'd be a minor curiosity and that's it. Gilkirk won't push it. He owes you and he knows it. He's a good man. Pays his debts.''

"I like being old news." Adrian thought about that. "But Sara . . .''

"Don't worry about Sara," Kincaid said softly. "She's my niece. I know her.''

"She's a woman," Adrian countered. "And she had a wild image of Wolf built up in her mind. What did you tell her about me, Kincaid?''

"Only bits and pieces. I was very concerned about you a year ago, my friend. I wasn't sure if the book was going to be the therapy you needed. I guess I had a few drinks with Sara one evening and talked. More than I should have, probably. She took the information and embroidered it a bit with her rather active imagination.''

"Did you really give her some idiotic story about the temperature, uh, dropping in a room when I walked in?" Adrian demanded.

Kincaid blinked. "I suppose I did. There are times when it's perfectly true."

Adrian winced. "No wonder I don't get many invitations to cocktail parties."

Lowell Kincaid howled with laughter. "Don't worry. The description only applies when you're working. If you're not getting party invitations, it's because people suspect you're not the party type. Not because they don't need an extra ice bucket."

"What about telling her I was a. . . a renegade?"

Kincaid looked surprised. "I never said that. I'm afraid she came to that conclusion on her own. I told her that I had trained a man who wound up with the code name of Wolf and that I was now worried about him. I guess she assumed—" He was about to say something else and stopped as Sara trotted back down the hall, tossing the crystal apple in her hands. "Ah, the apple."

"Yes, the apple." She pinned him with a mock-ferocious glance. "This is where the answer is, right Uncle Lowell? Clear as crystal?"

He nodded genially. "It's a microdot masquerading as one of the bubbles captured in the crystal. Pretty little apple, isn't it? I had one made especially for both you and Adrian. You each have half of the map. That's the wedding present, you see. Not the gold itself but the adventure of having a treasure map of your very own. And someday, someone in your family will be able to go after the gold. Maybe twenty years from now, when the politics and violence in that part of the world have changed. Maybe the next generation will get it. Who knows? In the meantime you'll have the fantasy."

"It was a brilliant gift idea," Sara said with a warm smile.

"I thought so. Just the thing for a woman with an overactive imagination. When did you figure out that the apple was the key?"

"While I was talking to Vaughn. I knew the answer wasn't in the manuscript." She slid a quick glance at Adrian. "*Phantom* answers other questions, but it doesn't tell where the gold is hidden. I just used that as an excuse to get Vaughn back here to the house. I figured out the role of the apple, though, when I put everything I knew together. The gold, you implied, was a wedding gift. Something to be shared. And you had given both Adrian and me an apple. It was a link between us. The key. Then there was your penchant for hiding things out in the open, the way you always say answers are crystal-clear. The apple itself has a gold stem and leaf and that was another clue. The gold on the apple was meant to be a connection to the gold in Southeast Asia, right? And you'd given us the basic clue when you told Adrian the legend. Last but not least, I knew you always like to cover your bases. You would have wanted the information available to both Adrian and me just in case something ever happened to you. It made sense that you had given us the answers. And you would have given them to us jointly. All we had to do was look around."

"And you realized that the only thing I had given both of you was the apple." Kincaid nodded. "Not bad, Sara. Not bad at all."

"Games," Adrian heard himself mutter.

"Better get used to them if you're going to marry into the family," Lowell advised lightly.

"I've played enough for one day. If you both will excuse me, I'm going to go to bed. Lowell, you can have the couch. Your niece has the spare bedroom." Adrian got to his feet.

Sara's head came up quickly. "Adrian. . ."

He stood still, looking down at her. "What is it, Sara?"

"I. . . I just wondered about your trip this morning." She chewed on her lower lip, obviously searching for the right words. "I mean, Vaughn seemed to think you'd gone to Mexico."

"That's what I wanted him to think."

"But. . ."

"I bought the ticket. But the plane made a few stops between here and Mexico City. I got off in L.A."

"I see," she said quietly. "You planned it that way to make Vaughn think you'd left the country to go after the gold yourself."

"I thought my leaving would draw him out into the open," Adrian explained very patiently. "I figured he'd make his try at night, thinking you'd be alone. I'd planned to circle back and be waiting for him. I had it all worked out. But you rewrote the rules."

"He tricked me," she protested. "I had a phone call from Uncle Lowell. Or at least I thought it was from him. Vaughn made a tape from the answering-machine recordings in Lowell's cottage and mixed up the words into whole new sentences."

"I know," Adrian said. "Vaughn told me."

Sara eyed him curiously. "Did he?"

"He told me a great many things," Adrian said. "Good night, Lowell. Sara." He left the room.

Sara watched him go, the smile fading from her eyes and being replaced by a wistful yearning. Slowly she lowered the apple into her lap as she sat down beside her uncle.

"He has a nerve accusing us of playing games," she whispered. "What does he think he was doing today when he fed me that song and dance about going off to find a mysterious contact who might know where you were?"

Kincaid swirled the brandy in his glass. "He wasn't playing games. Adrian never plays games. He simply didn't want you to know the truth."

"What truth?"

"That he didn't have any magic man to contact. The only one around he could depend on to protect you was himself. He had to make Vaughn believe he had really left town and the only way to do that was to actually get on the plane. Mexico City was the logical choice because it has a reputation in the industry. Vaughn made all the assumptions he was supposed to make when he discovered that was Adrian's destination."

"But why didn't Adrian tell me?" She sighed.

"He wanted to keep you from finding out the truth about him. In the end there was no way he could accomplish that. Not and save your life, too."

"What did you mean about Adrian never playing games?"

"Just that." Lowell took a long swallow of brandy and gazed up at the beamed ceiling for a moment. "You and I, Sara, we have a capacity for stepping back emotionally from a situation we don't like. You did it all the time in the corporate world. You treated it as a game when it threatened to get too serious or intense. I saw you do it in the academic world and when you played at being an artist. It was a survival mechanism for you. It works very well. I should know. I've used it myself. I could frequently put my work into that kind of perspective when things got too grim. I would detach myself and instinctively try to see all the moves and countermoves as just part of a great big chess game.''

"And Adrian couldn't do that?"

"No. For him it was very real. He gave everything he had to his work and it finally took its toll.''

"Phantom." Sara stared down at the crystal-and-gold apple. "The real truth in the manuscript isn't the hint about the gold that you put in, is it? It's the part Adrian put into the story. The reality of what he faced.''

"When he finally realized the job would eventually break him, he turned in his resignation. It wasn't accepted. They told him there was one last mission.''

"And he went on it." Sara shuddered. "I think he just barely survived, Uncle Lowell.''

"He did what he had to do. Adrian always does what has to be done. He was quite lethally serious about his work and that attitude made him the best there was in the industry.''

"Better than you, Uncle Lowell?''

"Better than me. But the violence and the frustration of that last job were the end for him. When it was over he simply disappeared. He showed up on my doorstep three months later, calling himself Adrian Saville.''

"That's not his real name?" Sara asked in astonishment.

Lowell Kincaid smiled. "It is now. I told you, Adrian doesn't play games. Everything is for real. He took another name and started a new life. He would have done anything to keep it real.''

"Well, it is real," Sara protested. "Nothing's changed.''

"Now you know the truth about him," her uncle pointed out quietly.

"But I don't feel any differently about him," she breathed. "How could he think—"

"Apparently you gave him quite a horror story about Wolf."

"That was all your fault. You're the one who told me the tale!"

"I was a little drunk that night as I recall. And I was genuinely worried about Adrian. I wasn't certain writing the book was going to work for him."

"That's no excuse. You told me things—"

"They were all true," Lowell Kincaid said, giving her a level glance. "But I will not assume responsibility for what you did to the facts with your imagination."

Sara grimaced. "When I found myself realizing this afternoon that my only chance for surviving lay with Adrian, I knew who he was. I also knew that whatever he had been, he was now the man I loved. You were right about him. He's the kind of man you can count on when the chips are down. Why did you sketch that wolf's head on the manuscript?"

"I was just doodling. It was natural that I'd be thinking about Wolf when I read the tale of Phantom."

"I suppose so. It put me on the wrong track altogether, though. I thought it was Wolf you had gone after." Sara fell silent for a moment. "I guess I'll go to bed, too."

"You do that," her uncle murmured blandly.

She shot him a half-humorous, half-rueful glance. "Going to throw your favorite niece to the wolf?"

"Wolves take care of their own." Lowell got up and headed across the room to the brandy bottle. "Good night, Sara."

She went over to him and hugged him affectionately. "Good night, Uncle Lowell. I'm so glad you're safe."

"Not half as glad as I am that you're okay. Guess I owe Adrian for that."

Sara said nothing. She merely smiled and walked down the hall toward Adrian's bedroom with a deep sense of certainty.

Lying in bed, his arms folded behind his head, Adrian stared into the darkness and listened to the sound of Sara's footsteps. He waited for them to stop outside her bedroom door, and when she didn't even pause he tensed.

It would be best if she stayed in her own room, he told himself. Quickly, silently, he ran down a list of why she shouldn't open his door tonight. Too much had happened today and she was inclined to be emotional. She was also inclined to be impulsive. She needed time to sort out her feelings. He didn't want her coming to him without having had time to absorb the full implications of what she had learned about him today. She might be feeling sorry for him. She might have convinced herself he needed her and she was too compassionate to deny him comfort. He didn't want her pity.

So many reasons, he thought savagely. So many excellent reasons why he should send her back to her own room if she dared to open the door.

She turned the doorknob and stepped inside. Adrian looked at her as she stood silhouetted against the light and knew that he could never find the willpower to send her back. He needed her warmth too badly tonight. It had been so cold today.

"Asleep, Adrian?" she asked softly, shutting the door and coming forward into the shadowed room.

"No."

"You must be exhausted."

"Umm."

There was a rustle of clothing as she undressed. He saw the pale gleam of her bare shoulder and then the lighter area of her hip as she stepped out of the jeans.

"I'm a little tired myself," she admitted softly as she walked naked to the bed.

"Sara..." He tried to say the words that should be said, tried to explain why she shouldn't be there. But she was pulling back the comforter and slipping in beside him and the logical phrases disintegrated in his throat. The warmth and softness of her as she reached out to hold him were a temptation that was far more difficult to resist than all the gold in Southeast Asia.

"Don't worry," she whispered huskily. "I won't be making any demands on you tonight. We've both had a hard day." She stroked her fingers through his hair, soothing the nape of his neck.

"Sara, it's not that, it's just... Oh, Sara, hold me. Put your arms around me and hold me."

She did, cradling him even as he pulled her tightly into the curve of his body. Adrian inhaled the familiar, enticing scent that was uniquely hers, knew the incredible comfort of her touch, felt the shape of her locked securely in his arms and relaxed for the first time since the day had dawned. Now he would be able to sleep.

Hours later he awoke to the light of dawn and the knowledge of what he must do. A part of him resisted the knowledge even though another side of him realized it was the only sure way. It was best to do things the sure way, he reminded himself. Careful, cautious, certain. He had spent the past year carefully, cautiously, certainly pulling himself back together. He knew about patience. He knew about being sure.

It would be tricky trying to teach those skills to the warm, frequently impulsive woman who lay curled so contentedly in his arms. But it was the only way. Above all else he wanted her to know exactly how she felt about him.

No games. Not even the kind played out of pity or compassion. Especially not those.

Adrian didn't move as he lay beside Sara. He was almost afraid of disturbing her because once she came awake he would have to explain his decision. He preferred to steal these last few minutes of closeness and warmth, make them last as long as possible. A wolf, he thought wryly, took whatever he could get.

Sara opened her eyes slowly, aware of Adrian's arm around her, his hand resting possessively on her breast. She lay still for a moment, letting herself realize fully just how good it felt to lie next to him. It felt right. A sense of deep certainty settled on her. It was unlike any emotion she had ever known. She was in love with Adrian Saville. She had known it since yesterday.

It didn't surprise her that love would arrive like this. Such an emotion, when it finally came into her life, was bound to happen in just this manner. For someone like her there was no other way. Quick, impulsive, but absolutely right. She knew real gold when she found it. Lazily she stretched, a serene, confident expression in her eyes as she turned to meet Adrian's steady gaze.

"Good morning," she murmured, touching her mouth lightly to his. "How did you sleep?"

He blinked, his features holding a trace of surprise as he thought about the question. "Solidly." His hand moved on her, following the curve of her thigh. "Thanks to you."

"Good." Feeling vastly pleased with herself, Sara stretched again, this time bringing her body quite deliberately against him. "I'm glad I'm useful for something. I felt like such a fool yesterday when I walked straight into Vaughn's hands.''

Adrian didn't respond to the invitation of her languid stretch. In fact, she decided, he seemed almost tense. Not at all like a man who'd had a good night's sleep.

"It wasn't your fault," he told her. "Anyone would have been fooled by the recording. I've heard tapes scrambled from other tapes. They can sound very real. But you kept your head. You got him back here.''

"I knew you would be coming back and that you could handle everything," she said.

"How long have you known?" He watched her with cool eyes.

Sara knew the coolness was deceptive. She also knew the real question he was asking. She knew him very well now, Sara decided. Reading *Phantom* had filled in many of the blanks a person normally encountered when learning about another human being. Her heart ached to replace what had originally occupied those blanks in his life.

"How long have I known that you were the man they used to call Wolf?" There was no point in not being totally honest. "Since yesterday for certain. When Vaughn told me that Wolf had been a legend at one time but had not made it back from his last assignment—''

"Because I'd cracked," Adrian put in bluntly.

Sara refused to acknowledge his interruption. "I began to think about Phantom. About a man who had been to the brink and hung on instead of going completely over the edge. A man who had forced himself to survive when by all logic he should have been crushed. And then I thought about the way I feel safe around you...."

"Safe?"

She nodded. "I realized it that day at the Pike Place Market when you showed up just as Vaughn was about to coerce me into his car. And yesterday when I found myself trying to think of a way to deal with Vaughn. Something told me I only had to get him back here. When you arrived I knew I would be safe again. There were lots of other little clues, of course. Your concern with the security of this house. The way you move. That sketch of my uncle's. Even the way you play checkers. So intense and cool. Then there was your recent conversion to vegetarianism. Somehow that seemed symbolic. Something a carnivore might do if he were trying to put aside that aspect of his life. It all fit. Especially once I knew for certain that Vaughn wasn't Wolf."

"You had such a terrible image of Wolf," Adrian began heavily.

"By the time I realized you had once been Wolf, I was ready to throw the image out the window. I knew the real you by then." She smiled dreamily, loving him with her eyes.

Adrian's face became remote. "I'm not so sure, Sara."

"Not so sure of what?"

"That you know the real me." He stilled the protest that rose instantly to her lips by putting his fingers against her mouth. "Listen to me, Sara. I rushed you into bed that first time. The second time was too intense, too emotional because you knew I was leaving and you weren't sure what was going to happen. We've been living in the eye of a storm ever since I walked into this house and found you in my study. There's been no chance for you to get to know me in a normal fashion."

Alarm flickered into life. Sara watched him intently. "Are you trying to tell me you aren't sure how you feel about me, after all?"

He shook his head once, a quick, violent negative movement. "I know how I feel about you. I've been wanting you for months. You've been growing in my mind every day, taking shape, tantalizing me, until I knew I had to have you. But your uncle was right. There was something else I needed to do first."

"Write *Phantom*."

"That book was a final step in freeing myself, Sara."

"I understand." And she did. Completely now.

"You were a goal, a treasure waiting for me after I had put the past behind me. I feel as though I've been getting to know you for months. Your uncle saw to that. But it didn't work that way for you. You've only known me a few days and that time has been too intense, too dangerous and too emotional."

"Falling in love is bound to be emotional!" she put in quickly.

"Are you saying you think you're in love with me?" He searched her face.

"Yes." She spoke the single word with gentle assurance.

"Sara, you can't know that!"

"You told me once that you would like me to love you," she reminded him.

His fingers tightened on her. "I want that very badly. But you have to be certain. You have to be sure. No games, Sara."

"I've never played games with you."

"How about with your own mind? Honey, it's just too soon. You can't possibly know how you feel. Not yet. Hell, up until yesterday, you've been thinking of Wolf as some kind of psychotic killer. Now you've learned that Wolf and I are one and the same. You can't tell me you've managed to adjust to that kind of news overnight!"

"I get the feeling I can't tell you much of anything," she tossed back. "You're not ready to listen to me. You've already decided the way things have to be, haven't you?" The alarm was coiling tightly in her as she began to see where his words were leading.

"Sara, I want you to have time to get to know me," he told her urgently. "This time around we'll do it right."

"I don't understand!" But she did and the realization panicked her.

Adrian continued forcefully, his certainty clear in every word. "Yes, you do, honey. We're going to do it right. I want you to have a chance to make absolutely certain of your feelings. The next time you tell me you love me I want you to have had plenty of opportunity to think through just what you're saying."

Sara pulled free of him, sitting up with the sheet held to her breast. Her hair swung in a soft tangle around her shoulders as she stared at him. "Are you sending me away?" Her voice sounded odd. She was clinging to more than the sheet. She was hanging on to her control with both hands.

Slowly Adrian sat up beside her, his eyes almost colorless. He was committed to finishing what he had started, Sara realized. She would not be able to reason with him this morning.

"We're going to start a normal relationship," he said.

"What's normal? Adrian, you of all people should know by now that life is short and highly uncertain. We've found something wonderful together. Why should we waste time? Please don't do this." The plea was all wrong, she thought. She was letting her emotions rule her tongue. Adrian wouldn't trust her to know her own feelings if she did that. He didn't trust emotions.

"I'm not sending you to Outer Mongolia," he said.

"No? Then where are you sending me?"

"I think it would be best if you went back to San Diego."

"San Diego! But I don't even have a job there!"

"You've got your apartment, don't you? It's still your home."

She groped for an argument. "What about you? Are you just going to sit around here until you figure I've had enough time to know my own mind? Adrian, that doesn't make any sense. I'm an adult. I already know how I feel."

"I'm going to come and see you. Call you. Sara, I'm going to court you, don't you understand? I'm going to give you plenty of time—"

"How much?" she challenged.

He looked blank. "How much what?"

"How much time, damn it!"

"I don't know." He frowned. "However long it takes, I suppose."

"That's not fair, Adrian. If you're going to sentence me to exile, you have to at least put a time limit on it. Give me a date. One week? One year? I want a date."

"Sara, you're getting hysterical."

The worst part was that she knew he was right. She was losing her self-control. It was the shock, Sara decided. The shock of waking up in love and being told by Adrian that he wasn't ready for her love. Sara gulped air, swallowing sobs of anger and panic. The more emotional she became, the less Adrian would trust her to know what she really wanted. For the sake of their future, she had to get hold of herself.

"Yes," she whispered, sliding off the edge of the bed. She looked around a little frantically for something to wear and finally saw her shirt on the floor where she had left it last night. "Yes, you're quite right. I'm getting emotional." Her fingers fumbled with the buttons but she managed to get the shirt on. Then she picked up her jeans with hands that still trembled. Adrian never took his eyes off of her.

"Sara, honey, listen to me."

She shook her head. "No, no, I'm all right. I understand. You don't fully trust intense emotions because you learned once that they can take you to the edge of disaster. I should have realized that after reading *Phantom*. That was the lesson you learned when you went through with that last mission and then disappeared, wasn't it? Your emotional response to your work nearly got you killed. You kept yourself so tightly leashed and under such control for so long that in the end you almost came apart when the explosion occurred. That's why you talk in terms of appreciating life's pleasures. Anything stronger than pleasure might be dangerous."

Adrian got slowly to his feet, completely unconcerned with his nakedness. "I just want you to be sure of how you feel," he repeated stubbornly.

She got her jeans zipped and lifted her head to meet his eyes. "You want to be sure of everything. Sure of the security of your house, sure of me, sure of your own self-control. Well, go ahead and make sure, Adrian. Being absolutely sure of things seems to be one of the few *pleasures* you get out of life. Who am I to deny you?"

Whirling, Sara fled from the room.

Chapter Eleven

Adrian's version of a courtship, Sara decided a month later, was going to drive her slowly insane.

Over and over again she told herself that he was the one who needed the time. Time to be sure of her. She would give him that. After all, she loved him; she would give him anything he asked. But how long would the farce continue, she wondered dismally.

"Farce" was hardly the most respectful term for Adrian's courtship, but it was the one that came to Sara's mind most often during the torturous, contrived, carefully choreographed weekends. True to his word Adrian flew down to San Diego every Friday evening. He spent Saturday and Sunday with her and then flew home to his island.

Sara's hopes for the first weekend were dashed when he checked into a motel near her apartment and continued to retreat to it every evening of his stay. The other weekends were no different. He took her to dinner, shows, the zoo and the beach. But he never took her to bed.

In fact, he rarely touched her with any intimacy at all. That was the part that was beginning to drive her out of her mind, Sara realized. She was left with a feeling of genuine panic every Sunday evening when she saw him off at the airport. Perhaps he wasn't capable of making the final step of total commitment. She knew he wanted her, knew he took pleasure in her company but he had convinced himself that she didn't understand her own feelings.

What she really feared, Sara decided, was that he didn't understand the depths of his own feelings for her. He was afraid to surrender completely to the force of his emotions.

They would be fierce and intense, the emotions of a strong man who had much to give once he had accepted the power of his own nature. But he had learned the hard way that there was a risk in losing some of his self-control. She yearned to set him completely free, to urge him to take a risk both on her and on himself but there was no way to break through the controlled facade. On Monday morning after the fourth weekend Sara acknowledged that Adrian had established the rules and he was going to force her to play by them.

Bad analogy, she told herself wryly as she fixed coffee with her imported Italian espresso machine. Adrian didn't like anything that smacked of game playing. She stared morosely out at the palm tree in front of her kitchen window and thought of the carefully restrained kiss she had received at the airport the previous evening.

Uneasily she tried to brush aside the worry that perhaps Adrian would never be able to relax and let himself trust both of them completely.

He did love her, she told herself with some violence. He hadn't said the words but that was all right. She knew him, understood him. She had complete confidence in his love. Her only fear was that he would never have the same confidence.

Somehow he had to learn that the iron control he held over himself wasn't necessary any longer. He was a whole human being now. He'd healed himself. He must learn to have faith in the health of his emotions and in those of the woman who loved him. He could live safely now without a perfect cover.

And she did love him, Sara knew. With every fiber of her being. One month of the stilted courtship hadn't changed that. Nothing on earth could change it. She had never been so certain of anything in her life.

She was at home that evening when he called. She was always at home these days. Not because she didn't have friends or invitations but because she was terrified that Adrian might phone and find her out. She wanted nothing to upset him or alarm him. She wanted him to know that she was simply waiting for him.

The conversation followed its by now predictable path.

"How was the flight back to Seattle?" she asked politely.

"Fine." He hesitated. "Have you eaten?"

"Oh, yes. I fixed myself a salad." Sara searched mentally for something to add to the careful conversation. "And I had a glass of wine."

"I went down to the tavern and had a beer."

At least you got to get out of the house, Sara thought irritably. *I'm forced to sit here from five o'clock on because I can't be sure when you'll call. And I'm terrified you'd use the evidence of my not being at home as an indication that you were right not to trust me.* "Sounds good," she said brightly. "How's the plotting going on the new book?"

"Okay. I'm trying to figure out how to untwist some things in chapter four without giving away too much information. This book is going to be a lot easier to write, though, than *Phantom* was."

Not surprising, Sara thought. This second book wouldn't be nearly so autobiographical. *Phantom* had been a form of catharsis. The next book would truly be fiction. She didn't have any doubt that it would be as good in its own way as its predecessor, however. The bottom line was that Adrian really could write. "Speaking of giving away information, Adrian," Sara heard herself begin quite firmly.

He paused before inquiring cautiously, "Yes?"

She floundered. "Well, I was wondering. I mean, it's been a month now and I was just thinking that you might have come to some, er, decision."

"About what?"

Sara very nearly lost her temper. "About us!"

"Oh. You still want a date when everything's going to be settled, don't you?"

"Adrian," she tried reasonably, "this is getting us nowhere. I've tried to be patient—"

"You don't know much about patience, honey."

"Don't be condescending. Just because people like you know all about patience, doesn't mean the rest of us—"

"What do you mean, people like me?"

Sara wanted to cry for having used all the wrong words. The forbidding cold was back in his voice. "I just meant that you seem to have developed a great deal of patience during your life. I, uh, I haven't been quite that fortunate. Adrian, I'm trying to give you the time you need, but—"

"I'm not the one who needs the time," he interrupted quietly.

"Well, I sure as hell don't need it! I know what I

want. I'm in love with you, and this past month has been awful. I feel like I've been in exile. You don't touch me, you're so polite I could spit, and you won't tell me how long it's going to go on. There are times when I really begin to wonder if you—" She halted the flow of words abruptly.

True to form, Adrian refused to be left hanging. "You wonder if I what?"

"Nothing," she mumbled.

"Sara, tell me what you were about to say."

She sighed. "I wonder if you will ever really trust yourself or me enough to love me." There. It was said. She hadn't dared anything that intimate before and she wasn't at all certain how he would react. She had been assuming a great deal, Sara thought bleakly.

Silence on the other end of the line greeted her statement. Then Adrian's voice came with rock-hard certainty.

"I love you, Sara."

She caught her breath, her fingers clutching the receiver. "You do?"

"You've been a part of me for months. I can't imagine life without you."

The simple words were devastating to her. "You never said anything quite that explicit before," she finally got out rather weakly.

"I don't think I've thought it out quite that explicitly until now," he admitted slowly. "You've just been there, a part of me."

She closed her eyes in relief. It was finally over. It must be over. "Oh, Adrian, Adrian, thank you. I love you so much and I've been going crazy down here waiting for you to be sure."

"I've been sure all along." He sounded vaguely surprised. "It's you who needed the time."

Sara's eyes narrowed as she picked up the first inkling that her waiting might not be ended after all. "I don't need any more time, Adrian. Please. I've been very patient. I could wait forever if there was a real need, but there isn't. There's no need for us to be apart."

His voice hardened. "I want you to have more time."

She heard the finality in his words and fury mingled with despair. "You think I'm playing a game with you."

"No, Sara, it's not that. I just—"

She didn't let him finish. "Adrian Saville, you don't know what real game playing is!" Quite precisely and quite definitely, Sara hung up the phone. Then she walked to the hall closet and found her shoulder bag. There was a chic, cheerful little tavern down the street and around the corner. If Adrian could have a beer in the evenings, so could she. Come to think of it, she needed it a lot more than he did tonight.

The phone rang insistently behind her but Sara ignored it. She walked to the door, opened it as the phone continued to ring, and then she stepped outside. It was a wonderful, balmy Southern California evening. The scent of the sea hovered in the air and the row of palm trees lining her street rustled lazily in the evening breeze. Sara walked briskly down the sidewalk, wondering what the trees looked like in Southeast Asia.

The tavern was only half full, with a crowd of people in their late twenties and early thirties. The women, with their cleverly casual hairstyles, their silk shirts and jeans, chatted vivaciously with men in equally expensive hairstyles and designer jeans. Several heads nodded familiarly as Sara took a lone seat in the shadows at the back of the room. She ordered an imported beer and sipped it thoughtfully when it arrived.

The trees in Southeast Asia. Images of menacing jungles and treacherous swamps came to mind. Not really her kind of place. Adrian had learned caution the hard way in such places around the world. Caution and patience.

But there was a time and place for caution and patience. Surely they shouldn't be allowed to stand in the way of a loving commitment. Love was so rare and so valuable it was a shame to make it wait on caution and patience. Sara took another taste of the expensive import and thought about Adrian's reluctance to release himself completely from the reins of his self-control.

He had let those reins slip on a couple of occasions, she reminded herself. The first time he had made love to her, for example. The second time as well. Of course, on those occasions he had been assuming that he could keep his past hidden from her. He'd had no need to fear her reactions to learning his full identity because he'd assumed she never would know of it.

But even that last night at his home he had been unable to send her away although he had already made up his mind to give her time. He had needed her that night, not in a sexual way, but in the way a man sometimes needs comfort from a woman. He'd let her comfort him to some extent, she reminded herself on a note of hope. He'd held her very tightly that night, even in his sleep. She'd been aware of the tension gradually leaving him. She seriously doubted that Adrian had ever risked taking much comfort from others.

Sara turned the matter over in her mind. He loved her and she loved him. And as she had told him, life could be short and precarious. Love was too important to risk losing because of too much caution and patience. She needed to find a way to make Adrian understand that.

she needed to yank him out of his cautious, patient, controlled world.

An hour later she walked home alone, opened the door and saw the gleam of the crystal apple as it sat reflecting the light of her desk lamp. She stared at it for a long moment, thinking of Vaughn's plans to retrieve the gold. Then, very slowly and very thoughtfully, she closed her door.

The phone rang just as she was about to get into bed an hour later.

"Hello, Adrian."

"Have you calmed down?"

"I've calmed down."

"I love you," he said quietly.

"I know. I love you."

"Just give it a little more time, sweetheart," he urged. "The waiting isn't easy for me, either."

"I think it's easier for you than it is for me," she told him.

"No," he said in a raw tone. "It isn't. Good night, Sara. Sleep well."

"Good night, Adrian."

She hung up the phone and trailed slowly out into the living room. Once more her eyes fell on the crystal apple. There must be a way to break the impasse. The apple held the key to the gold. Perhaps it held the key to unlocking Adrian's emotions.

Again she wondered what the trees looked like in Southeast Asia.

ADRIAN ANSWERED his phone on Friday morning with a sense of anticipation that he couldn't deny. Very few people in the world had his unlisted number. Sara was one of those people.

"Hello?"

"She's gone crazy, Adrian. I warned you this would happen. Don't say I didn't warn you!" Lowell Kincaid was one of the few other people who had the number.

"You didn't warn me," Adrian said patiently. Determinedly he squelched his disappointment that the caller wasn't Sara. After all, he would be seeing her this evening. He could wait. "Calm down and tell me what you're talking about, Lowell."

"You think it's a joke, but I can tell you from past experience, it isn't."

"Okay, it's not a joke. Now tell me what it is that isn't a joke."

Kincaid spoke grimly. "She's applied for a passport."

Adrian paused, absorbing that. "A passport?"

"And she called me up to see what I knew about getting in and out of Cambodia."

"This is a joke, right? You and she both have a very strange sense of humor, Kincaid. I've told you that on previous occasions." But Adrian's hand was like a vise on the telephone receiver.

"Believe me, I'm not finding this funny. Applying for a passport isn't the end of it, either."

Adrian sucked in his breath. "All right. Let me have it."

"She asked me for a second copy of your half of the map and she's put an ad in the L.A. *Times*. Want to hear it?"

"No. But I think I'd better."

"Listen to this." There was a rustle of newspaper on the other end of the line and then Lowell began to read: " 'Danger, adventure, financial reward for the right person. Applicant must be willing to travel out of the

country, able to take care of himself and willing to follow employer's orders. Personal interviews only, no
phone. Three o'clock on Friday.' That's today,
Adrian.''

"I know it's today."

"She goes on to name the hotel down in San Diego
where she'll be interviewing applicants. You know as
well as I do that every California bozo who's into fantasy violence is likely to show up. Adrian, this is all your
fault. I'm holding you personally responsible.''

"My fault? You're the one who gave her half a map
and a legend, for pete's sake!''

"And then I gave her and the map to you, damn it! I
thought you would know how to take care of both!''
Lowell hung up the phone with a crashing noise that
made his listener's ear hurt.

Adrian stood silently staring at the receiver for a very
long moment. The lady was playing games again. In her
usual impulsive, off-the-wall style she was issuing a full-
blown challenge.

She appeared to have absolutely no fear of him. Sara
must know that he would be furious when he found out
what she had planned. Everything she had done was
quite deliberate, of course. She'd notified her uncle just
to make certain Adrian would find out immediately
what was happening.

A challenge, Adrian thought as he yanked his canvas
overnight bag down from the closet shelf. She had one
hell of a nerve. He recalled the way he had walked into
his home that first night and found her casually searching his study. She'd had no fear of him then, not after
she'd found the apple. And she obviously had no fear of
him now.

But she had shuddered and gone cold whenever she

had mentioned the man called Wolf. And she knew he had been Wolf.

He had wanted to give her plenty of time to accept him completely once she'd learned the whole truth. He'd wanted to be certain she could handle the idea of what he had once been. He loved her. It would tear him apart if deep down she was unable to accept him and his past. A few more weeks or months and he would have been more certain she knew what she was doing.

But Sara had no patience for strategy. She had applied for a passport and put an ad in the papers. She was going to force his hand.

Adrian zipped the bag closed, checked for his keys and set the house alarms. It would take him several hours to get to San Diego and he didn't want to waste any time. There was a midmorning flight that he just might make if he moved quickly.

He was astonished to find himself suddenly very impatient.

THE LINE BEGAN FORMING outside the hotel room at two o'clock. Sara watched in growing trepidation from the lobby, trying not to be obvious. If any of the wildly varied assortment of men in the line realized that the potential employer was the lady in jeans who was hanging around the front desk, she would be mobbed.

She had never dreamed so many people would show up in response to that ad. What really alarmed her was that Adrian was not among the thirty-plus males lounging in line. Nervously Sara wiped her hands on her denim pants. In a few minutes she was going to have to start dealing with that motley crew. Several of them looked rather rough. One or two appeared to be ex-bikers. A few were probably ex-military and some appeared merely curious. None of them was an ex-wolf.

Reaching for a pad of hotel paper and a pen Sara tried to jot down a few interview-type questions. What did one ask a mercenary? Especially when one had absolutely no intention of hiring him? She needed a question or two that would definitely exclude everyone in that line. Desperately she searched her brain for something that would make each of the waiting men ineligible.

At five minutes to three Sara steeled herself for the task ahead. Adrian was nowhere in sight. She was going to have to start the interviews or risk a very discontented line of applicants. The hotel management would not thank her for starting a riot.

Chin high, she took hold of her jangled nerves and swept down the line of rather scrungy-looking males. Without glancing at any of them she opened the hotel-room door and said over her shoulder, "I'll see the first man in line now."

Five seconds later she found herself alone in the room with a swaggering young man who was wearing a much-abused military fatigue shirt. He took one look at her and grinned arrogantly.

"You the lady who wants to hire me?"

"I'm the lady who is looking for the right man," Sara said coolly. "Now, if you don't mind, I'm going to ask you a few pertinent questions."

"Go right ahead, ma'am," he retorted with mock courtesy. "I'm at your service."

The swaggering young man's grin was gone when he stomped out of the room five minutes later. He was grumbling fiercely under his breath. Sara beckoned for the next applicant.

She had sent fifteen of the men packing when there was a loud commotion in the hallway outside the room.

Angry voices rose in protest and a second later the door was shoved violently open. Sara looked up from interviewing candidate number sixteen and saw Adrian filling the doorway. Anger, a seething impatience and a vast masculine annoyance burned in his eyes when he looked at her.

But the room didn't go cold.

Adrian pinned her for an instant, then his gaze flicked to candidate number sixteen, a middle-aged ex-military type running to fat.

"Out."

The ex-military type examined the newcomer for a few taut seconds, then shrugged and got to his feet. "I was just leaving. Seems I don't fit the profile of the successful applicant," he drawled. He used the words Sara had just spoken a second before the door had been flung open. He sauntered past Adrian, a flicker of amusement in his expression. "A very interesting lady. Good luck, buddy. I think you're going to have your hands full."

Adrian ignored him and turned to confront the remaining candidates. "Everyone can go home. Interview time is over. The lady has already hired a man. Me."

"Now wait just a damn minute, pal...."

Adrian glanced over his shoulder at Sara. "Tell them, Sara."

She got to her feet and realized her knees were slightly shaky. She had seen Adrian in a lot of different moods, including the one that could chill a room. She had never seen him thoroughly annoyed. She summoned a polite smile as she nodded at the men in the hall.

"I'm afraid he's right. Mr. Saville is the perfect candidate. Thank you all for showing up today."

There were a few growls of protest but the cluster of men dissolved. A moment later the hall was empty and Sara was left to face Adrian alone.

He leaned back against the doorjamb, his arms folded across his chest. "What the hell kind of game do you think you're playing, Sara Frazer?"

She sighed and sat down again. It was easier than standing. "I didn't know so many people would actually answer an ad like that."

"This is California, remember? Put an ad like that in the paper and you're bound to lure a lot of nuts out into the open." He came away from the wall and stalked over to the desk, flattening his palms on its surface as he leaned down to glare at her. "Did you think I'd let you get away with a stunt like this?"

She smiled tremulously. "No."

He narrowed his eyes. "I'd have been here earlier but the flight was delayed. I've been amusing myself for the past several hours thinking of what I was going to do to you when I finally did get to San Diego."

"I can imagine."

"I ought to take a belt to your sweet backside."

"Sounds kinky."

"Damn it, Sara, what the devil do you think you're doing?" He straightened away from the desk and paced to the window. "I'm furious with you."

"Yes. I'm sorry about that part, but I—"

"Sorry about it!" He whipped around to stare at her. "Sorry about it!"

"I couldn't think of any other way to force you into realizing that this stupid courtship has to end. It's driving me crazy, Adrian." She sprang to her feet to confront him. "We're wasting time and love, and everyone knows those are commodities that are too valuable to waste."

"What makes you think you've achieved anything other than annoying the hell out of me?"

She faced him determinedly. "There's only one way you can keep me from going to Southeast Asia."

"Really?" he asked with soft menace. "And what's that?"

"You're going to have to marry me. If you don't, I'll be on my way as soon as my passport arrives."

He looked dumbfounded. "Marry you!"

"This is blackmail, Adrian. Pure and simple. I'm giving you an ultimatum. Marry me or I'll go off on my own in search of that gold."

Adrian continued to stare at her as if she'd taken leave of her senses. "You're serious, aren't you?"

"I'm serious. This isn't a game, Adrian. I don't play games with the really important things in life."

"And I'm one of those things?"

"Adrian, you are the most important thing in my life," she said with simple honesty.

There was a moment of profound tension as he regarded her with an unwavering gaze. Sara had the impression he was seeking the proper words to express his feelings. She waited in an agony of suspense.

"Sara," he finally said carefully, "I'm very angry. I can't ever remember being quite this angry."

"I know," she whispered. "And I regret that, but—"

"But you're not afraid of me, are you?" he finished.

"Are you kidding? I've crossed all my fingers and toes." Her mouth curved in wry humor.

"But you're not terrified, are you?" he pressed.

"Not the way you mean, Adrian. The room hasn't gone cold. The only time it ever did was the time you rescued me from Vaughn. And I knew at the time that the chill was my protection, not something I had to fear. I love you and you love me. How could I be truly terrified of you?"

He ran a hand through his hair and turned back to the window. "I've been scared to death," Adrian admitted starkly.

"Of loving me?"

He shook his head. "Of worrying that you couldn't really love me knowing who I am."

Sara stepped around the desk and walked slowly toward him. "I love you, Adrian. I love you so much that I'll do whatever I have to do to stay with you. I know all the important things about you. I read *Phantom*, remember? I told you after I read it that I'd fallen in love with the hero."

"And I told you that I'd rather you fell in love with me."

"You thought it would be pleasant." She nodded.

"I think," Adrian said huskily as he turned toward her, "that it would be more than pleasant. I think it's absolutely essential."

"Oh, Adrian," she breathed, throwing herself into his arms. "I love you so much. Don't send me away again. I couldn't bear it." She buried her face against his shirt, clinging to him.

"You do tend to dramatize, don't you? I never sent you away. This past month was supposed to be a courtship."

"It was a test and I hate tests. I trust you, Adrian. All I want is for you to trust me."

"Or else you'll blackmail me into marriage?"

Her nails bit into the muscled back beneath his shirt. "I've told you, I'll do whatever I have to do in order to keep you."

He stroked her hair, tangling his fingers possessively in the golden-brown strands. "I believe you, honey. After this fiasco today, how could I not believe you? I have to admit you're not exactly looking for a way out of our relationship. But I thought I had to offer you that escape if you wanted it."

"So that you could be sure of me. Well, I'm not looking for an escape, Adrian Saville."

"I love you, Sara."

She lifted her head, eyes shimmering with emotion. "I love you."

He smiled and wrapped her close. "Can we go home now?" Adrian asked.

"Yes."

"We can stop in Vegas on the way back to Washington," he went on thoughtfully.

"You really are going to marry me?"

"I thought I didn't have a choice."

"You don't," she assured him.

Adrian thought about being wanted so badly by Sara that she'd do anything to keep him. It was a novel idea. He discovered he liked it. He was suddenly very sure she wasn't playing games.

The phone was ringing in Sara's apartment when they walked in the door a few minutes later. Adrian reached for it.

"It'll be your uncle," he explained as Sara glanced at him in surprise. Then he spoke into the receiver. "Hello, Lowell. You can stop panicking."

"I knew you'd handle things once you got there," Lowell said in tones of great satisfaction. "What happens now?"

"We're going to get married in Vegas on the way up to Washington."

"The hell you are! Whose idea was that?"

"Sara is blackmailing me into it," Adrian explained, watching her as he talked.

"Blackmail, hmm? I always knew the two of you had a lot in common. You both know what's important in life and you'll both do whatever it takes to get the job done. You just approach things in a slightly different style, that's all."

"Umm."

"But that doesn't mean I'm going to let you two get away with a Las Vegas wedding. I've been waiting for years for Sara to find the right man. I demand a real wedding. With me there." Lowell paused and then said in tones of satisfaction, "I won't have to worry about shopping, will I? I've already given you your gift. That reminds me, I'll be expecting a thank-you note." Lowell Kincaid hung up the phone.

Adrian stood looking at Sara. "Your uncle wants a thank-you note."

"Don't worry, I'll write one."

"He's also demanding what he calls a real wedding. He doesn't approve of the Vegas idea."

Sara grinned. "He just wants an excuse to wear one of those dumb aloha shirts."

"Lowell always did like parties."

Sara smiled. "Well, much as I hate to admit it, we may have to accommodate him. I'm extremely grateful to him. But not for the map."

"I know what you mean. I feel the same way." Adrian moved, sweeping her up into his arms. "You're the real treasure. I will take very good care of you, my sweet Sara."

She nestled trustingly against him. "I know. And I will take very, very good care of you."

It was a long time later that Adrian stirred in the depths of the tangled sheets of Sara's bed and remembered the question he had wanted to ask earlier. He drew a hand playfully down her spine until he arrived at her derriere.

"Sara?"

"Umm?" She was rapidly adopting his characteristic response.

"What did you tell all those candidates before I arrived at the hotel? How did you get rid of them?"

"I told them that there was one important requirement the successful candidate had to meet."

"What requirement?"

"The successful applicant had to be a vegetarian."

There were a few seconds of startled silence. Sara turned over onto her back in time to see the laughter dawn in Adrian's eyes. A moment later it consumed him completely and she was left to marvel at the first full-throated laugh she had ever heard from him.

She decided that a laughing wolf was a very enthralling sight. She would make certain Adrian laughed a lot more in the years ahead.

THE WEDDING RECEPTION, held on the ocean-front terrace of the home of Sara's parents, was a loud and exuberant success. Mr. and Mrs. Frazer were pleased with their new son-in-law. For them, Adrian's cover was still nicely intact. They thought he would have a steadying influence on their beloved but often unpredictable daughter. They had several qualms about allowing Lowell Kincaid to act as best man, however.

"I knew he'd wear something ridiculous," Mrs. Frazer said with a resigned groan as she stood with her daughter near the punch bowl. "Just look at him in that silly shirt. Everyone else is in formal wear! I should have put my foot down right at the beginning and made it clear he would not be allowed to participate in this wedding unless he was willing to conform!"

"You wouldn't have had much to say about it, Mom." Sara laughed at her attractive, worried mother. "The best man was the groom's choice, not yours."

"It's not that I don't love my brother dearly, it's just that he's so...so..." Mrs. Frazer waved her hand helplessly.

"Have some more punch, Mother." Sara leaned over to pick up a fresh glass of the frothy red concoction.

"And that's another thing," her mother went on a little grimly. "Does this punch taste funny to you?"

"Spiked to the hilt, I'm afraid," Sara admitted cheerfully. She was watching her new husband as he stood talking to her father. The two men appeared to be involved in a very serious discussion.

"I knew it," Mrs. Frazer exclaimed. "I thought I saw Lowell fooling around near the punch bowl an hour ago! The champagne wasn't enough for him, I suppose!"

"Excuse me, Mom, I think I'd better go rescue Adrian before Dad sells him on the idea of investing all his royalties in long-term certificates of deposit."

"Adrian is a very stable, very intelligent man, dear. I'm sure he'll want to hear your father's advice. He's a man who will want to plan for the future."

"Adrian has me to help him plan his future." Sara swept up another glass of punch for herself and went off to join her husband.

The look in Adrian's eyes as she went to stand beside him warmed her from the head to toe. He loved her. Above all else, he loved her. His was a total commitment. Just as hers was to him.

"Your father's been telling me about the advantages of long-term investments," Adrian said, putting his arm around his wife's waist.

"I'll just bet he has." Sara smiled at her father.

"I'll go over some more details with you later, Adrian. So glad Sara found herself a man who has his feet on the ground," Frazer said easily. He nodded in a friendly fashion, leaned down to kiss his daughter and went off to have some more of the heavily spiked punch.

"Feet on the ground, hmm?" Sara tipped her head up so that Adrian could brush his mouth against hers.

"That's not where they're going to be in a couple of hours," he warned.

"No?"

"Nope. Unless we decide to try something really unusual in the way of wedding nights, I plan to spend the evening horizontally."

"Adrian, I must tell you that lately you've begun to develop an odd sense of humor."

"Any sense of humor is better than none," Lowell Kincaid declared jovially as he sauntered up to join them. He was holding a glass of champagne in one hand and a glass of punch in the other. "Nice party, Sara. Your mother can throw a decent bash when she sets her mind to it." He took a sip out of each glass.

"Glad you're enjoying yourself, Uncle Lowell."

"I always enjoy parties. Say, I'm glad I finally caught the two of you alone. I've been wanting to talk to you all day."

Adrian looked at him warily. "Is that right?"

"Yeah, you know, I've been thinking."

"I'm getting nervous already."

Lowell shook his head. "No, no, this is serious. I've been giving some thought to Vaughn's little plan for getting the gold out through Cambodia. After Sara put that ad in the paper—"

"Don't remind me of that ad," Adrian warned.

"I'm telling you, Adrian, it's given me pause. There just might be a way to do it." Lowell leaned forward conspiratorially. "If we put together the right team— and you know we've got some good contacts—we could slip in and out of the country without anyone even knowing we were there."

"Uncle Lowell!" Sara's eyes widened excitedly. "Do you really think so?"

"Well, it would be risky, of course. But it just might be feasible."

Adrian's gaze narrowed. "The only reason it sounds feasible to you, Kincaid, is because you've been drinking too much of that damn punch. Forget it."

Sara turned to him eagerly. "But, Adrian, just think. What an adventure it would be!"

"I said forget it and I meant it." Adrian lifted his champagne glass and swallowed deeply.

"But, Adrian, darling..."

"Don't 'Adrian, darling' me. I said no. That's the end of it."

Lowell chuckled. "How about this. Your first marital quarrel."

"And you started it," Adrian shot back.

"You know what I think?" Sara demanded, glaring up at her husband. "I think Adrian is taking his new sense of husbandly duties a little too seriously. He's starting to lay down the law and we haven't even left the reception."

"Start as you mean to go on," Adrian quoted blandly. "And speaking of going on, I think it's time we said good-bye to all these nice folks. We've got a wedding night waiting for us. Are you ready to leave, Mrs. Saville?"

"Yes, Adrian."

"I've never seen her quite so amenable," Lowell marveled.

Adrian grinned suddenly. "It won't last. I intend to take advantage of it while I can. Let's go, honey."

Sara caught her uncle's eye as she obediently turned to leave on her husband's arm. Kincaid winked. Sara laughed silently back at him. The gold could wait for a while. After all, legends lasted a long time.

Lowell Kincaid's sister drifted up to stand beside him. She smiled maternally after her daughter. "Well, Lowell, in spite of that idiotic shirt you're wearing, I have to admit that this time you really came through. I was beginning to wonder if my daughter was ever going to fall in love. But you seem to have found just the right man for her."

Kincaid raised one of the glasses he was holding and grinned. "The best. A legend in his own time."

November's
irresistible novels from
—TEMPTATION—

DUSKFIRE by JoAnn Ross

Collaborating with rakish Ryan Sinclair would be impossible, Brandy Raines knew. He wrote gritty detective novels; she penned sweeping romantic sagas. Joint authorship would *never* work.

Reluctantly Brandy agreed to meet with Ryan — and found herself immediately attracted. Ryan was so sexy, such a tease. And far more interested in collaboration of another kind. . . .

FOR THE LOVE OF MIKE by Candace Schuler

Limo service owner "Mike" Frazer preferred to spend her time tinkering with the engines of her prized fleet. So she was nonplussed when sexy Devlin Wingate requested that she personally chauffeur him around Dallas — at triple the going rate!

Reluctantly Mike agreed, and soon found herself utterly charmed by her roguish customer. Devlin was the epitome of the romantic hero — and a devastating lover. But when he attempted to speed them into marriage, Mike was forced to hit the brakes. . . .

FOR ALL TIME by Anne Shorr

When Callie Barnes inherited one of Sanibel Island's oldest newspapers, her first move was to launch a campaign against the "progress" marring her beloved home. As the most powerful developer involved, the dynamic and sexy Michael Brookstone was her primary target.

But the passion Callie brought to her crusade was tepid compared to the feelings Michael stirred in her. And she found herself wanting him as an ally of the most intimate kind. . . .

The 1987 Christmas Pack

Be swept off your feet this Christmas by Charlotte Lamb's WHIRLWIND, or simply curl up by the fireside with LOVE LIES SLEEPING by Catherine George.

Sit back and enjoy Penny Jordan's AN EXPERT TEACHER, but stay on your guard after reading Roberta Leigh's NO MAN'S MISTRESS.

Four new and different stories for you at Christmas from Mills and Boon.

Available in October Price £4.80